Death in delhi

A Melanie Eagleton Mystery

April Chloe Evans

Death in delhi

A Melanie Eagleton Mystery

Copyright © 2017 by Michael Braff, Sabra Elizabeth Brock, and Donne Gail Kampel.

ISBN-13: 978-1-946274-17-5 Paperback
ISBN: 978-1-946274-20-5 e-Book

First Edition Wordeee 2022

Library of Congress Control Number: 2022902054

Published in the United States by Wordeee, Beacon New York
Website: www.wordeee.com
Twitter: wordeeeupdates
https://www.facebook.com/
e-mail: contact@wordeee.com

Printed in the USA

Chapter 1

ADIEU MIO GAZEBO

Melanie tilted her hat to the right to block out the midday sun. Even the birds, flying from tree to tree, seemed to be seeking shelter from the unusually hot spring day. In her shaded gazebo, she sank deep into a comfy Adirondack chair, sipped on a cool glass of lemonade, and stared out at the brownish water nearer to her dock and the clearer, blue water farther out on the lake.

Some years before, Melanie had found her little bit of heaven in the small town of Newton, New Jersey, an hour and a half from New York City. The gazebo overlooking Lake Owassa was her favorite spot on the small property. For the past two years from self-imposed solitude, Melanie spent more time in Newton than usual. Ironically, this was where her last relationship had begun with such hope and promise but ended in disaster and tragedy.

Melanie closed her eyes and listened. Stillness. Peace.

Folding her legs up under her, she felt her heart race as she heard a motorboat speed past her gazebo. Every time one came close to her dock and cottage, she had the same reaction. Melanie could swear she could still hear a faraway voice calling out to her as she watched the boat pass by. Only that was two-plus years ago. That fated day, she'd peeked from under the brim of her hat to see a man in a funny-looking cap waving at her. As he came closer, the engine of his motorboat quieted down as he pulled up near her deck. He was wearing a silly hat that covered his beautiful eyes and partially hid his handsome face and his deep, dark secret, as she would later find out. Oh, how she'd loved her time with that man with the hat.

Melanie felt tears brimming. She still wondered how the man who'd motored into her life that day was able to deceive her so. He had been the hope, joy, and promise she'd wished for, and during their time together, she'd loved him with a powerful love. Some might have called it a naïve love, but to her, it was the best love she'd ever had. Yet, that love had shredded her heart to pieces and still to this day, she was at a loss for how a woman like her could've loved a man like Marco. There had to be a reason! Her Native American heritage taught that nothing happened by coincidence, and there was a reason for everything, yet even two years later, no answer magically appeared.

Melanie got up and began pacing up and down the small gazebo. After trying for so long to forget, she felt it wrong to go down memory lane. She still found comfort in the past, but this would be the last time. Once and for all, she scolded herself; she needed to find closure. Melanie permitted herself one final time to remember the good times and fairytale romance she'd shared with the man in the funny hat who had broken her heart. The man called Marco.

It had been a little over two years now, and still, her heart wept for her friend, lover and betrayer. In short, Marco had ridden up to her dock in his boat, saved her from a brown bear, prepared her his special gazpacho, and took her to a ball. Her Marco. The thought of him warmed her heart, and despite it all, she missed him. She missed his voice, his smile, and all the simple things she'd loved about him from the first time they'd met. The fact that this man, who'd become her husband, had poisoned two people, including her best friend Charlotte, all for scientific research, was something she'd only recently been able to accept. But how could she begin to forgive something like that? It was a question Melanie could not answer.

Melanie, a runner and student of deep breathing and meditation, straightened her back and got ready to start her daily routine. She'd been meditating for as long as she could remember. It was one of the ways she coped with things, both good and bad. When her iPhone ringtone chimed the notes of *Pachelbel's Canon*, her inclination was to ignore it, but she couldn't this time. It was Lars, her amazing assistant. She pressed the answer button.

"Hello, Lars."

"Hey, Mel, is everything on schedule?"

"Yes. I'll be heading back to the city later today. I only hope the traffic isn't too brutal."

"There is always Waze," Lars said. "It knows the best way when traffic is backed up. And don't forget to take your glasses."

"I won't," Melanie chuckled at his suggestion as she knew the various routes to the city cold. He was right, though, about her glasses. Though she could drive without her specs, she needed them to see up close. Usually a little vain, Melanie didn't want to risk getting lost because she couldn't see the GPS, so she'd put on her specs. She remembered once, because of horrific traffic on the George Washington Bridge, she'd allowed the navigation system to map her route without looking at the GPS. She'd ended up lost in Fort Lee, and it had taken her 20 minutes to find the bridge. "How are the plans for Delhi going?"

"Fine. Even with the wedding, I've had enough time to gather all the data and the stuff you'll need to take with you."

"I'm not surprised."

Melanie was set to begin a new chapter of her life with a new and special project to keep her occupied. She was ready to re-enter life with a bang starting with a prestigious design job in Delhi, India. Though the job wouldn't start for several weeks, for months now, Lars had been rigorously preparing for the redecoration of a Maharajah's palace. This would be one of her most important assignments to date, and she was looking forward to it with great zeal.

"Give the project a rest. Right now, Dale needs you more." Lars and his long-time partner, Dale, a music entrepreneur, had just married in a very small but lovely ceremony. Melanie had served as the combination matron of honor, best woman, and flower girl. As a special treat for the newlyweds, Melanie was loaning them her cottage on the lake for their honeymoon. Lars and Dale would fit right into the small town's culture, which was welcoming and diverse.

Most importantly, loaning them her cottage allowed her to thank Lars for all he'd done for her over the years. Mel knew that Lars could have left to open his own design business years before, but he'd stayed with her even when her life had spiraled out of control. While she was going through her bad patch, he'd held down the fort, requiring less input from her.

"I'll leave the car and cottage keys with Ed. I'm heading to Long Island early morning, but I'll see you before I leave for Delhi," Melanie promised and hung up the phone.

She was very glad to have Lars in her life. They were as close as two peas in a pod. They loved the same things, decorating and cooking. She was looking forward to her trip to India, always relieved that Lars was there and in charge. The cottage was great, but in the back of her mind was her offer to him to become her full partner in The Decorating Diva.

Melanie looked out at the view across Lake Owassa and the Kittatinny Mountains one last time before she left her beloved gazebo. She'd miss watching the sunset over the lake tonight, a ritual she enjoyed while having dinner on the porch, even in the winter months. Melanie strolled along the shaded wooden path that connected the dock and the wrap-around, enclosed porch of the cottage.

Though the small house dated back to 1945, Melanie had modernized it. Every time she walked through the door of her little cottage, she was delighted by the contemporary interior she'd designed as her home away from home. The stark white walls contrasted with the pastel furniture and light oak accents. Pieces of Cherokee pottery she inherited from her mother were perfectly placed and always made her smile. There was an Indian head bowl, a wedding vase, and a vase with a frog base. She loved them all.

Heading to the guest bedroom, Melanie made final touches to prepare for Lars and Dale's arrival. She put fresh towels in the bathroom, stocked the cabinet with soap, shampoo, and conditioners and changed the shower curtain. She'd always meant to get a shower door but just never seemed to have the time. Now she was more in action she might consider a little redo.

In the sunny yellow eat-in kitchen, she began preparing meals she'd freeze in case Lars and Dale were too lazy to cook. Lars wouldn't snub his nose at her cooking though he was as good a cook as she. Melanie sighed as she put the last batch of goodies into the freezer. She knew the job in Delhi would be a challenge, especially because it had to be completed in a relatively short period, and this wasn't exactly the kind of project she was used to, so she expected hiccups. To boot, her passion and natural proclivity were not for old-world palaces but more modern décor. Over the years, she'd come to enjoy mixing time periods, such as putting a Tiffany lamp into a starkly modern living room. This job would give her the opportunity to expand on the trend, and she welcomed the radical change her work in India would bring.

Her client, the heir to the Kumar Palace, was a young Rajah, born of noble blood, the last in a long line of Maharajah, now reborn as a Bollywood star. Rather than power, his title, money, and artifacts were all that was left of his family's noble past. The young Rajah's wish was to open a museum in a part of the old palace to preserve his family's history. The challenge the project posed was enough to bring her out of her two-year funk and back into her design mode.

Another venture on the horizon, less prestigious and much smaller, was closer to her heart. It was the pet project of her dear friend, Charlotte. Her dear, late friend, that is. Melanie still couldn't believe Charlotte had been dead for two years, always half expecting her to call at any moment. Since college at Mount Holyoke, the two friends had been together, both on the equestrian team. Before her untimely death, Charlotte had stepped up her commitment, her passion really, to a horse shelter on Long Island that was close to her summer home. In fact, it was one of the reasons Charlotte had bought a cottage in Baiting Hollow, a tiny town on the North Fork. The stables there were dedicated to caring for abandoned and abused horses.

The mission of the Long Island stable was to restore mistreated horses to health and ready them for adoption. If they were not adopted, the horses had a home for life right there. Unfortunately, there always seemed to be more horses to take care of than money to support. The stable's precarious financial situation, always a concern, its sustainability questionable, was why Charlotte had conceived of and decided on a project that would stabilize funding and expand the stables.

As an academic executive and wealthy socialite, Charlotte's short-term plan had been to fundraise yearly to keep the shelter running. Her long-term plan was to offer her East End property as a visitors' center and temporary residence for volunteers working for the horse rescue organization.

Upon her untimely death, Charlotte's will revealed she'd endowed the shelter handsomely and had given her property for their expansion. Melanie had been so positive that she and Charlotte would grow old together that not in a million years would she have believed her long-range plan would be implemented so soon. Her murder had changed everything. As executor of Charlotte's will, Melanie was responsible for ensuring that her wishes, including expanding the shelter, were carried out. Melanie believed she owed it to Charlotte to see this project through.

Melanie looked out the kitchen window as she drew the curtains. Spring was here again, and here she was, in the season when things were supposed to be in bloom. Being at Charlotte's cottage would again force her to face memories of her friend's death. But she had to do what she knew in her heart was the right thing.

Packing some of her New Jersey necessities, including several extra pairs of glasses, she covered the furniture with white cloths so they would not be dusty when Lars and Dale arrived for their stay at the cottage. Outside she inhaled one last breath of the Owassa air before driving down to Ed's Garage to swap her vintage car for Charlotte's smaller car, which had been housed there since her death. Melanie hoped all her stuff would fit into the little red car. Ed, her neighbor, the garage owner, was also the local deliveryman. He'd been the one who'd delivered the lilac-colored tulips that started her love affair with Marco.

"We are going to miss having you around here as often," Ed said as she stuffed the last packages into the small car.

"I'm going to miss it all too, but it's time to get back into the swing of things. And anyway, I will be back soon enough."

Ed nodded his head. Glad to see her smiling. He couldn't imagine how she'd endured the past two years.

"My friend Lars, you remember him, don't you?"

"I do." Ed nodded.

"He'll pick up the car. He'll be staying at my place for a week."

"I'll take good care of him," Ed promised.

"I know you will," Melanie hugged Ed and said goodbye.

Tonight, on her stopover in the city, she would try her hand at one of her favorite dishes, Spring Vegetable Medley with Bay Scallops. Melanie was glad to be getting back to her apartment. Since dusk was fast approaching, she planned to stay the night at her apartment and drive to Baiting Hollow early in the morning.

Spring Vegetable Medley
with Bay Scallops

INGREDIENTS

- Bunch (5-8) spring red onions, chopped into
- ¼-inch pieces
- ½ lb. spring ramps (rampions/leeks), diced
- 3 garlic scapes, diced
- 3 Italian plum tomatoes, diced
- 2 T olive oil
- ¾ C White Zinfandel wine. (Fish or chicken broth
- maybe substituted.)
- 8 to 12 oz small bay scallops, rinsed and drained

PROCEDURE

Add olive oil to a heavy skillet, and heat over medium heat. Add vegetables and sauté for 6–8 minutes until tender. Add scallops and sauté for 3 minutes more. Add wine, cover, and reduce heat to low and let stew for 5 minutes. Serve with quinoa, brown rice, or kasha.

Chapter 2

HI HO, HI HO, TO BAITING HOLLOW WE GO

When Melanie heard the jarring horns, swathe potholes, and saw traffic lined up for miles, she knew she was back in Manhattan. Before her life had gotten crazy, New York City was a place she loved, though sometimes the noise made her cringe. The energy seemed to pour life into her veins. As a designer, the sights, smells, and sounds, well, most of them, inspired her.

It was April, and Melanie loved seeing the bright spring colors, including the forsythias that bloomed along the sides of the Westside Highway. The sight of the huge cruise ship, berthed in the 50s, along the piers, one which was probably heading to the Caribbean, made her excited about being home. Coming close to another of her favorite neighborhoods, Melanie turned off the highway at 26th Street and headed down to 7th Avenue. As was now usual, many of the stores in the Meatpacking District had changed. Melanie mostly appreciated when part of New York City became something else because change was what made the city dynamic. A long-time resident of the District, Melanie had watched with great interest as the area transformed itself from a workplace for hardy butchers, men with blood-stained aprons who would wolf whistle at women and people going to small clubs that existed on the fringes of the city. Sometimes, in the early morning, you could see the club-goers leaving the neighborhood as the butchers arrived.

Gone were the alleys that smelled of meat and the local restaurants that served big food portions at small prices. Gone too were the westside sex clubs that dotted 14th Street. Change disturbed some city residents, but Melanie enjoyed the ever-evolving city. As a designer, she felt the changes made the city more dynamic—always becoming something else. And she welcomed the new art galleries, showrooms, restaurants, and even the High Line. The construction of this innovative New York landmark, created from the old westside elevated rail that used to bring food and materials to Manhattan, had served to erase the seediness of the left-over train tracks. Melanie loved change, but she was sure, like other die-hard New Yorkers, they'd miss the rail tracks that represented a New York history now lost forever. What replaced the tracks, she had to admit, was very special. A walk through the High Line Park special garden, curvaceous in architecture, offered unique views of the city. Around each bend are public gathering spots and coffee bars. The exceptionally pretty and popular park with planked walkways, wooden benches, and areas of native plants turned out to be a jewel.

Melanie was especially fond of the park in the winter when the number of people was greatly reduced. One could hear the wildlife and see the snow on the trees. And the icing on the cake was the relocated Whitney Museum of American Art to its south end.

Passing the High Line, Melanie looked across the street and saw one of her old haunts, The Well Hung Cow. It had somehow survived all the years of constant change. She smiled as she remembered the escapades she and her friends had behind those walls. Chowing down on 16 oz. steaks and guzzling oversized pitchers of beer with her old friends led to fun talks and activities. She regretted not seeing them in years, something she vowed to correct when she returned from India.

Melanie rounded a corner to a narrow street that led down the block where her garage was located. As she approached, she called the garage attendant. "Nathan, it's Melanie Eagleton. I'm pulling up in about two minutes. I'm not in my car but in a little red sports car."

The attendant was waiting as she pulled up. He helped her unload the perishable groceries into a cart so she could get them to her apartment half a block away. The rest of the stuff she left to take to Long Island. Melanie rolled the cart into her building and left it with the concierge, who would have it delivered to her apartment.

Melanie had been lucky to find her apartment. In a city filled with tiny, very expensive abodes, she'd found a small, fixer-upper penthouse in a sturdy old building that used to house blacksmiths. She'd fallen in love, at first sight, marveling at the tiny garden and very convenient kitchen. Better yet, was that the building had two modern elevators.

Melanie dropped the bags she carried inside the apartment and dashed toward the bathroom. As she rounded the corner, she came face to face with her favorite *objet d'arte*, a mask she fondly dubbed Mr. Creepy because of its horrible expression. Normally she didn't name her artwork, but Mr. Creepy, from the remote northern tribe of headhunters, was a Brazilian Amazonian *Wayana Aparia* mask she'd bought a few years before was the exception. Mr. Creepy was more than a piece of art. He was a constant companion that she missed when she was away.

There was a soft tap on her door. Melanie looked through the peephole and saw Oscar, her doorman, standing there with a big smile.

"Welcome home. We've missed you around here."

"It's good to be home, Oscar. How are you?"

"Good. I've been holding some packages for you. I thought I should bring them up since your hands are full. I also brought you the newspapers." He handed over the packages, mail, papers, and cart. "Good to have you back, you," his smile broadened as he closed the door.

*   *   *

The following morning, Melanie picked up her car, bundled in the goodies she made and picked up a sugar-free skim vanilla latte before getting on her way to the Island. It was just right and enough for the ride to the next coffee refill opportunity in River-head. Turning on the radio to her favorite oldies station, she set off for her two-hour-plus trip to Long Island.

Melanie pulled into Charlotte's driveway and stopped next to the cottage door. The pink cottage, its color inspired by the houses in southern Spain, was one of Charlotte and Mel's favorite places. Charlotte's recent changes were visible throughout the house. An old bathroom had been redone, and a small spa tub had been installed in the second bathroom. A bay window facing the west had allowed for magical views of the evening's sun setting over Long Island Sound.

Melanie rolled her suitcase into the living room and then went to the small open kitchen to put away the food she'd brought. When she reluctantly pulled her suitcase into the bigger bedroom, Charlotte's, memories of her friend intruded. She sighed and walked back into the kitchen, appreciating anew the bay window over the range that allowed her to cook and view the beautiful Sound at the same time.

Melanie changed into jeans and beat-up loafers to walk the quarter-mile to the Horse Rescue Shelter. The fresh air and spring sun warmed her along the path. As she approached, she could see the horses from the side of the road. A few, still too thin, showed the effects of a hard life. Melanie felt good about carrying out Charlotte's wishes. She'd work hard to improve the Shelter's operation and finances and ensure its financial stability could continue in perpetuity.

"Okay, Charlotte. I'm here, and I'm on the case," Melanie said aloud to the heavens and headed to the barn. Several healthy-looking horses were cantering around. Two recent and gaunt arrivals were standing unsteadily, but she was certain that though thin now, they would soon be on their way to better health. Melanie opened the corral, quietly walking over to the thinner horses. She gave them friendly pats and small apple pieces. The shelter seemed busy and looked as though it was doing well. They were saving more horses, and that would have pleased Charlotte.

Charlotte had been so committed to this particular shelter because of its missions, one of which was accepting carriage horses from Central Park. They had taken fifty-one to date. In addition, they received infirmed horses from across the state that they cared for and sheltered, often arranging adoptions for some of them to good families. Others who did not find a home could count on a lifetime of love and security at the shelter. Theirs was a mission of pure love.

Melanie walked over to a handsome brown horse who'd been rail-thin when he arrived, and they'd worried for his survival. He was on the mend. She moved cautiously, knowing that rescued horses could sometimes be unpredictable. Since she had interacted with this horse before, she felt comfortable patting his mane and spoke softly to him. "Hello again, Prince," She fed him one of her New Jersey apples which he ate eagerly. For dessert, she presented him with two sugar cubes. The grateful horse nuzzled her several times, and she nuzzled him right back. His name Prince fitted well because he looked regal and elegant.

Melanie had a few carrots hanging out of her back pockets. The nuzzling horse grabbed a carrot, pulled it out of her pocket, ate it, and then nuzzled her again. Melanie laughed. "Prince," Melanie again cuddled him, "that's the best kiss I've had all day. And to say thank you, here's another sugar cube." As she rose to her feet, she could feel some of her anxiety leaving. For Melanie, horses were therapy.

The shelter manager and a delightful man, Ralph Arrowhead was coming toward her. Today he rode his scooter, but sometimes he walked with the aid of crutches. As a boy, Ralph had contracted polio. Happy to see Melanie, the biggest smile lit up his weather-lined face. "I was beginning to think I'd never see you again."

"Oh, dear. Why would you think that?" Melanie scrunched up her face.

"I thought maybe it'd be too hard for you to come back. You were always here with Miss Charlotte." His smile disappeared.

"It's because of Charlotte that you'll always see me here. I'm the executrix of her will, and I've been charged with making sure this place is never in need."

Ralph Arrowhead smiled sadly. "I miss her a lot."

"Me too," Melanie whispered.

"Let's go inside and have some coffee or tea. You know Margie will be waiting."

"Yes, I'm counting on it," Melanie said, following behind Ralph.

Margie McClellan, the shelter's only full-time volunteer and someone committed to animal rescue, was a petite woman in her late sixties. She opened the door and began talking and never stopped. Margie was a talker. She told wonderful stories and could be counted on to help wherever she could. She had been with the shelter from the beginning.

Smiling at the sight of Melanie, Margie said, "Oh good, you're here just in time. I've just made the best potato leek soup. Ralph just loves it. Don't you, Ralph?"

Ralph enthusiastically nodded his head, looking around for the soup, cups, and spoons.

Margie was also a voracious eater, and Melanie wondered where she packed away all that food. Whenever she saw Margie, she was eating, and today was no exception. But Margie maintained a trim and well-conditioned body. An expert rider, the retired real estate agent lived alone in Riverside with her cats, dogs, and horses. She was committed to taking care of all animals, big and small.

True to Ralph's word, Margie had the table set in no time, and they sat down to lunch.

"Bread?" Maggie offered some beautiful Irish soda bread.

"No, thank you."

Margie handed the basket to Ralph and passed her a bowl of soup.

"Margie, this soup is delicious," Melanie said, which prompted Margie to offer the recipe.

"It's my mother's recipe. Shall I dish you another bowl? How come, no bread? This is the good stuff from Tully's farm. Hand-made this morning!" Continuing to talk, Margie's hand was already on the tureen, getting ready to ladle out more soup.

"Margie, I love bread, but I want to make sure my pants continue to fit. Bread does weird and awful things to my body. I eat it sparingly so I can look as fit as you."

Margie beamed at the compliment. "It's nothing I do. I think it's just the genes … and jeans that stretch.

"Good genes and jeans," Melanie chuckled, then continued before Margie got her babble going. "I'm going to be at Charlotte's cottage for a couple of weeks, so I can come up and help you out whenever you need me. Just give me a little notice and let me know what you need me to do. While I'm here, we should also try to interview contractors for the renovation. First, though, I think we should start with a few more staff members. What do you say, Margie?"

Margie nodded an enthusiastic yes.

That afternoon, Melanie placed a call to the Shinnecock Indian Nation Reservation located in Southampton. Though she believed in supporting all Native Americans, not just her tribe, the Cherokee tribe, she was particularly dedicated to the local Shinnecock Indian Reservation in any way she could.

Margie asked if they could send over people interested in helping run the shelter and who were good with horses. The tribe's staff was happy to help.

Thinking about the tribe brought Melanie back to her parents and the place where she grew up. Her family was not wealthy like Charlotte's, but her parents gave her whatever privilege they could afford. Melanie, an only child, brought up in Eastchester, New York, was doted on by her parents. Her architect father lived by his principles, preferring to work on projects he truly believed in rather than those that were more lucrative. Melanie was a true daddy's girl, the apple of his eyes, and she adored him. Her super-talented designer mother, Dyana, kept alive the great lore of Native American art and design, home cooking, and the culture. She seeded her daughter to know what one should be doing with one's life to make it meaningful. Melanie was devoted to her mom as well as the heritage that Dyana passed down."

Most of Melanie's Cherokee family originated in North Carolina. Growing up, she collected artifacts of her culture wherever she could find them. She haunted libraries and museums studying her heritage, and one of her favorite museums was right there on the Long Island Shinnecock reservation.

Dyana's seventy-five percent Cherokee ties to the Cherokee Nation and other Native American nations ran deep. Once a year, Mel's parents would take her to the Shinnecock reservation for the powwow. The reservation itself was quite old, dating back to the 1700s. It had an amazing museum, an old schoolhouse, and so much history that a young girl could wander around for hours and learn a lot. Roots and culture define a life Melanie would think as she visited each place. Melanie made it a point to go to the reservation often and to support the Shinnecock tribe in any way that she could.

Easy Potato Leek Soup

INGREDIENTS

- 1 large can (39 oz.) chicken broth
- 3 large leeks, tough outer leaves removed, sliced lengthwise and well rinsed
- 4 large baking potatoes, washed and eyes removed
- 1 medium red onion
- 2 carrots, orange or yellow

PROCEDURE

Cut all vegetables into chunks. Add them to a 4-quart pressure cooker. Add broth and salt, and pepper to taste. Cook for 5 minutes after pressure comes up. Cool pot under cold water to lower pressure to open. Use a hand blender and blend all the ingredients until pureed smooth.

Chapter 3

ON AND OFF THE WALL

"Mom, where's my bag?" said Steven Orville with obvious petulance.

She responded as she did every morning that it was in the front closet, where he had left it.

"Is that where you hid it?" Steven said sarcastically as he ransacked the small closet, angrily kicking a few things out of his way.

Steven had always been an odd child, quite brilliant and quite obviously mad. He never mixed with other kids and was often called anti-social. After his father left, things escalated, and Sarah had taken him to a psychiatrist.

When he was on his meds, Steven was a sought-after star, and for the past five years, they'd been doing very well on Steven's income. A computer genius at B-Capital, he daily received offers for bigger and better jobs, but Steven was the loyal type and never considered them. But recently, something had changed.

At work, one minute Steven could be charming, joking, and chatting with staff members, and the very next, he would go into a rage, blaming co-workers for mistakes, even if they were not on his team. In manic moments, he'd be impressed with himself, believing he was the most talented person in the entire department and that they just didn't understand. Another sign was when on his meds, Steven was a group leader who rallied his staff, but now he was becoming secretive about his life while others shared their weekends and outside the office activities. Steven's co-workers and managers tried to ignore his bizarre behavior because he was a solid producer on his better days.

In cutting him slack or ignoring him, they had missed the onset of even stranger behavior when he periodically began talking to himself and was becoming delusional. This was a sign that Steven had stopped taking his meds. Steven had been on a key project and felt the side effects of his medicine were dulling his senses, so he'd stop taking them to avoid the side effects during the project. The result ended in his instigating fights with other employees. Though nobody was hurt in the scuffle, the company let Steven go, to avoid a lawsuit.

Life had been fine until his psychotic break, and he'd been put on disability. Their cushy lifestyle soon came to a screeching halt, forcing them to have to move from their roomy apartment on the Upper East Side to a cramped 500 square foot, dark, airless basement tenement apartment in the least trendy part of the Lower East Side; too small for even the closest friends, let alone a mother and her grown son. To say that life at the moment for the Orville's was a challenge was an understatement.

These days, Steven was often angry since what his mother called his "trouble" and became increasingly belligerent and refused to go back on his meds. If only she'd been paying more attention, she'd have insisted he take his meds before things got this bad. She, too, was guilty of reveling in the cushy life her son's talents afforded.

"Mother," he whined, "I don't see the bag. The paper inside is very important." Steven never recovered from being fired and didn't trust his co-workers, boss, or mother.

"Of course, it's there, dear," Sarah tried to placate him so his anger would not escalate. "I'll be right there to help you." She was on her way to getting him back to a stable state, but it would be another month or two before the full effects of his drugs she'd been slipping in beverages would make him seem normal again.

Steven felt he had always been a disappointment to his mother and his father, for that matter. His father had deserted the family when Steven was a little boy, leaving no note or forwarding address. Steven believed that his father had left because of him. He wanted to do something big so his father would be forced to acknowledge him, but he'd messed up again.

Steven's mother, an optimist by nature, kept reminding her son that things could change again, for the better. And they had, but only slightly and temporarily as Steven had gotten a job at a call center, which eased some of their financial pressures. They even hoped to move soon. Unfortunately, he lost that spot when his new company began outsourcing tech jobs to India. Steven felt he had been gypped and betrayed again.

Unbeknownst to him, on his medication for several months, Steven was beginning to feel ready for the world, so he continued his job hunt in earnest. He was calmer, and many of his paranoid symptoms had stabilized. Along with the tempering of his moods, he experienced some dullness of his senses and slight headaches, but these side effects were something he had to deal with right now, and they were far better than his meds. He had to find a job, any job, to get them out of the dark, stale, acrid-smelling tenement as quickly as possible.

Steven didn't yet know that his luck was about to turn. While poring over the newspaper for job opportunities, Steven read about a protest group called the "Concerned Citizens for Corporate Conscience," known in the States as the 4Cs. This group had made it their mission to convince Americans that jobs in the U.S. were for Americans, not "foreigners" who now, more and more, were taking them away. And certainly, he despised the "offshoring" of business that some U.S. companies were undertaking.

In Manhattan, Steven, somewhat normal, made his way to the office of the largest chapter of the 4Cs. They had no paying jobs but needing to be useful; he joined them. Within a few weeks of being at the 4Cs, Steven had reorganized the company and armed them with powerful technology for recruiting. His enthusiasm for the cause was palpable.

Ruth, the head woman in charge, encouraged by Steven's enthusiasm and the rapid progress they'd made being technically enabled, was impressed by the boy wonder and kept him close by her side. She asked his advice on everything. Steven, talented in mathematics and computers, was an asset to the 4Cs, and Ruth considered him an essential, if somewhat eccentric, worker.

Feeling on top of the world, Steven went to the kitchen and took two of his mother's cinnamon buns. Fattening but fabulous. His mother reminded him of the calories right before she reminded him to take his pills. He had found his niche, albeit for no pay. Because Steven himself could not get the good jobs he wanted, he felt personally offended by the outsourcing of American jobs overseas. He fit well into the 4Cs. In this group, he could become important, and what he didn't get in salary, he got in accolades.

America's current chaos worked for Steven. In the 4Cs, he found people just like him, people whose jobs had moved to foreign countries. Some were zealots, some were loners looking for purpose, and some were just ordinary people who had lost their jobs and could not find work.

Using his excellent organizational skills, Steven quickly became an important part of the 4Cs and their success. The 4Cs rewarded him with positive publicity, hailing him a genius. The group rapidly grew, and their cause, due to his efforts, had reached the ear of government. In fact, the 4Cs had even been written up in *The New York Times*.

As Steven rose in the 4Cs leadership, he began advocating for more radical action, something he had read about from the 1960s and '70s. Once a less organized ragtag group, the 4Cs had grown in strength and stature with Steven's skills, more organized and purposeful. To boot, they were bringing in some sponsorship from anonymous donors who believed in their cause. He soon found himself one of the top leaders and the only one allowed a modest stipend. His education, ability to orate, and seemingly bottomless energy, made him invaluable.

The 4Cs knew all the facts about job loss and had data on every country where jobs were being outsourced. They were razor-sharp on all statistics about worker displacement, including the psychological, emotional, and financial toll it took on individuals and families. This became a new source of income for the 4Cs as they sold the data to government entities and others to police the activities of companies.

Steven also believed there could be no real revolution without consequences and casualties. As far as he was concerned, the call centers, particularly those in India, were the enemy and had to be eliminated. Granted, there were call centers in Ireland and other places. He wanted those jobs back, too; however, Asia, especially India, sucked the life out of the American call center industry and industry in general. Steven wanted some heads to roll both in Corporate America and in countries like India. He pulled out a list of offenders he'd compiled and added a few names.

Steven began looking through the paper and reviewing his to-do list as he walked to the subway. He needed to leverage his popularity and rising star status; top of his list: get a job so he could get back to living the good life he already knew. Next, step-up adverse activity against companies that wreaked havoc on the lives of people like him.

On the subway, Steven read an article about a horse rescue organization on Long Island and was encouraged. There were always "bleeding heart liberals" who were ready to throw money at causes. His group needed rescuing too. People's livelihoods and lives were at stake. If he could get more of these socialites to invest, he would win his fight and get a real job too! He studied the picture and the people in the article.

Steven's Mother's "Homemade" Cinnamon Buns

INGREDIENTS

- 1 package unbaked dinner rolls
- 1 C plus 1 T light brown sugar
- 2 T cinnamon
- ½ C raisins
- 1 stick butter, melted

PROCEDURE

Open the package of dinner rolls. Roll out the dough into a foot square, about a ¼-inch thick. Cut into 1-inch strips. Dust with 1 T brown sugar and 1 T cinnamon mixture, and scatter about a ½ cup of raisins on top. Roll the strips into spiral buns and place them on a greased baking sheet pan about 2 inches apart. Mix the remaining 1 T cinnamon, 1 C sugar, and butter. Cook over low heat and stir for 5 minutes until smooth. Pour over rolls. Bake according to biscuit package directions.

Chapter 4

MEMORIES OF THE LIVING NIGHTMARE

To air out the house that had been locked up for more than two years, Melanie opened the doors and windows. It wouldn't be a stretch to clean. Thank goodness, it had only four rooms. There was no denying the charm and style of the home. Melanie walked out the back door to the tiny garden planted on a small patch of land beside the house. To her surprise, it showed evidence of spring—the perennial Hydrangeas were sprouting! Though Melanie loved her cottage in Newton, she could see how one could fall in love with this picturesque petite house on a bluff. The views were spectacular. Life was in full bloom, with boats in hangers and bathers dotting the shore. Even the neighbor noises sounded melodic in the bucolic setting.

Charlotte, once a diehard Southampton girl, had surprised Melanie when she and her husband Jason had bought the weekend cottage on the North Fork of Long Island in the small village of Baiting Hollow. Although only a dot on the map, Baiting Hollow, near Riverhead, was well-known for its vacation homes, strawberry picking, and, best of all, wineries. Lots of wineries.

At first, Melanie didn't think the cottage fit Charlotte's style. But for sure, it didn't fit Jason's high society taste. Jason and Charlotte's styles and values were completely different, and Jason was not even tempted by the view of the Long Island Sound from their back deck. He rarely came to the cottage. Charlotte loved it. But Charlotte had reasons to buy the cottage, other than she loved it.

Charlotte and Melanie had decorated the cottage to blend in perfectly with its environment. Perched high on the bluff, the intimate rooms were comfortable and pretty. From a terrace of the master bedroom overlooking the water, one could hear waves lapping small stones on the beach far below. The house was quiet when one needed quiet. Melanie often came for weekends to spend time with Charlotte and the horses and enjoy the peace, open spaces, and wineries of the East End.

Though she was sure she'd enjoy her week at the cottage, Melanie's heart became heavy. She'd never been there without Charlotte. Maybe this trip would bring her final closure. To be honest, she liked the idea of going to a place where hardly anyone knew her, and those who did were circumspect. She could wander freely around little forested areas, vineyards, the fresh fruit and vegetable stands, the riding paths, and the beach without having to talk to anyone or answer questions about Charlotte's death. With Melanie's and Charlotte's mutual friends in Manhattan, the conversation nearly always veered toward Charlotte, her remarkable life, and death.

After airing out and cleaning up, Melanie pulled out a jar of apple butter she'd brought from New Jersey and the granola muffins she'd made a few days before. She loved baking anywhere. She poured a glass of orange juice and scrambled some eggs. This kitchen was small, but the windows gave it an open feel. While making a pot of coffee, she started a list of other things to bring from the city for future stays—like a one-cup-at-a-time coffee maker and candles, in case the lights went out.

Melanie set the table tucked in a little corner near a tiny bay window in the living room. As she ate, she watched the sun slip out from under the clouds over the water. A spring squall was long over, but the trees still had a light dusting of snow—yes, even in April. As she knew firsthand, life can be so unpredictable. Outside the window, robins and gulls seemed unperturbed by the unexpected snow, while in the distance, she could hear waves rolling against the pebbled beach below the deck.

"I could stay like this forever," Melanie said to herself as she fell asleep in the comfortable armchair.

She was running, yelling something. "Marco. Marco," she was running faster and faster to catch up with him. When she caught him by the waist, she wrestled him to the ground and smothered him with kisses.

Melanie could not believe how a man she'd met only a few weeks before could make her so deliriously happy. She'd called him her prince.

As they'd collapsed on the beach, still laughing as dark clouds began moving in, from the frantic townspeople milling around, the news had reached them that her dearest friend, Charlotte, had died. At the news, Marco became agitated.

"What's wrong?" Melanie asked.

Pulling no punches, he admitted, "I am the one who killed her. I can't stay here. I am going to Brazil."

Melanie couldn't believe what she was hearing. It was like a bad movie. "But why?"

"It was all for my experiment. I was so close, but it all went wrong."

"No, Marco, no. Don't leave. Not now. We can find a way." She heard herself screaming even though Marco was no longer in sight.

The dream shook her body awake, and Melanie bolted upright from the horrific dream drenched in sweat and with tears streaming from her eyes. If only it could remain just a dream…but it was real. Very real. Her Frankenstein was real.

Standing up, holding on to the chair for support, she walked slowly to the small, enclosed deck and stared at the water below. She recalled her dream vividly, as well as the living nightmare behind it.

"Marco," she whispered into the wind.

Their courtship had been a whirlwind and intense. Melanie hadn't known Dr. Marco Ferri, a research doctor and botanist, long but knew she loved him from the start. And even after he'd fled the United States, having killed one person and making another critically ill, and he becoming ill, she'd followed him. It turned out that Marco had been administering the same drug to himself that killed Charlotte, trying to find the right dosage that would be medically effective, but all had gone wrong. Flying to Brazil to be by his bedside, Melanie cried with him as he talked about his experiments and the many regrettable acts he'd committed in the name of science. Melanie, believing herself deeply in love, had convinced herself that Marco loved and needed her, so she'd flown to Brazil to nurse him back to health. Upon his discharge from the hospital, not only would she stay, but they would marry. They would rent a small place on a quiet street in Rio de Janeiro, just for the two of them and figure out what to do next. Thus, did her dreams go.

But she wouldn't wait to become his wife as it might help his case. To put their plan into action, Melanie found an elderly pastor from a nearby church to perform their nuptials. Despite the odds, he was quite taken that such a beautiful couple wanted to marry. He conducted a simple ceremony at

Looking annoyed, McKerny finally said, "Go to yesterday's newspapers and track him from there. Hopefully, he is local to New York. Everyone is findable with technology!"

*   *   *

Steven walked down the dark hallway of the dingy apartment to check to make sure his mother wasn't home. She wasn't. He made himself a cup of coffee and sat down at the kitchen table. He pulled out a list of people and companies and scanned it. The biggest job outsourcer was Aurora Technologies right there in New York. Just as he was about to do a deep dive into the company, his phone buzzed.

"Hello."

"Is this Mr. Steven Orville?"

"It is. Who's this?"

"This is Sally Denney from Aurora Technologies. I am calling on behalf of Mr. Albert McKerny, president of the company. He would like to make an appointment to see you. Are you available to come here tomorrow at 2 p.m.?"

How serendipitous. The person sounded all business, and Steven hesitated. "Are you serious? Is this a joke?" He asked after a moment. After all, he was just thinking about the said company, and now they're on the phone? What are the odds?

"Mr. Orville, this is not a joke. I am Mr. McKerny's assistant, and he's asked me to call to see if you're available to come in to have a chat with him. I have no idea why or what about."

Steven was taken aback. Why should someone from Aurora Tech want to see him? Talk to him? About what? Just about this time, in the middle of his doubt, his ego kicked in, and he said to himself, *why not. I am the best there is and a free agent.* It was worth an hour of his time to see what this guy had to say...*what could he say?*

Steven answered slowly and cautiously, "Yes, I probably can be available, but I'd still like to know why he wants to see me. And how you got my number?"

"I was lucky. I found you in the newspapers. So how about it, can you come in tomorrow? Will you take a chance that this meeting is a good thing? Is 2 p.m. good?"

She could hear him breathing and hoped she'd convinced him. Finally, Steven responded. "Yes, I'll come."

Sally was relieved that she didn't have to give McKerny bad news. He could be overwhelmingly harsh. "Great," she said. "See you at 2 p.m. Our address is 1643 Broadway, on 51st Street between 7th and 8th Avenues. On the fourth floor. Oh, and by the way, the security desk downstairs will ask you for identification. See you then."

Steven was baffled but knew his curiosity would force him to keep the appointment. He wondered how they got his telephone number. Steven's paranoia kicked in a little, but the thought of something good happening quieted him. Perhaps it was those newspaper stories about the 4Cs, but they wouldn't have given out his number. Steven ruffled his hair in confusion but walked himself away from the edge since he was back on his meds. Still, he wondered why Albert McKerny wanted to see him. He didn't have long to wait.

*   *   *

The following day, Steven was in a better mood. He dressed in his best-looking suit from his Wall Street days which, luckily, still fit, if a bit tight. He'd leave the buttons undone. Too many of his mother's sweets? Or perhaps the medication? Steven hopped off the C train at 1:40 and headed toward Aurora Technologies.

The building was big, with a busy, very well-appointed lobby. Upstairs, the waiting room was nicely decorated with oil paintings, flowers in huge vases and little tables for setting down one's coffee. Looking at the luxurious way the place was decorated, Steven felt his anger bubbling to the surface. He couldn't help thinking that this company, apparently swimming in luxury, was firing people, forcing them into poverty just to outsource their jobs to other countries. People like him had a mother to support.

"I am Steven Orville," he announced, walking up to the desk and doing his level best to be calm.

"Mr. Orville," welcome to Aurora Technologies. I am Sally Denney. I made your appointment. It's a pleasure to meet you." Sally had to admit that he was not what she'd imagined. He was taller, good-looking and better dressed than she'd expected. With an ever-so-slight paunch, there were no six-pack abs for this guy, but he looked healthy and happy. His brown hair was neatly cut, and his nails trimmed and tidy. After looking him up and down a few times, Sally said, "I'll let Mr. McKerny know you're here. Would you like coffee, tea, or cucumber water?"

Cucumber water! *What the hell was that?* Steven refused any beverage and sat down to wait.

In-person, Albert McKerny was more imposing than his picture implied. He stood six feet two. His thick black hair was slicked back. His grey pin-striped suit was fashionable.

"Steven Orville," Albert rose as he walked into the office. "How are you? Nice to meet you."

"I'm fine. Why am I here?" Steven said abruptly.

A little taken back, Albert grabbed his hand in a firm grip and began pumping it up and down. "I've been watching you and the 4Cs as well as reading about you in the newspapers. They say you were a major force in turning that ragtag group into a formidable influencer and that you are a genius. The papers seem impressed.

You are packing some kind of intelligence there, my boy." A wide yet ironic grin spread over his face.

Steven wanted to protest the 'my boy' bit but had to admit he was a little flattered that his brains did not go unnoticed. "Thank you."

"Can I get you anything? Coffee, a drink? "

"No," Steven said evenly. "But you could tell me why I am here."

"Of course." Albert moved back to his desk and opened a folder. "A Harvard man, huh? I'm a Stanford guy myself."

Steven just stared, waiting for the man to tell him what he was doing there.

"Look, I know you are passionate about the 4Cs. But we are not happy either about having to export jobs. Unfortunately, the competitive landscape is brutal, and business is business. We would like to bring back jobs to the United States if we could find a way. We have talent here. We know that. But again, this has never been personal. It's just business."

Steven looked at McKerny with a withering look and said nothing. He figured this guy was on a roll, and he knew eventually he might get down to business.

McKerny continued, "We at Aurora are working on a plan to bring jobs back to the USA. It's a three-year arrangement. We are looking for someone to help us implement our plan. I read about you, saw what you accomplished while on Wall Street, and what you have done with the 4Cs in a short time. I have a proposal for you that could be lucrative for both of us."

This got Steven's attention. "I'm listening," he said.

"The position is Director of Technical Relations. You would need to spend some time in India, learning their processes, what they do and how they do it and, how they handle employment issues. How to maneuver the way they do is what we need to begin to move technology jobs back to the States. It is an expatriate assignment, so you and your family would live in U.S.-standard housing and fly first class for the length of the three-year contract and, of course, get paid in U.S. dollars.

Steven looked at him and asked, "India? You want me to go to India? Right now, that's not my favorite place. They took our jobs and our livelihoods. And you want me to live there?"

McKerny continued, "Yes, if you want to bring back the jobs, we need to bring back the technology and the know-how."

"It's not technology and know-how. It's cheap labor."

"We are aware of that, but there is more. More info we can't get by waving a wand. Listen, I have read that you've had some issues—you know, stress and stuff like that. Life in India is way less stressful than it is here. It may do you some good."

Steven's mind was racing. How did McKerny find out about him? He knew the web was not private, but he'd scoured it and removed all the negative stuff. Well, there is no point dwelling on it, and it may be for the best.

McKerny continued, "You'll have a house with a car, a driver and servants. We will pay you very well, say 300K a year, and we have an excellent international benefits package, including medical. Good, right You'll stay two, maybe three years max. And you will be helping us figure out how to get back and keep technical jobs in America. Right in keeping with your philosophy, correct? That's what your group wants, right?"

McKerny stopped talking and stared intently at Steven. He did well in business because he was a master of understanding what made people tick and how to clinch the deal.

Steven's mind ran a mile a minute, especially when this guy mentioned the 4Cs, but he jerked himself back to the offer. "Is this a temporary job? What happens when I get back to the U.S. after the two or three years?"

"When you get back, we'll take care of you. We'll find a position worthy of your talents. What are you thinking now?"

Steven began to wonder again where he'd gotten this information. He would have to do some hacking tonight. He knew he was brilliant and appreciated McKerny's acknowledging that fact, but why him? Then again, he was very smart, so why not him? That they knew all about him and wanted to hire him anyway was a relief!

Steven began to fantasize what it would be like to live like a normal guy again, with money and security. With this position, maybe his mother would finally stop complaining. Maybe he could get her an apartment for herself. He would love to live alone for a change. Without even realizing it, he began nodding his head. "I need time to think this over, and I would like to see the agreement in writing. I will need to discuss this with my family. It's not just me, sir."

McKerny knew his answer. "Take all the time you need. We just need an answer by the beginning of May."

"You haven't told me why you selected me? There are other smart people in the world."

Without missing a beat, McKerny said, "Because there are not too many people like you in the world."

Steven took the compliment and reddened a bit. "How do you know so much about me?"

"The Feds know everything about agitator groups, another reason to be on the right side of change."

The Feds? It must be a government contract.

McKerny stood up, and so did Steven. McKerny said, "First of May or before, Mr. Orville."

Steven nodded, shook McKerny's hand and left. Albert McKerny smiled as he shut the door.

Steven spent the time on the subway thinking of ways to tell his mother they would be moving to India. He had already made up his mind, and she would have to go along or stay in New York. He could afford to put her back on the East Side with his new salary.

Two hours later, over dinner, he told his mother that the work with the 4Cs had paid off because he was offered a position at Aurora. "It means, however, that if I accepted the job, we'd have to go to India for two or three years."

His mother was adamant about not going. "It is too hot, dirty, and crowded with strange foods. The streets are particularly dirty." That's what she said, but her biggest concern was about where he'd find a doctor and what about his medication? For the most part, Dr. Carrington knew his history and had kept her son safe.

Steven was ready for her. Quite firmly, he said. "We are going to India so that we can live like humans. We are getting out of this slum. Isn't that enough, mother?" I need to take a job. If you can't or don't want to go, you can stay here. I'll be able to afford a better place and cover food, clothes, and the other stuff you need to live."

"But Steven …" she was petrified of him being there alone.

"So, we're going to India? It's for a few years, and then, hopefully, we'll have enough money to come back and live like decent people for a very long time. Mom, I can save all the money I make, so we never have to live like this again. It's a real opportunity."

Finally, his mother agreed to go. She hoped that their life would be better, the way he said.

After further negotiations with Albert McKerny, Steven accepted the job at $400,000 a year plus benefits. He would be on his way to India.

*   *   *

It had not been easy convincing the 4Cs that this was a good move for them. They believed Steven was selling them out for his own career. They feared it was a trap, and it would not be good for the group and American jobs in the long run. Steven, however, swayed the leadership group that he would still be a strong ally of the 4Cs and that he would be bringing jobs back to the United States. "As an inside man," Steven emphasized, "I can be more effective." Steven persuaded the members and wound up believing himself that he could do all that he promised.

Cucumber Water

INGREDIENTS

- 1 Cucumber
- 1 Quart purified water

PROCEDURE

Slice a whole, unpeeled cucumber into a quart of purified water in a pitcher. Chill covered for at least 20 minutes.

Serve with a slice of cucumber as garnish.

Chapter 6

ON THE ROAD AGAIN

Once home in the city, Melanie looked forward to a quiet week of planning and packing. She was thinking about the horse shelter and her trip to India, but especially about the challenges of redesigning a palace.

"Guess who?" Lars practically sang on the phone.

"Hmm, let me see."

"Let's talk about the Rajah."

By his tone, Melanie wondered what was up. Ready to take him up on his mystery, she said, "Yes, let's do."

Lars continued. "Now, don't be upset, but the Rajah wants you to arrive in Delhi this week. His film wrapped early, and he is free to begin the palace redo and wants to begin right away."

Melanie practically shrieked, "Please tell me you're kidding!"

"No can do."

"Damn! This is annoying. I was looking forward to a quiet week of thinking and doing."

"Best laid plans," Lars said. "Anyway, it is time for you to get back in the game of life. Etihad or Emirates?"

"Neither. Or I don't know. I know I don't want to stopover. I want to go straight through. How about KLM? How about a direct flight from JFK or Newark?"

"Not to worry. I will find a non-stop to New Delhi. There must be one, right?"

After settling on a nonstop and praying there was one, Melanie said goodbye to Lars, who'd called back with the details and breathed a deep sigh. It must be nice to have people at your command. She started thinking about the young Rajah. The Rajah title was an honorific, but Shiv Kumar's movie star status was real. He's impatient as he was very anxious to learn about the renovation she'd been planning. This was the twenty-first century, so she wondered why she couldn't have sent him a file and Zoom instead of rushing to India. She understood that this project was very important to the Rajah, but….

It was obvious he'd retained all the entitlement of his heritage, one of the last heirs of the powerful line of Rajahs who ruled India before England colonized it. So, what choice did she have? It was important to him to preserve the history of his grandfather's palace, and she was the one he'd chosen.

Young and flush with money from his starring roles in Bollywood hits, the Rajah spared no expense or effort to bring Melanie to Delhi as quickly as possible. She found herself becoming excited, despite the hurried-up departure date. Bollywood, she thought. How magical. Before taking on this design assignment, she didn't know much about Bollywood, except superficial public information. On her first visit to India, several years before, she'd been in Mumbai, Bollywood central and the home of the largest film-producing studios in the world but never made it to Bollywood. Now, because of the project for Rajah Shiv, she wanted to know more about the glitz and glamour of India's film industry.

The Rajah had promised to give her a personal tour and thought it would inspire her as a designer. The name Bollywood, he had explained, was a combination of Bombay (now Mumbai) and Hollywood and referred to the Hindi movie industry. Early Indian producers, directors, and actors hoped that Bollywood would become their Hollywood, where their stories were brought to the screen and where people became stars. This had certainly happened, and Bollywood, the number one moviemaker globally, produces almost a thousand movies a year. Shah Rukh Khan, the reigning star of Bollywood, had made her client, the Rajah, the new face and heartthrob of Bollywood Cinema in his latest Red Chili Production, *Chulta Hai.*

Shiv, from his pictures, was a very handsome young man who had surprised his family and the public with a talent for acting. Now he'd joined the ranks of Hrithik Roshan, Amir Khan, and the legendary Amitabh Bachchan as a movie idol. He was single, and industry gossip was that he was shopping around for a *rani*— a wife. Melanie wondered whether he would take multiple wives, which she thought was still permitted in Hindi. She could never understand why anyone would want more than one spouse. To her, even one was hard to handle.

A day later, as she waited in the first-class lounge at JFK, Melanie pulled out the photos and AutoCAD drawing for the palace to study them. It was a rather small structure, at least for a palace, less than 100,000 square feet. Most of the architectural renovations had already been completed, and they would be the foundation of her interiors. After finding her glasses, Melanie sketched and filled in colors as she sipped a glass of merlot. Starting with a base of black, ochre, and white marble, she added brightly colored tones and shapes that echoed India. It was indeed one of the lands where color permeated the landscape and the culture, from the colorful spices and saris to the Mughal buildings in deep, burnt oranges.

"Madame," a sophisticated Indian woman said as she passed by Melanie. She was peeking over her shoulder. "That is a most striking rendition of the Kumar Palace? The old Rajah, bless his soul, has died and left everything to his only grandson."

Surprised, Melanie looked up, masking her slight annoyance at being interrupted. However, this woman looked so sophisticated and seemed knowledgeable about the culture of the Rajahs that she wanted to hear what she had to say. "Yes, are you familiar with it?"

The woman continued, "Indeed, I am. "I went to many wild parties there. Are you to have full access to the palace?" Melanie wondered if the woman had used the rendition to connect with her regarding the palace. "I'm Lata," she continued. "I understand the palace will be going through a major renovation. It really needs it. But someone must document what is referred to as "the glory days of India. I'm glad Shiv is doing so."

The woman sat down in an empty chair. She gave Melanie the historical highlights of India from the 1700s until the 1940s. The 40s being a period of dramatic change that ended Great Britain's rule over India, ushering in its independence and division into India and Pakistan. She said, "Indian kings, back in the days much like other royalty, adopted elaborate dress and rituals that conveyed their wealth and power. Their palaces were filled with the finest artwork and luxury goods made in their palaces, or commissioned by the court."

She went on to explain that the word "Maharajah," which meant "great king," was rooted in the concept of "king above kings." Use of the title Maharajah was formally adopted in the nineteenth century. After 1858 when India became a British colony, it came to be used as a generic term to describe all of India's male royalty.

Melanie enjoyed the history lesson but wondered if Lata had some other business to discuss with her. She seemed ready to begin another conversation, but the plane began to board. The women were separated, and Melanie knew that rather than talk with Lata, she had work to do as well as some much-needed sleep to catch up on. Melanie wanted to thank the woman for her informative story as they boarded, but Lata had disappeared. She didn't see her as she boarded the plane and didn't see her when the plane landed. Just a bit strange. She must be a historian.

As she settled into her seat, to get her in the right mood, Melanie plugged in her headphones and selected music by A.R. Rahman, the famous Bollywood music composer. His use of drum lines was inspiring. She began working as the plane departed and continued until dinner was served. Once dinner was over (including her polishing off the cool raita she couldn't resist), Melanie released the button for the bed. This made her feel wonderful about the world and new inventions. She switched the channel to her favorite relaxation music, golden oldies. Going back to her old-fashioned, sentimental roots, she started with vintage singers crooning Italian love songs before moving on to her lullabies and classical. An hour later, she donned her cool eye mask. She liked overnight flights and, thanks to her dose of Melatonin, had little trouble sleeping.

Melanie awoke in the middle of the night with a little start. The plane was quiet and dark. She was alone with her thoughts and found herself thinking about her life. Up until a few years ago, she thought she had an ideal life. She loved her work, her friends and colleagues. She was financially stable and had even loved and been loved. However, she did wonder why the people she loved seemed to leave her so early?

Her mind drifted to her parents. She felt their loss keenly and still missed them. Losing her father Nicholas to an aggressive and virulent cancer in her late twenties was shocking, and then her mother dying a year later nearly killed her. Nicholas and Dyana Eagleton seemed to have been made for each other in life and death. Melanie was comforted by a fact she believed with all her heart that they'd found a way to be together even after death.

Then came another cruel blow. A few years after her parents' deaths, the woman she considered her best friend and sister, and the man she had married, died. It seemed too much to bear. Had it not been for Lars's consistent support and encouragement, she may never have found her way back into the world, much less be on her way to Delhi.

Approaching the middle of her life, she had experienced more than her share of loss. She hoped she'd get to a ripe old age before she had to face death again, including her own. Melanie chided herself for having dwelt on the past for so long. She had accepted sadness as a part of life back then and would now try to embrace the life that had yet to be lived. No looking back would be her new mantra. Thanks to all the breathing, meditation and Lars's care, she had snapped back. Perhaps one day, love would find her again, but right now, she had to keep her wits about her and her mind on her business and this fantastic opportunity.

Deep breathing to the bells on her phone drew her back into sleep. Melanie pulled the soft white comforter over her. After that, nothing, until the pilot's voice announced they would be landing in New Delhi in about two hours. Thank goodness for Melatonin.

Once awake, Melanie went to the bathroom and splashed water on her face, brushed her teeth then dabbed on a bit of makeup. She managed to change her clothes, a painful exercise requiring her to twist and turn in the tiny bathroom to put on a pair of straight-legged black trousers with a shiny grey cotton shirt and suspenders. She changed into loafers and tied her hair into a ponytail. At the end of this changing experience, she felt like a pretzel.

Mel ate the light snack of chapatti and curd and tea. She stretched her arms over her head and was extremely happy to hear that their landing time was a mere one hour away. The landing was smooth, and once on the ground, as if choreographed, 300 people grabbed their iPhones. Melanie watched the chaos as the Apple "zombies" checked for messages and texts. To her surprise, her phone dinged. It was Lars wishing her lots of luck with her India project. She smiled and walked forward into her new journey.

Her journey began with intense heat, which was, for some reason, something she had forgotten about from her last trip. Here it was April, and the heat was already so intense that Melanie donned her wide-brimmed hat and sunglasses and wished that her pants were lighter and shorter with every step. She wiped herself off with a sweet-smelling towelette and ran towards the air-conditioned arrival building. She was trying to figure out why the plane didn't connect to the airport building as here she was trekking across the blazing tarmac.

The new Indira Gandhi International Airport was a welcome surprise. On her first visit, the airport was barely functional, and the service was dismal. But here before her, this gleaming airport with high-tech options and great service was very functional and comfortable. Flush with well-trained computer scientists, engineers, and cheaper workforce options, India became an attractive place to do business over the years, and it was visible in the economic strides the country had made in the past twelve years, at least here at the airport.

Melanie made her way to baggage claim. As she waited for her luggage, she saw a man in a turban holding a card with her name. Melanie approached him, "I'm Melanie Eagleton," she said, pointing to the card.

"Ah, yes. Welcome, madame. I will collect your luggage." He asked for her baggage claim tickets, and after retrieving the bags, he escorted her to a waiting limousine, got her comfortably nestled in the back seat, and handed her a bottle of water. She never realized how much she took water for granted until she guzzled the water in three gulps. Her escort handed her another, which she gratefully accepted.

On their slow-moving ride through teeming Delhi, Melanie again wondered how on earth so many people fit on the streets. It remained a mystery to her. Engaged by the sights, sounds, and the most extraordinary colors of this city, her imagination and creative juices fired up. Melanie couldn't wait to begin this new and exciting project. After miles of maneuvering in and out of bottlenecks, the driver finally pulled up to the hotel, and she was soon being escorted to her top floor suite in the Delhi Taj Mahal Hotel. Melanie was used to opulence (she was a designer after all), but this was on another level. The Taj Mahal brand, recognizable no matter where in the world one was, obviously paid special attention to cultural details here, and it was exquisite. The new building echoed the same grandeur of the original Taj in Agra, with lots of marble, columns, fountains, and spaciousness everywhere one looked. The fabrics, tapestries, and art spoke of India's grander days and proud heritage.

Melanie loved her suite. It was quite lovely. The small stained-glass details on the windows added to the lush drapery, exquisite furnishing, and the king-sized bed draped with a satin duvet. She immediately checked and was glad the sheets weren't satin. She was always afraid she would slip and slide out of bed. On the coffee table was a goody basket of tropical fruits, including mangoes and guava, as well as crackers, nuts, and chocolates by the House of Grauer. Attached was a note for her to call the rajah as soon as she arrived. If this luxury kept up, Shiv would quickly become her favorite Rajah. For some reason, her mind focused itself once again on Lata, the smart, attractive woman from the airport lounge in New York who was curious about the palace's happenings. Would she see her again?

Looking longingly at the bed and fantasizing about the cool sheets and fluffy duvet, Melanie picked up the phone and dialed the number on the card.

"Welcome to India," the young voice that answered the phone was that of the Rajah himself. Did he really answer his own phone? Of course, he was a modern Rajah!

"It's good to be back," Melanie said. "Delhi has changed a lot since I was last here some twelve years back, but I can't believe you answer your own phone?" Melanie laughed, and so did the Rajah.

"Yes, I do. Why not? And yes, Delhi has changed a lot. Was the flight tolerable?

"Yes. Thank you."

"Good. I'll have you picked up around 8 p.m."

"Tonight?" Melanie sighed, looking lovingly at the bed. "But Rajah, I've just traveled for 15 hours, and I'm exhausted."

"You can call me Shiv, Miss Melanie. Sometimes it's just better to stay up to help your internal clock along. Tonight, I have put together a wonderful soiree, but it's six hours from now, so you have plenty of time to unpack and rest. You will be fine, and I promise it will be an unforgettable night."

Melanie, who'd wanted to keep her schedule light on her first day to minimize the effects of jet lag, sat on the welcoming bed. Oh well, so much for plan A! Plan B now included unpacking, a shower, sleep, and lots of water.

"Oh, by the way," the Rajah continued, "look in your closet. I have sent over some Indian formal wear. I believe you would like it. Tonight, you should look like an Indian woman for a change!" When he heard Melanie laugh, he chuckled too. "I know. I know. You're Native American Indian. Indulge me. See you at 8 p.m. then," the Rajah signed off.

Melanie opened the closet and stood spellbound, just staring at the regalia. Inside the closet were some of the most beautiful saris and accessories she had ever seen. And by gosh, the colors, the fabrics, sheer luxury! It just blew her away. Her first thoughts were, of course, how had the Rajah gotten access to her room, and how did he know her size? It could only be Lars. She bet he had everything to do with this, and once again, she blessed him.

Melanie rifled through the rack and chose a burnt orange sari with a lavender *choli*. Removing it, she hung it on a hook behind the door smiling at how pretty it was. She adored the way Indians mixed colors. Quite different from New York's uniform of basic black on black!

Melanie called the front desk and asked to be awakened at 6 p.m. After a quick shower, she and a couple of glasses of water, she slumped onto the welcoming bed, hoping to get some rest until it was time for her magic pumpkin to arrive. Climbing between the luxurious 1,200-thread count sheets and cool satin comforter, she could feel her body immediately drifting to sleep.

When the wake-up call buzzed, she frowned, turned over by no means ready to wake up. She pulled the cover over her head for a few more minutes then forced herself out of bed. "I can't wait to get back to you, my love," she patted the mattress dragging herself to the palatial bathroom that smelled divine from soaps and lotions. She tested a few, deciding on the lavender and sandalwood shower gel. Hopping into the hot shower for a refresh, she promised herself that in the morning, she would take the longest bubble bath ever, something she never had enough time to do because of her hectic schedule at home.

After showering, Melanie took a few minutes to unpack and hang up her clothes. She couldn't believe how unwrinkled everything was, and a good thing too because she hated to iron. Still a little groggy, she pulled out some beautiful sandals and ordered coffee. Promptly, there was a knock on her door, and a pot of coffee on a lovely silver tray appeared. Good, she thought. This will wake me up. And maybe next time, I'll order some cookies.

In the Air Raita

INGREDIENTS

- 1 medium cucumber, peeled, seeded and diced
- ½ medium onion chopped fine
- ¼ t salt
- 1 green chili chopped fine
- 1 small firm tomato peeled and diced
- 1 T chopped coriander leaves
- 1 C yogurt

PROCEDURE

Mix cucumber, onion, and salt together. Let chill for at least 5 minutes. Mix remaining ingredients and add to the cucumber mixture. Whip with an electric beater, chill again. Before serving, sprinkle with chili powder. Cool and serve.

Chapter 7

GILDING THE LILIES

Steven had been in Delhi a few months now. At first, he had a hard time adjusting to the bustling crowds, the live animals in the streets, the food, and the oppressive heat. While his mother cooked most of the time, they were provided a cook, a housekeeper, and a chauffeur. Life had gone from miserable to exciting and new in a short time. Now he was quite content for the life of luxury, which included his weekly massages. Then again, Steven always knew he was meant to have this kind of life. It just took some time to acquire it.

Steven was anything but a tourist. He didn't like sites, museums, buildings, stores, stories, any of it, so for the most part, he stayed in his office and at home, in the air conditioning and avoided everything, not to his liking: people, heat, street noise, food, and other foreign annoyances. Most of his coworkers were aghast that he didn't want to travel on weekends to see world-renowned wonders such as the Taj Mahal in Agra or the glitz and glamor of Bollywood in Mumbai, the Red Palace right in Delhi, and the others all a short plane ride away.

To his surprise, Steven got along with his co-workers and enjoyed his new work. The hardest part was trying to get used to the Indian-accented English and the wobble head movements which seemed to have some meaning he didn't understand. To his further surprise, he could even make out a few words in Hindi and found the Indians a friendly lot. Feeling satisfied with life, Steven had started skipping a few meds here and there. Still thinking about his promises to the 4Cs and McKerny, he observed every process and every procedure the Indians implemented. He now, too, understood why the people here worked for salaries no American would as they were working stiffs simply trying to feed their families, a fact he'd communicated to the 4Cs. He also assured the group that he'd find a way to make America win again. For a while, things seemed to quiet down on both continents.

Not a single soul at the call center could tell that Steven was different from any other expat. Even his mother had to admit that this move had been a good one. Perhaps they didn't ever have to go back. She could get used to this life without poverty and strife and with a calmer son.

Startling him, a voice behind him said. "Good morning, Mr. Orville." It was Vijay, his office assistant. "I have scheduled lunch with Mr. McKerny, who you remember is coming to the office this morning. I booked that restaurant famous for the curried eggs you seem to like. And here is the report you asked me to prepare."

"Thanks, Vijay."

"And don't forget, you and Mr. McKerny will probably be accompanying Mr. Victor Gupta to the Rajah's party tonight at the palace."

Steven nodded his head in acknowledgment though the Rajah's party was the last place he wanted to be. Hanging out with these well-heeled guys might be good for some but not him, especially since Victor Gupta, a well-known and wealthy call center owner, was one of the biggest offenders to the 4Cs cause. He owned the greatest number of call centers and had taken away the most jobs from America. In fact, he was one of the people Steven had steadily marched and picketed against. Though Steven rarely interacted with Gupta, he found him arrogant, privileged and entitled when he did. If Steven for a moment forgot his mission, all he had to do was remember that from Gupta, he needed to find a way to bring American jobs back home from India and make a name for himself.

Steven flipped through the report Vijay had given him. Humm, his brows knitted realizing his first report to McKerny would not be that encouraging. Based on his study, it would be far less costly to relocate Americans to India than bring the jobs back to America. With salaries, taxes, and health care costs, the average American worker would have to be earning four times what the Indians were earning to meet American laws and standards. He wasn't sure that claiming patriotism alone would work with McKerny. He needed to find more of a win-win situation. Still poring over the report, he was surprised when Vijay reentered his office to remind him it was time to get ready for his lunch meeting. He hurried to the washroom to freshen up. Steven had taken to using the bathroom in the executive wing.

*   *   *

McKerny and Gupta were talking in hushed voices. "We are prepared to renew our contract for another five years," said McKerny.

"It would be in my best interest to sign a ten-year contract."

"Things move too fast in technology for that, Victor. I am doing my best now to extend from three to five. Our CEO is under fire for outsourcing jobs as it is. This means I am on the line to deliver, so we need a ten-year priced contract for five years."

"I suppose I can understand since he sent you, the President, to negotiate." Victor could be quite persistent.

"Yes," McKerny said quickly, steering at the conversation in a new direction. "How is my new guy working out?"

"From what I hear, he's okay. Bright and intense." Gupta continued, "But, Albert, why on earth did you bring him here? Is he going to take over from your other guy? I can understand that he's tired of making these trips every six months, but some young guy with little call center experience?" Victor said provocatively.

Furtively looking around, McKerny lowed his voice further. "To be frank," McKerny said, "the reason he's here is because we had to get him away from America. He was a leader in the 4Cs group protesting American companies outsourcing jobs. He has actually protested against your company quite blatantly. You remember, they have picketed this location and the one in Mumbai twice so far, and it was all under his direction. Once he became a leader in the group, they became more confrontational. So, I figured that getting him out of the States before his success went too far would help us avoid the chaos and bad press. Orville thinks I brought him here to discover a way to bring jobs back to America." McKerny chuckled.

"You're kidding? He really thinks he's here to figure out how to bring jobs back to the States?"

McKerny nodded, and Gupta could not stop laughing.

"Not kidding. He was definitely stirring the pot, and because he is smart and people are angry, his followers took him very seriously. He was getting quite a following. He is our decoy. It's worth the money we pay him just to get him away from the protestors. And it's working. He's even working on a report for me."

Victor was serious again. "And just what will you tell him when he finds out that you were just trying to shut him up?"

McKerny was about to respond when his assistant buzzed him. He looked at his watch and hurried Victor to the door.

*   *   *

Their luncheon conversation was a little bit strained. Steven felt his dander rising as he was uncomfortable around the top executives and these two in particular. He did his best to maintain an ongoing conversation while outlining some of his ideas on bringing jobs back to the United States. Albert did his decoy bit by constantly steering the conversation to the night's festivities at the palace. They made it through lunch, Steven aggrieved.

After lunch, Steven told Vijay he was not feeling well and would head home for the afternoon to rest before the party. Vijay clucked around him like a mother hen, "Perhaps you are dehydrated. These air conditioners are as bad as the sun, you know. Drink lots of fluids. I have everything under control, so not to worry, sir. See you tomorrow?"

"Yes. Tomorrow."

By the time Steven left the office, he felt exhausted and slightly off-centered. But now he was looking forward to visiting the palace and the party tonight! Steven ran his errands and made his way home to prepare for an evening of palace festivities, as Albert McKerny had said.

Kerala Egg Roast

(Bess Chazhur)

INGREDIENTS

- 2-3 Vidalia or yellow onions sliced
  (the sweeter, the better)
- Canola or olive oil for greasing pan
- 1 green chili pepper, sliced into thin strips
- 1-inch ginger chopped fine
- 1 clove garlic chopped fine
- 6 small plum tomatoes, diced (or more if wanted)
- 4-6 hardboiled eggs, shelled
- ½ - 1 t red chili powder (adjust to your spice level)
- 1 t turmeric powder
- ½ t black pepper
- 1 ½ t garam masala powder
- Chickpea flour
- 2 t coriander powder
- Salt to taste
- 1 sprig of curry or basil leaves

PROCEDURE

Start by caramelizing onions in a well-oiled, non-stick skillet on low-to-medium heat, stirring every few minutes to ensure that browning doesn't happen too quickly. Once the onions get going, add the chili pepper, ginger, garlic, and diced tomatoes. Let get golden brown, and then add dry spices. Bring heat down to low; you don't want to burn the spices, just toast them. Add salt to taste and give a few minutes for the spices to "cook" and lose their raw taste. Add the hardboiled eggs whole or sliced, garnishing with the curry leaves or fresh chopped coriander. Serve over toast. Spices and leaves are available at any Indian/Pakistani/Bengali grocer.

Chapter 8

DINNER IS SERVED

Under most circumstances, Melanie loved parties, and even though this one was part of her work, it was an adventure, and she was looking forward to it. Unfortunately, she was still jet-lagged from her trip. Once she was nearly dressed, Melanie wrapped her hair into a bun and weaved a colorful hairpin through it. Dabbing her lips and her cheeks a burnished red, she looked in the mirror and said, "I'm done." In her best model pose, she was satisfied that even as tired as she was, she'd transformed herself into the consummate professional designer/world traveler. Then she yawned and ruined the entire moment. To no one, in particular, she said, "Too many miles, too little rest, go-team," and with a quick fist-pump to nobody, sprinted out the door.

Down in the lobby, she was greeted by one of the concierges, "I almost did not recognize you, Ms. Eagleton. You look like a beautiful Indian princess."

Melanie laughed out loud and said, "But kind Sir, I am. I am a Native American princess."

"Excellent," the elegant, well-dressed man said with a big smile. "We are honored, and your driver is waiting for you. Please let me escort you out," the man gave her his arm and escorted her to a waiting limousine. He held the door open as she slid into the car.

Bowing, he brought his palms together in a namaste gesture. "Goodnight, and please give my regards to Rajah sahib." Melanie recognized the more formal title and remembered that the Rajah sahib had told her to call him Shiv. She was honored.

At the palace, Melanie was greeted by a middle-aged man dressed in formal traditional Indian attire, as were all the staff. He pointed to a waiter holding a tray of champagne. "Shall I bring one over, or would you prefer to take it yourself?" Melanie thanked him and said she would wait until later, after which he escorted her over to another middle-aged Indian gentleman. "Miss Melanie Eagleton," the first man presented her. Then bowed. This was better than Downton Abbey, she thought.

"Welcome to the House of Kumar. Please follow me. The Rajah has asked that I give you a quick tour before dinner. On the way, I'll tell you a bit about what to expect tonight," he gave her his arm. Melanie, a veteran New Yorker, was not easily impressed, but she was blown away by Kumar Palace's staff graciousness. From the moment she entered the great halls, she'd observed the stunning architecture. As they started up the stairs that led to the palace's main floor, mirrors reflecting the candlelight from the sconces lit their way. Underlaid by quiet, hypnotic drumming, a single flute's haunting tune was beyond ethereal.

Melanie admired aloud the dramatic, traditional Indian floral hand-painted dhurries that hung from walls. She was crazy about flowers of any kind—fresh flowers, flowered patterns, anything floral, for a good reason. American Indian decoration venerated the flower in tiles, wall hangings, and rugs, especially in the first nation's ornate architecture. Back home, she'd buy an assortment of fresh flowers in different colors at the green markets to put around her Manhattan apartment and her cottage in New Jersey.

As they walked this "small" palace which was quite big, it was easy to envision the personal lives of Indian kings, their marriages, family relationships, and pastimes from the history she'd read. The old palace was not just a residence for extended royal households, but as a small city, it was intensely public and political and was where the state's business was conducted and court held. It housed troops as much as it maintained artisans' workshops.

As they entered the large garden surrounding the palace, a breath caught in her throat. Abloom everywhere was a kaleidoscope of flowers, from fragrant jardinières, bougainvillea, and night-blooming cereus to marigolds. It was a sight to behold. Melanie's love for flowers was fully satisfied. Benches surrounded the fountains in the four corners of the garden so one could sit and appreciate the absolute beauty of nature. In a smaller but stunning water garden, even in the dim light, Melanie could see reflections of the beautiful pink and white lotus flowers shimmering in the moonlit water. "Magnificent!" She said out loud and tightened her grip on her escort's arm.

"Now I understand my friend's love of the Lotus flower." She said to her companion. Melanie's looked closely at the flower, recalling the story her Indian colleague had told her about the lotus flowers. Several New York City designers had been invited to the New York Botanical Gardens in the Bronx. Melanie and her colleague Chitra had stopped to look at the lotus blossoms growing in the aqueduct of a picturesque building. Melanie had been staring at them when her colleague explained that the lotus was the national flower of India.

"Its beauty symbolizes divinity, fertility, wealth, knowledge, and enlightenment, yet it grows out of the mud."

Melanie had never forgotten her lesson on the lotus and its deep meaning. She was glad the memory surfaced so that this important symbol of India could be incorporated into her design for Rajah's palace.

Soft wafting music accompanied Melanie and her escort as he took her up another flight of marble staircases. Off to the right, Melanie stopped for a moment, prompting her escort to do the same. "That's amazing," she pointed to a balcony overlooking the palace garden. It hardly looks in need of repair."

"That is because most of the new renovation has been completed."

"Ah yes. I see," Melanie said, then asked. "Where will the proposed museum be?" She thought it would be a shame to take apart an edifice this grand.

"Part of that has been completed, too. The outer structure, that is. I am sure you will see it later, but right now, Rajah Sahab Kumar is awaiting your arrival. You must not keep him waiting." He released her from his arm and began walking backward.

Melanie turned to thank him for the tour, but her escort was gone when she looked back. She walked a few steps and saw the Rajah at the center of a group of young, bubbling Bollywood starlets. If Melanie had been up on her Bollywood stars, she would have immediately recognized among them Priyanka Chopra, a stunning beauty who'd been Ms. Universe, Indian royalty Kareena Kapoor of the famed Kapoor family, and Salam Khan. Shiv had flown them in from Mumbai. What beautiful women, Melanie thought, looking from one to the next. If Shiv was looking for his *rani* to ensure his family linage continued, he didn't have to look too far. Melanie wondered which ones were intelligent, funny, and perhaps a combination of all the qualities a Rajah could want. Would he marry someone he handpicked, or would his be an arranged marriage? She was intrigued. Right now, to take the edge off, she could use a drink, champagne. Refocused, Melanie shifted her attention and went towards the Rajah Shiv. And the champagne.

Rajah Shiv was a fine figure of a man. Tall and erect, he looked elegant and every bit a royal. His thick black hair, nape length and his smokey eyes flecked with specs of brown were captivating. His sharp features were alluring, and he seemed charming and likable. He was wearing an elegant gold-trimmed, white embroidered Nehru jacket (everything old is new again) and *black dhotis*, loose slacks wrapped around his legs knotted at his waist, which made his star-quality radiance shine even more. His velvet slippers were the latest style.

Rajah Shiv looked up just as Melanie approached. A big smile spread over his face as he walked across the room to meet her. He reached for both her hands and kissed each one with a delicate little peck on the dorsal side. Melanie was charmed. "Miss Melanie Eagleton, you look even more beautiful in person. You don't know how much I've endured waiting for you," he said dramatically as he once again planted a small kiss on each of her hands and led her back to his group of stars. "Now that you have arrived, all the important people are accounted for," he winked, and the party can begin. Come let me introduce you to my friends."

Melanie accompanied him to the circle of friends milling around.

"This, my friends, is Melanie Eagleton, straight from New York. It is she who will be designing the interior of our palace. She is the best of the best designers in the world."

Melanie was sure she was turning several different shades of red.

The Rajah continued, "While at Columbia, I went to a few New York homes so exquisitely decorated I broke protocol and inquired about the designer. It was always Ms. Melanie Eagleton who had done them all! So, I tracked her down, and now I am looking forward to what she will do with Kumar Palace and Museum."

Melanie thanked Rajah for his appreciation of her work.

To the Rajah, she was perfectly charming. She could have been a contender for his rani if she had been of childbearing age.

There were hellos all around except from one beautiful woman who stared at Melanie for a few seconds before tentatively extending her hand. Melanie felt like she was being examined. Shiv quickly took her hand and said as he moved Melanie's away, "Do not mind that young starlet. I dated her once, a few years ago. Not now. Not ever again." Shiv continued, "Come, I want to introduce you around."

The Rajah led Melanie to another group of people laughing at a story someone was telling. Shiv introduced her to a Mr. Victor Gupta. As they moved down the line, Rajah whispered, "Stay away from him. He is considered a 'playboy of the Eastern world.' You might have heard about him. He's a big deal in India and owns many call centers here, you know, the ones America and all the other countries seem to hate. Except for India, that is." He laughed, knowing that there was truth in his statement.

Playboy Gupta and other owners were being threatened because of what was considered greed and avarice connected to the operations of their call centers. Melanie had heard that many of the center's workers were overworked and underpaid and that Victor Gupta owned the most call centers. The Rajah introduced the other people standing around, but the group broke up when waiters with champagne began circulating.

Melanie was overwhelmed by the enthusiastic reception, but she was happy to be welcomed. Though the group had splintered, Shiv and Victor were still hanging around. Though not wanting to stare, Melanie couldn't help but notice that Victor, about forty, was an extremely good-looking man. He had a disarming smile and a dazzling sex appeal. Melanie couldn't help herself; she felt a fluttering in her heart. She looked him up and down and decided that he was even more handsome than the young Rajah. He also projected a more grownup air and a spellbinding charisma that shouted danger. She was torn between the feeling of moving toward him or keeping her distance. She decided to move forward.

They shook hands again. Victor, like Shiv, took both of Melanie's hands and planted small kisses on them. However, unlike Shiv, he did not immediately let go. When Melanie looked up, she was captivated by his full-on gaze and found it hard to look away. Their gaze and hand-holding were interrupted by the approach of a young man and an older man. "Ah, here come some colleagues from America." Victor turned to shake the hand of a Mr. Albert McKerny.

"Albert McKerny," meet Rajah Shiva Kumar, our host, and Ms. Melanie Eagleton, his esteemed designer." He then turned to Steven, "and this is Mr. Steven Orville, who works for President McKerny and is here to help figure out the best outsourcing options."

Both men greeted the Rajah and Melanie, and the Rajah further engaged with Mr. McKerny. Melanie, in turn, spoke to Steven, who had not taken his eyes off her.

"How are you adjusting to India?" Melanie asked.

"Quite well," Steven answered, and the timbre in his voice surprised her. He had seen her somewhere, but where? As they chatted, he remembered…she was one of the people pictured in *The New York Times* article about the horse shelter in Long Island.

Melanie was glad to have fellow Americans in her midst, and she smiled warmly at the two men. The young man addressed himself to the rajah, "I am grateful for the invitation to this wonderful party."

Melanie could tell he was a bit nervous though he sounded sincere. At his age, she, too, had been intimidated by these kinds of surroundings. Recognizing the look of unease, she gave him a calming smile. Even with her experience, she found herself somewhat awed by the grandeur and luxury of the palace.

Steven smiled back and was glad he'd come to the party after all.

Victor led them over to a large, round table near the entrance, where he and his guests added their gifts.

"Did I make a faux pas? Answering Melanie's curiosity, Victor explained that a "gift table" was customary to acknowledge the host for their hospitality. Melanie nodded and remarked that this was also a custom in the United States, but she didn't think a bottle of wine from the hotel was appropriate.

"My dear, you are the gift."

Steven felt a bit agitated with how Victor was dominating Melanie's time. He loved the way she was animated and friendly.

Albert handed Victor a gift. "Since you leave tomorrow, we wanted to show our appreciation for all you do for our company."

"And for taking care of me," Steven added one of his own, which Victor dispatched to his room.

Melanie took a mental note of the very elegant "gift" marble table, deciding she'd keep it as a part of the redesign. "An amazing table," she was saying to the Rajah, as their attention shifted to a plumed man who appeared at the door with his gong to announce that dinner was served. Victor Gupta slid over to Melanie, took her by the elbow, and escorted her into the dining room.

*   *   *

To say what she saw impressed would be an understatement. The elegance was breathtaking. The elaborate and ornate table was set with the most beautiful gold-edged dinnerware and flanked by a splendid silver service where every detail of its design gleamed. These place settings looked like they had been in the family for generations and should be displayed in the museum. How wonderful! Melanie wondered how Shiv felt being the last Rajah of this magnificent heritage. After this party, the palace would be forever transformed as a legacy.

Melanie wondered too, how Indian royals, in general, felt about the Brits who had made their legitimate sovereignty only a legacy. The British who'd colonized India mid-eighteenth century had stripped away the enormous power of the Rajahs, transferring it to the "white" Rajahs of the crown. Though most had kept their titles and even their lavish palaces, their political power over India had drastically diminished. Melanie understood only too well this transfer of power and subjugation. Her people had been similarly undermined by the coming of the Europeans to America, so she understood displacement as much as Shiv, and she felt a tad sad. This was not the time to ask Shiv. Perhaps of some comfort was that his family still had all the trappings of their once opulent life—silver and gold, ornated artifacts, lavish clothing, an indisputable history, and so much more to show for his family's long reign over India. Her forebears, on the other, had either been killed by disease and firearms, run off their land, assimilated or marginalized. Those who resisted were confined to reservations.

Melanie admired the Rajah for his preservation work on the palace. Building a museum was the right thing to do. He had a right to feel very proud of his family and that their history could fill a museum and tell an admirable story to leave behind forever. The museum would showcase the power and pride of a dynasty and never let it be forgotten. Shiv, not one to lament what could not be changed, had added the whole Bollywood star dimension to his new legacy. Melanie was happy to be a part of the process.

Twenty-six people were gathered at the table, arranged "boy-girl, boy-girl." The men wore old-world Nehru jackets in various colors atop black dhotis. The women were all dressed in Delhi-style couture. Melanie particularly loved an electric blue sari that flared at the waist one of the guests was wearing and which flattered her stunning figure.

Before sitting down, Melanie walked over to the lovely woman. "I hope you don't mind, but I just had to tell you how amazing you look. That's a stunning sari."

The woman smiled at Melanie, and they shook hands. "Many thanks for the compliment, Miss Eagleton."

"You know who I am?"

"I've only heard the Rajah say your name a few dozen times in the past few days. We are all very excited about your work and how it will influence the palace's redesign."

"Thank you for your kinds words," Melanie smiled.

"The sari, by the way, is by Massaba. They are designers of the most luxurious sarees in India. Your sari is by Ritu Kumar, and may I say how lovely it is too?"

Melanie would have told her about Shiv's part in choosing her sari, but it was time for everyone to take their seats. Unsure of the reference to Massaba and even Kumar, she'd check out the designers online as she doubted she'd find them in the markets.

Thanks to Shiv, Melanie had fit right in, sparkling in her orange and lavender Kumar sari.

A server came around with pink champagne. Melanie could not, and did not, resist. She didn't think champagne was in great supply in India, so Shiv must have imported it and wondered what would happen if she asked for bitters to make a champagne cocktail. She imagined it would be promptly provided, but the soup arrived as she was mulling this over.

Melanie loved Indian food, but her palate was used to it as prepared in the United States. She didn't want to appear provincial but knew she would pay the price if she ate spicy dishes. She'd found that out on her last trip. The food looked and smelled divine, and because she'd taken Lars's advice and brought plenty of antacids and Pepto Bismol, she added a smidgen of each to her plate.

Melanie had barely finished her delicious mulligatawny soup (she was trying to figure out how to get the recipe for her soup collection) before a parade of never-ending steaming foods began. Melanie loved the puffy paratha bread, and even knowing it was going directly to her waistline, it took her no time to polish off a few squares. The main courses were so numerous she lost count, so she kept eating sag paneer. The spinach dish, her favorite food, was so fabulous she couldn't stop herself, but she was quickly reaching her limit. Her stomach felt like it was popping out from under the sari. She passed on the enormous panoply of desserts and fruits but accepted a cup of spiced chai tea. When served, she weakened it and added two teaspoons of the incredible rosewater custard served in a small Limoges ramekin. She just couldn't resist.

Table conversation was spirited. Melanie's eyes kept being drawn to Victor, who seemed always to be looking at her at the same time. So too was the young American who barely said a word. She wondered why he kept looking at Victor when the Rajah clapped his hands and rang the silver bell beside his plate.

Troupes of dancers twirled their way into the room to lively music from sitars, tablas, and tambourines. They led the guests like the pied piper into the garden and began throwing handfuls of colored chalk.

"What's all this about Rajah Shiv? I thought Holi falls between the end of February and the middle of March?" Melanie showed she had done her homework!

"It does, but we are extending it just for you. Isn't it lovely?"

"Beyond."

Holi, the jubilant Indian celebration to welcome spring, had been something Melanie had wished to see. Most colorful and exotic, the visual stimulation would normally spark her creativity, but she was getting a bit tired and didn't feel like doing anything but sleeping. Melanie had intentionally parked herself away from Victor Gupta, who seemed to be having a lot of fun, but once he spotted her, he dashed over to where she was standing, half-hiding behind Shiv.

"Are you going to be stuck to Shiv all night? His *rani*-to-be might get jealous." He again greeted her with such enthusiasm that one would have thought they had known each other a lot longer than two hours.

"And who would that be?" Shiv asked, leering at Victor.

"I just made that up," he said sheepishly, "so that I could dislodge Melanie from your side." Then he turned to Melanie. "Shiv talks so much about you. I think I fell in love before I met you. On a more serious note," he winked, "I wonder if you'd help me out with a little project. Really little." He sized it up with his thumb and index finger.

"What would that be?"

"I bought a few art etchings a couple of weeks ago. I want to know if they are as good as the dealer who sold them to me insisted they are."

First, Melanie smiled and then said, "Etchings? Are you kidding? I haven't heard that line except in really old movies."

They laughed, and then her designer's brain kicked in. She said, "Did he give you authentication papers?"

Victor and Shiv both smiled in appreciation of Indian reality. Victor said, "Yes, but in India, that's like getting an expensive brand watch from the Stanley Market in Hong Kong."

Not so good, she thought.

"Why didn't you get them appraised before you bought them?"

"It wasn't that serious, but since you are here."

Melanie's cell phone dinged. She had forgotten to turn it off. "I am so sorry. Excuse me," she stepped away just in time, missing the color bomb that landed on Victor and Shiv.

"Hello," she shouted over the din, making her way to a quieter place. She ducked into a room just off the garden, "Who is this? Colin? Colin who …" she said aloud. Then it clicked. It was Colin, the detective. The English Colin. Melanie was blown away with surprise. "Detective Colin Saint James Smythe. Is this really you? What in the world?" Melanie could not have been more surprised.

"Melanie. It is good to hear your voice. How are you? You sound fine."

"Colin, it's great to hear from you. I am fine. And I am back in the world of the living and working and happy to be doing so. How are you? What are you up to lately? And why, may I ask, are you calling? Is someone dead?" Melanie was sorry she had added that last line, but she was a New Yorker after all.

"Nothing is wrong, and nobody's dead. I'm well, thanks. Still in jolly old England."

Melanie loved his dry sense of humor. Dry and funny.

"I heard you were back to work. I called your office to see how you were and spoke with Lars. He told me you are working on a project in India."

"I arrived today. In fact, I am at a party with my client, the Rajah, at his palace."

"Incredible. Really, a palace. We have those here too", he joked. "Then you are busy. That's good. Get back to the Rajah. Shall we talk tomorrow to catch up? Shall I call you?" he laughed. "I just thought to check in, but we can chat another time."

"Colin, I don't know my schedule yet. Can I call you back tomorrow? How's that? I might be less jet-lagged then too."

"I was just checking in. We haven't spoken, except for a few short 'how are you' calls since I returned to England. For some reason, you popped into my mind. Probably because I am now undertaking a new project."

"Let me get back to you tomorrow so we can talk. I will bring you up to date. Okay?"

Colin agreed, and they said their goodbyes and disconnected.

Melanie was more than curious about why he'd called. But that would have to wait until tomorrow. They'd met in the States where he was working on a special assignment, which happened to be her best friend's murder case. His work was focused on Marco, but he had been very kind to her. Melanie remembered that even after he had discovered that her husband was the killer, he'd been most understanding. She had grown close to him during her time of grief, and when he returned to England, he'd checked up on her once or twice. Melanie suddenly found herself going down memory lane and quickly snapped back to the present.

Seeing she had completed her call, Shiv grabbed her by the elbow and proffered his arm. She laughed, dropped the phone in her purse, and looped her arm through his arm. As they were walking back inside, Victor cut in and said with a smile and a wink, "Rajah, please take care of your other guests. I will attend to this one."

Before she walked off, one arm looped through Shiv's and the other through Victor's. Melanie noticed the woman who had hesitated to meet her and the younger American talking.

"Well, well. Isn't this very nice," Melanie said as both men walked her back to the dining room where the other guests had reassembled. A glance into the courtyard, and Melanie noted the mess they had made for Holi had magically disappeared. The dining room table had been reset for their even more elaborate desserts and spirit's course. On the back of each attendee's chair was a flowing white garment for guests to slip on over soiled attire from the Holi extravaganza. The Bollywood crowd had changed attire completely.

While the guests enjoyed the festivities, the household staff was busy arranging gift boxes on the marble table that previously held Shiv's gifts. She'd never seen a more efficient staff.

McKerny and Orville, the Americans, graciously accepted their gifts, said their goodbyes and left the party. Other guests expressed their gratitude, as did Melanie, who was given a tiny box. Victor proceeded to open his box, and Melanie didn't know how he managed it, but he popped what seemed like a dozen candies in his mouth all at once. The chocolate high was instantaneous and contagious for both him and Melanie as they laughed their way somewhere.

Mulligatawny Soup

INGREDIENTS

- 2 T butter
- ½ C chopped onion
- 1 clove garlic chopped
- 1 t curry powder
- 4 t flour
- 1½ C light cream
- 2 10-oz cans chicken broth
- 1 C chopped sour apple
- 1 C chopped, cooked chicken

PROCEDURE

Sauté onion and garlic in the butter until translucent (about 10 minutes). Mix in the curry powder, flour, cream, and broth. Stir over low heat till slightly thickened, then add the apple and chicken. Continue cooking 10 minutes, and serve.

Chapter 9

INDIAN ETCHINGS?

Melanie's long plane ride helped along by the champagne and food was catching up to her in a big way. As she walked, she stifled a yawn and declared her departure imminent.

"What about the favor, I asked?" Victor said innocently.

"What favor?" Melanie stifled another yawn

"Looking at the etchings," he said, bound and determined to have her examine his artifact.

"Victor, I truly cannot stay. I am exhausted beyond words and need to go back to my hotel."

"But the night is still young, and so are we."

Melanie looked at his lovely face and gorgeous eyes and said, "But, I am falling over my feet. I need to get some rest if I am to be of any use tomorrow."

Looking disappointed, Victor said, "But it won't take long, I promise. Please. I do want you to see them. I would love your opinion, really I would."

Melanie looked at him pleadingly and said, "Oh Victor, I'm tired and jet-lagged. Can't it wait until tomorrow?"

Shaking his head, Victor said, "No. Please. I'm headed to New York tomorrow to see my biggest client. If they are authentic, I want to take him one of the etchings. Please, just for a few minutes. It won't take much time. I'm staying at the palace tonight, so you're already here, and my room is only steps away. I would truly appreciate it."

Melanie sighed, as only a kind woman can do. Trapped again. Victor led the way to a small elevator at the end of the hall. Dragging herself slowly behind, she was so slow that Victor turned around, grabbed her by the arm and led her into the elevator. Melanie thought to herself, how relentless he was. No wonder he was so good at business.

Glad to have the extra support, Melanie leaned heavily on his arm as they walked down the hall to his room. They entered the guest room, and Melanie was immediately sorry she hadn't taken Shiv up on his offer to spend the night. This was a bedroom! Glorious, plush and exquisitely appointed. The colors of the room were bright and inviting. The furnishings were light and airy. There seemed to be dozens of pillows in a rainbow display propped up against the large pillows against the bed's headboard. Vases of fresh flowers in a variety of sizes added to the beauty of the room, and the floral aroma was soft and subtle. Not only was the room huge, darn near the size of a football field, but it was dominated by the most inviting and enormous four-poster bed she'd ever seen. She thought, if Victor would only disappear, she would gladly crawl in and get some much-needed sleep!

Victor walked to a nearby table, marble, of course, and looked at the beautifully wrapped gift that had been delivered. On the table were also what appeared to be several of his etchings. Melanie said to herself; he really does have etchings. It wasn't a pickup line!

"Ah, the etchings," Melanie said, teasing him.

Victor was anxious to show them to her. "Yes, here they are. Before I take one of them to New York, I want your frank opinion. Shiv said you had exquisite taste and knew a lot about art."

"I do about some."

"And, if I am allowed to say, you are a lovely woman, and Shiv didn't exaggerate, which he is sometimes prone to doing."

"Well, thank you for the compliments. But Victor, I am exhausted, and I am not an appraiser. I will do my best."

"Who is the artist?" Melanie asked.

"Haren Das? He was a master of Indian etchings, actually drypoint etchings. According to the dealer, they were done in the early twentieth century. He was not just a great artist; he was a teacher, and here's something you will appreciate. He was one of the first Indian artists to include women among his students. His work is hanging in many museums, and I am lucky enough to have an art dealer who acquired three of his incredible etchings."

Melanie opened her purse and put on her reading glasses. She picked up one of the etchings and looked at it for several minutes. Even though she had only seen one or two works of Das's work, she immediately knew it was genuine.

The etchings were superb, and as she pored over the other two, she said to Victor, "these are in really good condition. Whoever had these before took very good care of them, and they are wonderful examples of Das's work. You are fortunate to have them. They will make a wonderful gift to your client. I hope they'll appreciate how lucky they are."

Victor was smiling from ear to ear. He dropped the etchings and took Melanie's hand, and kissed it. As he started to move his lips up her arms, Melanie pulled her hand from his and laughed and said, "Victor, please. Even if I wanted to, I don't have the energy to kiss you back."

Victor was quick with his return. "I know exactly what will give you a second burst of energy." He walked to the other side of the table and opened one of the delivered packages, seeming to know what was inside—delectable-looking candies. "Here, have one. They are very special. Gilded chocolates. From my clients, who came tonight and why I had them sent up to my room. I am a certified chocoholic, and this is the best money can buy."

"I have a box of my own, thank you."

"But not these. I assure you." Victor said, popping a few into his mouth. Back to his more serious self, Victor held up one of the etchings, "I am so pleased that you are impressed by these."

"Thank you for insisting I see them. This was quite a treat." Melanie said, glad she had taken Victor upon his request to view his etchings.

"Anyway, I must go." Fifteen minutes after her arrival, Melanie was ready to take her leave. Before she could take a step, she felt Victor leaning into her, holding her from behind. Melanie, too tired to fight but wanting to keep the moment light, said with a laugh, "excuse me, sir, my back is not a bed." When Victor didn't move, Melanie, now quite annoyed, spun around to confront him.

"Help me," his voice was weak.

Melanie immediately realized that Victor wasn't joking.

"What's wrong?" Melanie held up a collapsing Victor.

"I think I am sick." He was barely audible, then lost his balance, grabbed his stomach, and fell to the floor. He writhed in pain and kept repeating, "help me." Moments later, he tried to stand up to head to the bathroom but vomited before he could get there. Melanie looked over at the heaving man and saw what she thought looked like blood coming from his mouth. Then he fell over again. "Victor, Victor, tell me what's the matter? Is it your stomach?" She grabbed him in time to break his fall.

He doubled over saying, "You must get me some help. I am in a great deal of pain. I don't know what's wrong. Please help me,

Melanie." He grabbed her arm with what little strength he had, and then he collapsed on the floor and was still.

With seconds and minutes passing, Melanie didn't know what to do. Melanie grabbed her phone and called Shiv. When he picked up, she screamed into the phone. "Please hurry to Victor's room. He is very ill. Bring help and hurry. Hurry!"

By the time Melanie turned her attention back to Victor, she was sure he'd stopped breathing. She began screaming at the top of her lungs, "Help us, please. We need help here." Victor did not move.

Gilded Chocolate

INGREDIENTS

- 10 oz bittersweet chocolate, finely chopped
- 1 14-oz can sweetened condensed milk
- 2 t vanilla extract
- Pinch of salt
- Sheet of edible gold leaf (available from www.gold-leafcompany.com)
- Sharp knife
- Clean, dry paintbrush

PROCEDURE

Prepare candy by combining chocolate, milk, vanilla, and salt in a heavy saucepan. Cook over medium-low heat, stirring, about 5 minutes until melted. Transfer to a shallow 9-inch x 12-inch baking pan lined with plastic wrap and spread evenly. Chill until set.

Cut away the desired portion of gold leaf with your paring knife or a sharp razor. You can use the brush to anchor the leaf down in an opposite corner so that the cutting motion does not tear the entire leaf.

Lay the gold leaf on the candy's surface and use the brush to push it down and get it to attach to the candy, and detach from the blade.

Use the brush to gently pat down the leaf and press it onto the candy so that it is in a smooth, even layer.

Cut the gilded chocolate very carefully into pieces. You can also cut it into pieces before gilding.

Note: Gold is inert, so it just passes through digestion.

Chapter 10

Help Is on the Way

Melanie was still screaming when, a second later, she heard someone rattling the door. She ran to open it, realizing then that Victor had locked it,

"Something's wrong with Victor," she shouted. He's not moving."

Shiv shouted, "What happened?"

"I don't know. He held his stomach and then just collapsed." She was still staring at Victor to see if anything had changed. Shiv leaned over and was quietly talking to him but got no response.

"Is he dead?" I inadvertently put lines through it probably shouldn't have said that, but she couldn't help herself. Victor looked dead.

Shiv dialed emergency. "No. His breathing is very shallow, and he is unresponsive, but he's not dead. Stay with him, please. Help is on the way."

He didn't seem to be breathing to her, but if he was, it was very, very shallow. Melanie felt as though she was in the middle of a very bad dream, again. Then all of a sudden, Victor moved slightly. "He's moving. Thank goodness, he's moving. He's not dead." Melanie grabbed Shiv by the arm and whispered.

Then there was what sounded like an army of footsteps, and suddenly, the room was filled with people. Mass hysteria broke out as some of Rajah's party guests began screaming. Then the room became a revolving door of people in and out. A young servant pulled out his cell and called emergency again, as Shiv had said they'd already been contacted. Just then, the faint sound of a siren could be heard. Victor was groaning and still clutching his stomach. He seemed to be turning a shade of blue.

Within a minute or so, three white-coated EMTs entered the room. Two of them began examining Victor, and the other approached Melanie and Shiv. He shook his head and said something Melanie did not understand. Shiv translated. "They are putting him on oxygen and getting him downstairs quickly. They say he is not in good shape."

Melanie said, "Well, I could have told them that. What's wrong with him."

"Do you know what happened to him?"

"I don't know what happened to him. It happened so fast." Melanie went on to explain about the big dinner, the etchings, and the candy. "Can't we do anything to help him?"

The technicians worked on Victor for several minutes before one said, "We can't do anything here. We've got to get him to the hospital." The technicians bowed to Shiv, hoisted the gurney, and wheeled Victor out of the room. Melanie and Shiv watched from the window as they put him in the ambulance.

As though seeing her here for the first time, Shiv said, "Melanie, what are you doing in here? I thought you were going home?"

"I was on my way, but Victor insisted I see the etchings he'd bought." She pointed to the marble table. "I agreed to see them for a few minutes because he was supposed to leave for New York tomorrow and wanted to give one as a gift to his client."

"Then what happened?"

"Nothing. After looking at the etchings, he tried to ply me with sweets, which I refused. There were two other etchings in his portfolio, and we looked at them. I was commenting on how elegant and valuable they were when Victor suddenly grabbed his stomach, my back and collapsed to the floor. He said he was dizzy. Then he threw up. There was blood."

"Maybe he ate too much or drank too much."

"This couldn't be indigestion, could it?"

"I doubt it." Shiv seemed truly baffled, as was Melanie.

"Maybe he's reacted to something that was served. But no one else seems to have gotten ill."

"Or to the chocolates. It was right after he ate them that he collapsed."

"Looks as though he ate a few too many of the *Soan Papdi.*"

They sat staring at each other, speechless and deeply worried. "I should go to the hospital," Shiv said. "Let me drop you home on the way."

Soan Papdi

INGREDIENTS

- 1 C garam flour (very fine chickpea flour)
- 1 C all-purpose flour
- ¼ C ghee (clarified butter - melted with solids skimmed off)
- ¼ t cardamom powder
- ½ C water
- 1 C sugar
- 2 T rose water
- Generous pinch saffron, crushed
- ¼ C grated or finely chopped pistachios
- ¼ C grated or finely chopped almonds

PROCEDURE

Combine both flours together in a wide bowl-heat ghee in a frying pan. Add the flour mixture and roast flours to a golden brown. Add cardamom powder and mix well. Remove from heat to the wide bowl. Allow to cool with occasional stirring. In a separate heavy saucepan, prepare sugar syrup by dissolving sugar and water. Continue heating with stirring until it reaches thread consistency.

You can check this by adding a drop of syrup to cold water. It should form a ball, which can be flattened easily when taken out of the water (Soft ball stage 234° to 241° F). Getting correct sugar syrup consistency is the secret of the softness of this treat. Now add the crushed saffron threads and stir.

Mix and pour the hot syrup into the flour mixture. Beat well with a fork until it forms flakes. Add grated almonds, pistachios and rosewater. Transfer it to a greased tray, cover it with plastic wrap, and pat it to 1-inch thickness. Allow to remain for 30 minutes. Now cut into pieces and serve.

Chapter 11

REFLECTIONS

Melanie was still sitting on the bed. She felt dizzy, and her knees were weak. Shiv helped her up. "This is all so dreadful. And on your first day here."

On the verge of collapsing herself due to shock and lack of sleep, Melanie rose to her feet. Before they could take a step, Shiv's cellphone rang. He looked at the text message. "Hmmm, it seems we are not leaving right away. The police are downstairs. I suppose, as per protocol, the techs called them. I need to go downstairs to see them. You should come too." He held her arm as they walked to the small elevator that took them back downstairs. Two detectives were waiting.

"Good evening, Rajah." They bowed deeply and made a namaste gesture. "We received a call from the technicians that a man was seriously ill. And that that man is Victor Gupta. This is an unfortunate turn of events, especially since we have been protecting him. Like many of the call center owners, his life has been threatened. We can't rule out foul play, so if it is okay with you, we'd like to have a look at the location where this happened."

"Did the techs say how Victor was? We were just on our way to the hospital."

"Give us just a moment, and then we'll all go to the hospital."

They took the small elevator back up to Victor's room, and with Melanie's help, Shiv explained the chain of events. The detectives asked about everything that happened at the party, the people who attended, the food and wine served, and anything else that might have been relevant to Victor Gupta's sudden illness. Shiv said that the kitchen staff would give the detectives samples of the elaborate dinner, including the alcohol served.

"That would be great," the men slipped on gloves putting all that could be evidence into clear plastic bags—the box of chocolate and even the etchings.

Once done, the men asked Shiv and Melanie if they would accompany them to the hospital or drive separately.

"I'll take my car. Miss Eagleton just arrived in India this morning, and she is terribly jet-lagged and in a state of shock. I will take her back to her hotel and join you at the hospital." Unfortunately, the detectives explained that that could not happen as a short statement from Rajah and Ms. Melanie had to be given tonight at the police station. He assured the Rajah that immediately after, she would be driven home.

"Very well. My driver will follow you. Then we'll take her home."

"So, we shall go to the police station before the hospital." The senior inspector informed his colleague.

"Yes," Shiv said, and the inspector nodded. "I'll join you at the hospital once I've taken Melanie home."

The police station was too warm and too dark. Melanie and Shiv were put in adjoining rooms. The rooms they inhabited were right out of 1940s American film noir. Still, he was Indian royalty, and she, as his friend, was treated with the utmost respect. Since this was a questioning, to Melanie's chagrin, they had to be separated.

Melanie's room was stuffy and lit with a single bulb dangling from a cord. The uncomfortable wooden chair was wobbly, so Melanie tried not to move too much.

An officer brought in a tray of hot tea and some biscuits. Melanie thanked him. Fishing an antacid from her purse, she drank the tea, hoping to settle her nervous stomach. While waiting to be questioned and knowing nothing of Indian law, it occurred to her that she was a foreigner caught up in something awkward. Melanie didn't know what to expect, though she felt confident Shiv would protect her. It was then that the potential seriousness of the case dawned on her. Worse, she was at the mercy of a foreign government with no legal support.

Feeling the constriction in her chest, Melanie though overdramatizing, couldn't help it! She could be a suspect! A man she was alone with became so sick he could be hanging on to his life by a thread. "Oy, this was not good." She hadn't realized that Victor's life could've been in danger because he owned call centers. Back in the U.S., she'd read in the papers that call center directors and owners, especially those in India, were often threatened, but she hadn't connected the dot that this could be foul play. How? How could all this be happening? Melanie truly hoped that foul play wasn't the case.

Perhaps Victor had suffered a heart attack or aneurysm. He seemed far too young and vibrant for those conditions. Melanie had just finished her tea when a sergeant walked in.

"Miss Eagleton," his smile was genuine, "I want you to know we are still waiting for information from the hospital. We hope that whatever happened, an illness or an attack, Mr. Gupta will recover. Once we have your statement, there will be no further need for your assistance tonight. The Rajah said, you will be staying in India, so we know where to reach you if we need to ask you anything further. Now, can you tell me what occurred?"

Melanie took a deep breath. "Here is what happened," she began repeating the story she'd told Shiv, the EMS and police. "I feel so awful for Victor."

Melanie finally came up for air, and even the detective felt sorry for her. He told her to take a sip of tea and relax if she could. He didn't want her any more upset than necessary. His Rajah, Shiv, had told them to treat her kindly, and they meant to.

"Yes, it is a sad situation. The hospital is checking for all the common conditions and for food poisoning and allergic reactions. They will do a complete workup, and we should know more soon enough. We are grateful for your cooperation. Rajah said that we need to let you go back to your hotel. He was adamant." The officer smiled to let her know that she was safe.

Melanie stood up and was led back through the dark hallway where Shiv's car was waiting.

The police thanked them for their time, and Shiv took Melanie by the elbow and steered her to his waiting car. They compared notes as the driver sped along. Melanie was grateful it was still dark.

"Are you going to be okay, or do you want to come back with me?"

"No, please. I want to go back to the hotel." Shiv nodded and directed the driver.

Melanie slumped back against the plush leather seat, exhausted. Shiv held her hand, and she dozed off the moment the car pulled away from the curb. When the car finally stopped in front of the hotel, Shiv gently tapped Melanie. She awoke with a start, looked around disoriented, said a quick good night and thanks and jumped from the car before he could move. Thankfully, the doorman led her inside.

Melanie awoke the following morning, fully dressed. She felt awful. She sat up staring at nothing in particular, the events of the night before swarming around in her head. If the phone hadn't rung, she would still be staring straight ahead.

"Hello, it's Shiv. How are you? Did you get any rest?"

"Shiv. I am still a bit groggy but tell me, how is Victor?"

"He is on a ventilator."

"That can't be good."

'I am at a loss," he said after breaking the bad news. They spoke for a few more minutes and hung up.

Melanie couldn't go back to sleep. She disrobed, took a shower and thought about popping a Melatonin but instead just got into bed. Between Victor's illness and her ever-worsening jet lag, her brain would not shut off. She tossed and turned for a few minutes before giving up. She got out of bed and began pacing from the window to the bed and back. What could she do to calm her anxiety? Melanie immediately thought of her maternal grandmother, who, when Melanie was anxious as a child, would bake bananas with cream to calm her down and make her feel better. She needed something like that now. Her eyes turned to the fruit basket gifted by the hotel. She pulled a banana from the basket, sliced it through the peel, added a package of honey from the tea service condiments, and put it into the microwave in her penthouse kitchenette. Five minutes later, she added a cream substitute from the condiments tray and took her anxiety buster to the balcony, where she sat down with a great sigh. Spooning the sweetness into her mouth, the memories of home helped her, and she could hear her breath slowing down. Melanie snuggled under the cool silk spread strewn over the chair and once again tried to recall the events of the past twenty-four hours.

Baked Banana

INGREDIENTS

- 1 unpeeled ripe banana
- 1 T honey
- Dash cinnamon or nutmeg if desired
- Heavy cream if desired

PROCEDURE

Slice the banana end to end through the peel. Open the peel enough to drizzle the honey end to end. Bake 3 minutes in the microwave on high. Spread opening and pour cream over the banana.

Chapter 12

Breakfast for One

Steven and several of his colleagues arrived early to work. The place was in a state of chaos as people milled around whispering news about Victor Gupta's unfortunate event. Steven and his co-workers didn't seem overly distraught about the tragedy that played out at the Rajah's palace, and they did not join in the conversation. Steven went to his office and thought about the chain of events. This India was quite something else. Then his mind turned to the beautiful woman at the party. At first, he thought she was the only white woman there, but it turned out she was an American Indian with violet eyes! She intrigued him, and what a stunner! Steven was beginning to appreciate that India afforded him a significant change of fortune all around. One that had him in company like the Rajah. His mother would never believe it, and he did not tell her.

Today, his anxiety stemmed from not knowing what would happen to the company and that his contract would end sooner than he'd like. However, a few call centers less were part of the plan. His co-workers were directing their anger at their bosses, locked in a conference room, trying to figure out the next steps.

Steven walked back to the break room. Workers, sipping their coffees, we're taking comfort in each other. When Steven mentioned that he had been at the Rajah's party, everyone asked questions. He told them the truth. He had no idea what happened after he and Mr. McKerny left the palace. Making his coffee, Steven retreated to his office. When alone at last, sipping his strong coffee, Steven mulled over the Rajah's party. He had never been in a home like the palace and was immediately impressed with the powerful Rajah. Envious of his lifestyle, riches, power, and youth, he thought of all the dismal days and nights he was forced to live on the Lower East Side after he'd been fired. He believed he was owed all the luxury for his suffering and humiliation. Finding the 4Cs had allowed him to direct his anger into a productive outlet and the opportunity he now had to improve his lot in life. He'd even met the beautiful and unforgettable Melanie Eagleton.

Finally, he picked up the daily newspaper and, on page one read, the headline: *CALL CENTER TITAN RUSHED TO THE HOSPITAL*. He had it coming. Little did Victor and McKerny know that Steven had overheard their conversation about why he was there. It truly galled him. Here were these people living in the lap of luxury while qualified Americans were barely able to eke out a living. He wondered what the company would do next if something really bad resulted from this debacle. The article was vague after the roaring headline, giving no further details. Steven drained his coffee cup and leaned back in his chair.

*   *   *

Across town at the LaLiT Delhi Hotel near the Jantar Mantar area of Delhi, Albert McKerny sipped his black coffee. He needed coffee this morning because today was the day he would be renegotiating the contract with Victor's people. He was surprised at how little he felt when he'd heard the news that Victor was gravely ill and there was uncertainty about his survival. He'd been annoyed for a long time that his CEO had felt he, the President of the company, needed to handle the renegotiations himself because Gupta insisted. His Vice President would have done just fine.

Picking up the report Steven and his team had submitted, he flipped through the pages and had to admit that Steven's team was smart. Their clever analysis suggested that instead of just outsourcing jobs to India, there could be a compromise and a collaboration that made sense. Why not rotate American workers every three years to work alongside Indian workers in a 1:1 ratio. It would be cost-effective, which even McKerny couldn't deny. A fifty percent labor cost savings would be sufficient to make a healthy profit. This solution had social currency, too, something the company could use. He flipped through the proposal again. Hell, it would be more like seventy-five percent savings as living in India was far cheaper than in the USA.

Additionally, if he kept Steven and his team on until the project planning was finished, he wouldn't have to keep coming back and forth. Once Steven was replaced by a steadier, more senior man, all would be finished. This proposal had legs.

McKerny sipped another mouthful of coffee and dug into his breakfast of roti and dosas with spiced potatoes. For dessert, he popped several candies from his gift box into his mouth. A few minutes later, he felt his head pounding and pains becoming more severe by the minute shooting through his stomach. Was it the Indian's rich and spicy food? McKerny went into the bedroom, his intent to take a couple of aspirins and some antacids to settle his gut. Before he could open the bottle of pills, McKerny fell to the floor.

*   *   *

Melanie was startled by the sound of her phone. She answered and heard Shiv's voice. "Hello, Shiv. I am beginning to 'un-jetlag' and feel better."

"I waited as long as I could," was all he said.

From the tone in his voice, Melanie knew something was wrong." "What's happened?"

"Victor died a few hours ago."

"Oh, dear God." Melanie's right hand flew to cover her mouth.

"He had a hemorrhage that caused him to have major convulsions, and then he died. Just like that! I wanted to call the moment I found out, but…" his voice got wobbly. "I just can't believe it myself. We've been friends for a long while. They don't even know what's going on. That's the hard part. I don't know what to say to his family."

"Shiv. I am so sorry. I liked Victor." Melanie always tried to think of words of consolation at times like these. But there was nothing to say.

"The doctors are perplexed. I suppose now they'll do an autopsy and try to get to the bottom of this. The police haven't ruled out anything, including foul play. I find that strange, but it's a known fact that Victor and the other call center owners have enemies."

Melanie listed without saying a word. Shiv needed her ear.

"Victor always knew how to make money. He was a genius at it, in fact, and equally as good as a philanderer. It's not hard to imagine a man in his position making enemies in business and his private life. I understand that a lot of his ex-girlfriends are riled. Now I think back to something he'd told me recently. He'd received death threat letters. I remember us speculating about which of his women would go that far. Victor had taken the threat serious enough to contact the police, and as we found out, they were protecting him. Not so well, it seems." Shiv's voice dipped at the end of that sentence, and then he said quietly, "Melanie, you were the last one to see him alive and well. Any ideas?"

"I can't think of anything. Not a single thing. But then again, I'd just met the man. I can't believe he practically died in my arms. Frankly, I am still stunned." A very scared Melanie asked the next question, "Shiv, if I were the last to see Victor alive, do I need a lawyer? I am a foreigner in a foreign land. What should I do?"

Realizing how frightened she must be, Shiv reassured her that she most likely did not need a solicitor. "I can't imagine how anyone could suspect you of anything. And, as you said, you'd only met Victor on the night of the party. What would be your motive? Victor was still very much alive when he was moved to the hospital, so I don't think you have a thing to worry about."

Then the Rajah changed the subject. "This may sound crazy, but if I don't keep my mind occupied today, I will go mad. Are you up for doing a small bit of work on the palace?"

"Absolutely. Work is always a good option for people in shock."

Melanie thought she could hear him smile, and she asked quietly, "Shiv, are you going to be all right?"

"I am not now, but I hope I am going to be once time passes and we have some answers."

"Okay. I'll need a bit of time to gather myself so should we meet for lunch here at the hotel at 1 o'clock? I'll review the drawings with you then. I may even have some other ideas from the photos I took at the party."

Melanie decided against room service breakfast. Today, she needed to be around people, so she threw on some clothes and headed outside. It was still early in the morning, and the lobby was empty. She nodded to Mr. Rashid, who'd escorted her to her car on the night of the party. He waved back. Melanie made her way to the only restaurant in the hotel serving breakfast. How she wished for something familiar, but pancakes, eggs, and bacon were not on the menu, so she ordered coffee. At this moment, she wished she could blink herself back to the States. Fishing about in her bag to find her phone, to her delight, she found something comforting. Homemade granola bars she'd made in New Jersey to take on the plane. Hurriedly, she unwrapped one and took a generous bite, savoring the familiar taste of home.

After some more coffee, Melanie wondered if it was prudent to have a lawyer anyway despite Shiv's reassurance. At a minimum, some legal advice couldn't hurt. Mulling it over, her intuition, which she always trusted, told her she wouldn't need one at the moment. No one knew what happened to Victor, but she could use some expert advice to make sure she did things right. She decided to call Colin. She owed him a call anyway, and since he was a Scotland Yard detective with international experience, he would be able to advise her.

Melanie scrolled her address book on the phone, and there Colin was on her contact favorites list. Melanie and Colin were friendly acquaintances and trusted him, but why had she put him on her favorite list? Huh, she paused before punching out his number. Since the restaurant was empty, she wouldn't disturb anyone.

She let the phone ring two or three times, then did she look at her watch. *"Oh, good grief,"* she said to herself. *It was 7:30 a.m. in Delhi, which means it was 3:30 a.m. in London.* Bad etiquette on her part. She was about to hang up when he answered.

"Smythe here. How may I help you? And, at this time of the morning, this had better be good?" said the calm voice.

If someone had called her at 3:30 a.m., she wouldn't have been that calm. Melanie supposed that being a detective, he was used to calls at all hours of the day.

"Colin, it's Melanie."

"Well, it's early, but you did say you'd call," he deadpanned.

"I am so sorry to call you at this hour, but I need your good advice."

"Really. I just spoke with you a little while ago. What could have happened in such a short time that you need my advice?"

"Colin, someone died at the palace event I was when we spoke. I was the only one in the room with him when it happened. Nobody is sure whether the death was of natural causes or otherwise, and I am not being accused, but I'm not sure what's the right thing to do legally. Do I need a lawyer? Indian or American? Help."

"Are you all right?" Colin's voice was serious.

"I am."

"Who died? Not the Rajah, surely?"

"No. A man named Victor Gupta. A mogul who operated call centers." She explained some of what had transpired since she had landed. She ended the explanation with, "I am sure I am not in trouble, Colin, but since I don't know yet what happened, I want to make sure I cover my bases."

"I understand. But what has happened with the incident so far that makes you think you need a lawyer?"

"I thought about it only when Shiv said, and correctly, that I was the last one to see Mr. Gupta alive. I was with him when he became ill and collapsed."

"Melanie, Shiv is the Rajah. And I am sure he knows that just because you were the last to see him alive does not mean you were responsible for his death. Plus, in so many cases like this, it's often someone close to the victim."

"Oh, he knows that and told me as much and that I don't need to take on that worry…but I'm American, you know, and I can't ….

"You should take one step at a time." He cut off her ramble. "Right now, it's too early to do anything. They will do an autopsy and many other analyses in an unexplained death. These things take time, especially in Delhi, so you must try to be patient."

"I know you are right, but you, of all people, know my history. Two years ago, what I went through left me sensitive about death, especially this kind of death. Perhaps this sounds childish, but the thought did occur to me, wild though it is, that it's me who's cursed or jinxed or whatever." When the garble spilled from her mouth, she knew it sounded nuts, but she was still a little sensitive.

"You may think you are cursed and all that, but I doubt it. Besides, my dear, you are still alive, which means the jinx didn't work!"

Finally, Melanie smiled. "Oh, Colin, how practical you are. But a man has died. And I was the only one there."

"Melanie, that's just being in the wrong place at the wrong time. It doesn't make you guilty of anything. However, I can certainly understand your sensitivity given the past, but when you look at the facts, those occurrences had little to do with you either."

Colin did admit one thing. "This does have a sort of *déjà vu* feeling about it, so please keep your wits about you." After a brief pause, he continued, "Let me do this. In my capacity as an international professional, I'll call the police and see if there is any reason for you to be concerned. If there is, I can fly over. I will call you when I have some news."

After they hung up, Melanie felt a little better. At least a professional crime solver believed she had no reason to worry. Would he fly over if there was a need? For her? Melanie didn't know why he would, but she felt comforted. With her appetite now completely gone, she signed the check for her coffee to her room and headed back.

Feeling more composed and less anxious, Melanie climbed back into bed, wearily fluffing the down pillows under her head. And she did sleep. The next thing she knew, it was four hours later, and her phone alarm was blaring. Emotionally drained as she felt, she knew Shiv was expecting her to be ready for work, so she hurriedly dressed, made herself up, and met him downstairs in the hotel's private business center to go over the plans for the palace.

Homemade Granola Bars

INGREDIENTS

- 2 C rolled oats
- ¾ C packed brown sugar
- 1½ C wheat germ
- 1 t ground cinnamon
- 1 C all-purpose flour
- ¾ C raisins (optional)
- ¾ C chopped walnuts, pecans, or almonds
- ¼ t salt
- 1 egg, beaten
- ½ C honey
- ½ C vegetable oil
- 2 t vanilla extract

PROCEDURE

Preheat the oven to 350° F. Generously grease a 9- x 13-inch baking pan. In a large bowl, mix the oats, brown sugar, wheat germ, cinnamon, flour, raisins, and salt together. Make a well in the center, and pour the honey, egg, oil, and vanilla. Mix well using your hands. Pat the mixture evenly into the prepared pan. Bake for 30 to 35 minutes in the preheated oven until the bar begins to turn golden at the edges. Cool for 5 minutes, then cut into bars while still warm. Do not allow the bars to cool completely before cutting, or they will be too hard to cut.

Chapter 13

IS NO NEWS GOOD NEWS?

Steven Orville and his team watched the news stories on repeat about Victor Gupta's death. This morning the hubbub caused more chaos than the day before. People were running around; some were shaking; others were crying, and others were sitting silently trying to process and accept that Victor Gupta was dead. Just as disturbing and scary was the latest news that rolled across the screen. Albert McKerny, a client of Victor Gupta and who was also at the Rajah's party, had died. There was a great and collective sigh from Steven's team as they sat stunned, staring at the TV screen. Both their bosses were dead.

One of the assistants filled in the details left out on the news ticker. "I believe they found him in his hotel room. Mr. Gupta had collapsed at the Rajah's party the night before, and Mr. McKerny died at his hotel just this morning."

*   *   *

That following day, Melanie awoke and shook her head to physically clear her mind. They had worked late into the night, and by the time she'd left Shiv, he was feeling better. She, too, was feeling better and hungry. She dialed room service.

"Good morning, Miss Melanie."

"Good morning. I'd like some yogurt with fruit and coffee, please."

"Madame, that is a wonderful choice. There is a hotel specialty called Tropical Yoghurt Parfait. Would you like to try that?"

"Great. Bring it on up."

Since the food wouldn't arrive for at least 30 minutes, Melanie decided to get ready for the day. The dial turned to warm; she stepped into the refreshing water. The scent of the frangipani soap wafted, bringing Melanie's anxiety level down a notch. That was wonderful, Melanie said out loud as she grabbed the warm towel and then wrapped herself in a fluffy bathrobe. Sitting on the dark maroon velvet bench in front of the mirror, she inhaled the steamy air in the bathroom. Breathing in deeply and focusing on her breath within ten minutes, she'd recentered and was ready to face the day.

Breakfast arrived almost on the dot to the thirty minutes she'd predicted. The staff wheeled a beautifully appointed table covered in the most vibrant yellow linen tablecloth. A stem of yellow orchids in a small vase sat dead center and completed the ensemble. An assortment of tropical fruits surrounded a tall parfait glass of yogurt. Melanie signed the bill, tipped the young waiter, and was eager to satiate her hunger. As she got ready to leave, the server said to her. "You were the lady at Rajah's house when one of India's big shots died."

Melanie just stared at him and was going to say something, but the young man beat her to it. "I know, Madam because I was working at the palace for the evening. I offered you a glass of champagne." He smiled, thanked her for the tip, and disappeared. Melanie looked at the closed door and was a bit taken aback. She didn't remember him at all.

Melanie was pouring a cup of coffee when the telephone rang. It was Colin Smythe, sounding a bit muffled.

"Hi, Colin."

"Hello. How are you this morning? Better, I hope."

"Much. I finally got a good night's sleep."

"Good. I spoke with the Indian authorities."

Nothing like getting right to the point, Melanie thought.

"And?"

"Did you know an American called McKerny? Someone who worked with the dead mogul?"

"McKerny? No. I don't think I know him. Should I?"

"He was at the Rajah's party."

"Oh, maybe. He could have been one of the Americans to whom I was introduced. Why?"

"He was discovered dead by a maid at the LaLit Hotel early this morning." Colin continued, "McKerny was a close business associate of Gupta's."

"Oh, my God," Melanie said before being struck silent. Then she continued. "I met two Americans who worked with Victor. Of what did he die?"

"No one has a clue."

"This is getting crazy."

"Seems like it, but right now, I don't believe you have anything to worry about. No one seems to know anything about anything yet. However, it just so happens that I have some work to do in Mumbai, so I can hop over to Delhi before heading out there. An Air India flight is leaving early tomorrow morning, and I will be on it. Would it be an imposition to ask you to book a room for me at your hotel?

"None at all," Melanie said, thanking Colin over and over again.

Five minutes later, the hotel phone rang. It was Shiv with the news that she had just received from Colin. McKerny was dead.

"Wow. I just met him."

"Yes. He was the older of the two American guys Victor introduced us to at the party."

"Same therapy as yesterday," Shiv asked.

"Yes."

They arranged a time to meet. Melanie downed a much-needed cup of coffee, finished her yogurt and dressed. She decided to walk to calm her nerves and clear her head. She missed her morning runs, and for three days now, hadn't done any exercise. She needed to find an exercise substitute that fitted India.

Melanie stopped by the registration desk and reserved a room for Colin on her way out. Walking out into the crowded streets, Melanie began to think over recent events. After a splendid party with so many important and well-known individuals, two men died—two businessmen from the same industry. One of the companies is being accused of stealing jobs from other countries. Were these deaths connected? Coincidences?

Melanie tried to distract herself for a little while. Remembering from her last visit, she turned in the direction she believed would lead to some of the most interesting Indian markets in Delhi.

Yoghurt Parfait

INGREDIENTS

- ¼ C each diced papaya, fresh pineapple, mango, and lychee
- 1 C yogurt
- ½ t bourbon vanilla
- 1 T jasmine honey
- 1 T granola
- 1 t chopped pecans

PROCEDURE

Mix yogurt with vanilla and honey. Layer with fruit in a parfait glass and top with granola and pecans.

Chapter 14

THE SPICES OF LIFE

Without a map or a guide, Melanie decided not to venture too far from the hotel. As a precaution, she'd tucked the hotel card into her small leopard purse in case she got lost. If her sense of direction failed, she'd hop a cab instead of roaming the streets. Switching to shopping mode, she wondered why she'd brought such a small tote when she expected to make purchases. As a New Yorker, the city of schleppers, she was sure she would be schlepping today.

The Delhi of years before had changed a great deal, and the once resplendent city of Maharajahs had from their technology economic boom landed solidly in the modern age and was now a city of shopping malls. Delhi boasted the early stages of gentrification: empty, abandoned shops—a sign that the city, not unlike New York, was pushing the poor further away. The once diverse city neighborhoods now gone, Delhi felt no shame. Old and charming indigenous stores had been turned into small museums while others had given rise to western-style shops for tourists. Melanie hastened her steps past the tourist stores, preferring to trek areas of town that still held onto its history of outdoor markets and small personal stores that had once been so popular.

One thing hadn't changed. The streets were teeming with cars, bikes, wagons, pedestrians and occasionally, farm animals. After walking for a while in the blazing sun, Melanie found herself at the western end of Chandni Chowk, the main street of Old Delhi, very close to one of her favorite spice markets, the Khari Baoli (pronounced "curry bowly"). She knew she was going in the right direction when she saw the elegant Red Fort and another landmark, the Fatehpuri Masjid Mosque, at one end of the street. Gone were the hideous government offices and the beyond dreadful bus depot and nondescript shops. Melanie faced the mosque entrance and turned right. Remembering from her last trip, she followed the corner to the left.

At last, she was, among the narrow streets with little shops and stalls displaying the fruits, nuts, and seeds of the India she loved. The market areas were, as usual, full of everything from snake charmers to vendors with incredible and unique wares. Elegantly attired business-people and tourists with their ever-present camera phones, mingled in these areas for a taste of the old and splendid days, as well as the new and modern.

Melanie continued walking until she saw the vendors selling spices. She passed displays of Indian cinnamon, cardamom, cumin, anise seed, coriander, hot peppers, and ginger. Melanie was again mesmerized by the vivid colors—oranges, yellows, deep red, shimmering browns and all the earth tones and scents she loved so much. and scents. She wanted to buy everything.

A visceral memory surfaced as Melanie thought back to her mother's Cherokee-American kitchen, where spices added to the joy of cooking and the warmth of the special dishes made with love. Dyana Eagleton was a fine cook, blending traditional Cherokee recipes such as bean bread, grape dumplings, and corn pones with Indian pudding. Her Indian pudding was Melanie's favorite, and she made it often. Melanie smiled and made a mental note to come through again and mail back supplies for her kitchens before leaving Delhi.

These were the colors she'd use in her design of the palace, and she began snapping photos on her phone. With her excitement and the heat, she was sweating profusely. Reaching into her purse for a scented wipe, she mopped her forehead and neck. Why had she not remembered to bring bottled water?

A bit cooler, after a few more pictures, Melanie looked at her watch and realized she needed to get back to the hotel to meet Shiv. She passed a few food carts and was drawn by the intriguing aroma of what promised to be an authentic Indian meal. Maybe when she had more time.

Hurried as she was, Melanie couldn't help stopping at a window with an amazing display of antique and new jewelry. She forced herself to move on only to stop again at the window of an elegant sari shop. She made a mental note to come back to both stores.

Hoping not to be late, Melanie quickened her steps, reaching the hotel faster than expected. Unfortunately, she couldn't get close to the entrance because of a mob of screaming young women. Police, in hard hats with sticks, were holding them back. Melanie wondered what was going on. It looked like a scene from her attempt to see Bruno Mars. Then she spotted Shiv. All this was for him?

Melanie was impressed. The star himself exited his white stretch limo for just a few moments, waved to his fans, and went right back into the car. Melanie waved, thinking he would stop to pick her up. He did not. Confused but thinking he probably hadn't seen her, she walked toward the hotel.

As the crowd dispersed, Melanie was stopped at the door. She pulled out her room key to show a police officer, and he escorted her into the hotel. As she entered the lobby, she was met by two police officers who escorted her to an office. Her phone pinged with a text from Shiv. Laughing to herself, Melanie thought, what a burden stardom must be.

"Ms. Eagleton," the cop said. "Please come with us. We will take you to the Rajah."

From the office, Melanie followed the officers to a nondescript building a block from the hotel. Inside, Shiv was there looking tired and sullen.

"I'm sorry about this," he said. "I forgot the movie trailer dropped today. Usually, the Taj is where celebrities go when the movie drops. It's always that way."

"It's okay," Melanie said, smiling. "Fame is fame everywhere. But what are we doing here?"

"I know we were supposed to meet, but in light of Victor and Albert McKerny's deaths and the fact that both men attended my party, the police would like to talk with us again."

About five minutes later, an inspector arrived. He said, "Good day Rajah Shiv and madame," in a most respectful tone. He turned to Melanie and smiled. Shiv nodded, and Melanie smiled back. She'd grown fond of Shiv, even though she had known him for only a few days.

The inspector sat in a chair facing Shiv and Melanie and got straight to the point. "Do you both know the man who died at the hotel? Mr. Albert McKerny?"

Shiv was the first to answer. "No, I didn't know him personally. He came to my party with my friend, Victor Gupta and another American, an employee at the call center, I believe."

"The second American? Did you know him?"

"I did not."

"Did you, Miss Eagleton?"

"I am afraid not. Like Shiv, I was introduced to them at the party."

Shiv, looking like he remembered more information, said, "There weren't a lot of people at the party. Victor's guests were the only people I didn't know personally."

The inspector continued. "We do not know if the deaths are coincidental. Both men died within hours of each other. They were colleagues, and they both went to your party. We have a list of the people who attended your event, and we will be interviewing all of them to try to piece together what happened."

After this conversation, Melanie assumed the police would dismiss her and Shiv. What she didn't expect was what turned out to be several young people from Gupta's office walking through the door, including the young American she'd met at the party. He smiled at Melanie, and she smiled back reassuringly. All of them acknowledged Shiv with the familiar namaste greeting and said, "Hello Rajah Shiv."

As the inspector introduced himself, Melanie and Shiv were escorted out. With the door where the questioning was taking place open, Melanie and Shiv could hear some of the discussion. The inspector began by asking the group, which Melanie thought was a little strange, "Are you all aware of Mr. Gupta's death?"

Indian Tapioca Fry
(Sabudana Khichdi) Yogini Joglekar

INGREDIENTS

- 1 C tapioca (sabudana)
- 2 medium potatoes
- Ground peanut powder from 1/2 cup peanuts
- 2 T ghee
- 3 small green chilies
- 1 T cumin seeds (jeera)
- 1 T fresh or frozen coconut shredded
- Salt and sugar to taste
- Cilantro and lemon wedges for garnishing

PROCEDURE

Soak tapioca overnight in 1.5 cups water. The grains should be completely covered and be moist the next day. (If using Minute tapioca, soak for 30 minutes.)

Roast the peanuts, peel off the skin and then grind coarsely.

Finely chop the green chilies cut the potatoes into small cubes. Wash and chop coriander leaves.

Heat ghee in a pan. Add cumin seeds and chilies. When cumin seeds crackle, add the potatoes.

Add soaked tapioca and peanut powder, add salt and sugar.

Roast the mixture on low flame until color changes to light brown.

Cover with a lid and cook for 3-4 minutes.

Add coconut, garnish with cilantro and lemon wedges, and serve piping hot.

Tip: for extra soft khichdi, add 1/4 cup milk before covering with lid.

Chapter 15

BACK IN THE PALACE AGAIN

As they say, the show must go on, and work was work. Work would keep them busy while they pushed through the next few days. When Melanie arrived at the palace the following day, Shiv waited to escort her to his large, elegantly appointed office. Melanie immediately loved his beautiful and colorful space, furnished with a mixture of the old and the new pieces. The office overlooked a small garden where peacocks strutted around beds of orange marigolds and yellow and white roses. Melanie couldn't have designed the room more beautifully. She looked at the Rajah and said, "You have done a splendid job here. Why on earth do you need me?" She laughed.

"Ah, Ms. Melanie, this room was done with my mother, the late rani. If she were alive, I might not have needed you, but alas, as you see, she made sure to lead me to you. She was like you in many ways, an artist and a pragmatist. Art, beauty and comfort all in one room was her signature. You are here, because like mother, you are the best."

Melanie blushed as Shiv continued.

"Aren't they delightful?" Shiv said, stepping out on the balcony and pointing to the peacocks in the garden.

"That they are."

"These are our Indian peacocks. You can tell by the iridescent blue and green plumage. Before they were exported, you could only find them in India, Sri Lanka, and Pakistan."

The green peafowl is the second Asian species. You find those in Myanmar, Indochina, and Java. There is also an African species, native only to the Congo Basin."

As though they understood they were being talked about, one of the peacocks spread its tail displaying the flamboyant colors and the iridescent eyespots of its plumage. Another began the loud, distinctive peacock birdcall. Though Melanie liked peacocks, their strident calls echoed in her ears after a while, and she reminded herself that beauty had a price. Still, their beauty was unmatched. Retreating inside, she closed the soundproof French doors of the balcony.

Shiv laughed. "That's why the doors were made soundproof. They make a racket when they want to show off. Would you like some tea?"

"Definitely. Chai?"

Shiv called the kitchen and asked for chai and eggplant appetizer to be sent up.

"These events are unfortunate, but to stay on schedule for the opening of the museum, we do have to continue working through the chaos at the moment. By the way, tonight I must do some promo shots for the film when we are done. Would you like to come along?" Shiv asked.

"Do I get another closet of saris to choose from?"

"Of course." And they both laughed. There was no more room in her closet.

Melanie began to review with Shiv her ideas for the palace and museum. She displayed her renderings on the table. "I see the theme as Indian royal combined with earth tones and many splashes of color. We will take advantage of the lush marble already here. We will add life and serenity and embellish the space with bold peacock-blue accents, highlighting the rare, blue-veined marble. I believe the combinations will be magical and represent well the magic of all India. Your opinion, my Rajah?" Melanie bowed, trying to keep him in a cheery mood.

"Hmm," he said as he held up the designs. "These designs are excellent. I appreciate how you've worked the contemporary culture with old-world India. We are definitely on the same page."

"I'm glad." Melanie spread a new drawing on the table.

"I am hoping you will have one room where I can display some artifacts from my movies."

"I think you are reading my mind."

Melanie pointed to another drawing in the portfolio. She completely understood his sentiments of showing the evolution of power in a changing society. "Look at this." She pointed to the drawing. "I've reserved one room as a gallery of you. It will house your awards and memorabilia as a living museum of the present and future. It will also be the museum of the illustrious past of your family. Reminiscent of Lon Chaney, you know, 'The Man of a Thousand Faces' kind of thing. And we'll make a small tearoom on the balcony overlooking the gardens where guests can order small meals and enjoy the beauty of the grounds." Melanie had designed the outdoor tearoom while thinking of her favorite tearooms, many of which had closed like the one at the Plaza and the ones that still survived, like the one on Irving Place, not far from Gramercy Park.

"Remember the peacocks. They like to show off for the guest, you know." Shiv poured the tea that had arrived, handing her a cup.

"We'll use white noise in the space."

He sat across from Melanie, quietly observing her. He now understood why she was so beloved by her clients.

"What?" Melanie looked up at his stare.

"I was just thinking how pleased I am with your drawings of the palace. It seems you can get into your client's heads, and that's why they love you so. You've captured exactly my vision. What I want to do is indeed for posterity, but I also wanted to share with my fans how committed my family remains to India. You captured that beautifully. I think this project is for everyone and is so much better than just being a Bollywood icon with a lavish beachfront showplace in Mumbai who appears on the balcony once a week for adoring fans. Don't you?"

Melanie responded, "Without question. You will be honoring your heritage and sharing it with your people. Now all you have left to do is to hurry and find a *rani* so the next Rajah can keep your story alive for generations."

"You're right. I must find a rani. Do you want the job?"

"Shiv, all jokes aside, what about that beautiful woman I saw you with at the party. The one in the royal blue sari who looked like she could kill me? She was stunning." *Oops, after Victor, that was a bad reference.*

"Ah, please. Definitely not! Women in India today are very independent. I am not sure that many professional women would trade their careers for "first lady" status. Being a *rani* with all the ceremonial tasks is not an easy life. But I bet you could handle it, Ms. M."

"No. I think you are wrong. I am way too independent, and truthfully, I like my "smallish" life. Wouldn't trade it for a grand lady title."

Shiv raised an eyebrow.

"No offense, of course."

He raised it higher.

"Stop Shiv, don't look at me that way."

They both laughed. Melanie was glad the Rajah had a sense of humor. As Melanie was putting away her drawings, Shiv approached her quietly.

"Melanie, Victor's family is preparing his funeral. I wanted to ask if you would attend with me. What do you think?"

"I want to say this so you will understand. Would you think me heartless if I said I just couldn't take the reality of another death? Can I keep Victor in my mind's eye the way I saw him laughing?"

"You have had a recent death?" Shiv asked.

Melanie hesitated before she answered him. Should she go into all that? "Yes. I lost my husband and my best friend two years ago. It was quite traumatic, and until recently, I have felt surrounded by death. I am only now beginning to recover fully. I would rather not attend Victor's funeral. I hope you understand."

"I am so sorry. And I completely understand why you prefer not to go." Shiv continued, "Victor was a good guy, you know. He always used to say, 'If anything ever happens to me and I can't chase pretty girls, or eat chocolate, let me go." Shiv's face broke into a smile. "Victor was quite the ladies' man. But for the past year, he surprised me by talking about settling down. He even mentioned children. I, frankly, was stunned."

"The police, do they know anything yet? Such as was this natural causes or foul play?" Melanie asked.

"At first, they thought natural causes. But the second death has put them on another track. Foul play seems at the top of their list. They don't yet know how or why. And they believe the deaths are connected. Perhaps poison."

The idea of poison hit Melanie like a bolt of lightning. Poison, again! But how and where? As she mulled the news over in her mind, words fell out of her mouth, "Poisoned? By whom? And why?"

"They think that the poison could have been in the food at my party. Or in the drinks."

"If that's true, why are there not more victims? Like why aren't you and I and your other guests not stricken? We should have been victims."

"None of this makes sense, and I have been meaning to tell you. If it's foul play, Victor and his colleague were not the first call center casualties. There were two deaths before Victor."

"You are kidding. *That's probably why Colin is coming to India.*"

Melanie then remembered something from the party. She opened her purse and took out the tiny box of candy that had her name on it.

Shiv looked and gave a low whistle. He said, "Really? Wow, we should probably get that to the police. Though I doubt anything will come of it, but it was at the scene of the accident."

Melanie agreed. "Shiv, I should let you know that I have a friend, Colin, who is connected to Scotland Yard. He's coming to Delhi before a stop in Mumbai. He left London this morning."

"I see. That's why you didn't answer me about accompanying me to my promo shoot."

"Nothing like that," Melanie felt the need to provide a few more details about her reaction to the idea that poison killed Victor and how Colin St. James Smythe became part of her life.

Shiv listened to her story and said when she was done. "What an ordeal to have gone through." He then gave her a quick hug. "Not to worry, Ms. Melanie. I will protect you. After all, you are a guest in my country."

"With you and Colin, I am invincible, I hope."

He looked at her closely and smiled at the beautiful woman with the violet eyes, feeling sad for the sorrow she had known and wanting to lighten things up for her. She was a good woman and, he hoped, a good friend forever.

Melanie finished packing her drawings and asked Shiv if she could be driven back to her hotel. Before leaving, she outlined the next steps in the project, "First, I will secure fabric and paint samples and start working. I will run them by you before I begin. Do you want to keep my portfolio overnight to consider further?"

"No, I trust your judgment. Sorry, you won't accompany me to my shoot but let's meet again tomorrow before you go shopping."

"Okay." Melanie squeezed his outstretched hands in gratitude as she stepped into the waiting car. Once inside, she was glad to have some alone time to rest and speak again with Colin.

She went to the guest desk and asked for more towels and hangers for her room. The concierge smiled and said, "Did you have a good day? There is a note in your box," he said, handing her the paper.

Melanie opened the note and laughed to herself. Dear, dear Lars. With all going on, she had neglected to call. She knew he'd probably left a few voice messages on her phone that day but being Lars, he'd left one in her inbox. Back in the room, she looked at her phone, which had been dialed off. Sure enough, there were two messages. In the room, there were two others. She called Lars.

"Am I in the doggie house?"

"Hello, Melanie? How are you? It is so good to hear from you," she could hear admonishment in his tone but also his chuckle.

"It's been crazy." Melanie thought about telling Lars what had happened but decided against it for the moment. He would only worry.

"The Rajah is very pleased with our rendering. Melanie said. "Thank you. Lars, this might not be the most appropriate time and over-the-phone to boot, but I wanted to make this offer to you before things get any busier here. I would love to offer you a partnership in Designing Diva, making it Designing Divas. What do you think?"

For a single moment, there was silence. Then a torrent of words, "What? Oh really, Melanie? I couldn't be happier. You know how much of a diva I am. And how much I love you and *our* company. Yes. Yes. Thank you, Melanie. Thank you. I can't wait to tell Dale."

"On the contrary, thank you, Lars. Now, we are tethered together forever," Melanie laughed. She was genuinely happy, and she knew Lars was too.

"How is the honeymoon time together?"

"It's as perfect as your cabin. If you didn't call soon, I promised I would be calling."

They spoke for a few more minutes, and Melanie ended the call with a promise to check in again soon.

Melanie felt happier and more positive than she had in days. Lars was her official partner, and Colin was supposed to arrive soon. She was sure he had said he had a morning flight and was going to call her to give her the exact details once he'd confirmed everything. Since she hadn't heard from him, she decided to give him a quick call. Her call went immediately to voice mail.

Figuring he was busy, she left a quick message and went to her room to wait and nap while she had the chance.

Eggplant Appetizer

INGREDIENTS

- 1 large eggplant (about 2 lbs)
- 1 medium onion diced
- 2 cloves of garlic, pressed
- 1 small can of tomato paste
- T olive oil
- ¼ C water

PROCEDURE

Slice eggplant into half-inch thick slices and place on a tray and sprinkle salt on top and leave for 10 minutes. Meanwhile, sauté onion and garlic in the oil in a heavy skillet over medium heat until they start to turn brown. Rinse the salt off the eggplant, blot dry, and chop into half-inch cubes. Add to pan and sauté for 5 minutes. Add water and tomato paste, cover and cook for 10 minutes until tender. Mix all ingredients and mash until 5r6smooth. Serve with warm chapattis, cut into quarters.

Chapter 16

PLAN B

Steven was filled with anxiety as he sat down with coffee and his mother's pumpkin cake. Though he had taken his pills this morning, the erratic skips in his medication must be catching up because he had a headache and was feeling down. When he was down, he ate. He wasn't required for any more questioning by the police, but he couldn't leave the country, so Steven worked through his Plan B. As a dutiful employee, he spoke to Victor's company's acting CEO. This plan would get him back to the States for a bit to sort himself out from under the glare, but he'd have to get police clearance.

"It is the right thing for me to accompany Mr. McKerny's body home. His wife and children will be grateful, and I would like to show my respect and attend his funeral. I hope I will be able to get permission to leave India."

"It is." The CEO said, "Let me reach out to the officials."

The cause of death had not yet been ascertained, but the Chief approved his request and even commended Steven on his loyalty and thoughtfulness. Still, he made it quite clear he was to return to India as soon as possible.

"Yes, sir. Thank you."

While making plans to take Albert McKerny's body home, Steven forwarded his report to his company's CEO. In his cover letter, he offered to take McKerny's place in India permanently and suggested if he were available, they could meet to discuss while he was there. Steven thought it was an excellent thing to make a bold move and move his agenda forward.

*   *   *

Detective Colin St. James Smythe had just heard the bad news. Unforeseen weather delays. He'd rushed around, rearranging his schedule to meet Melanie in Delhi and now this. It hadn't been easy to change so many appointments, but for some reason, he was just beginning to understand, he wanted to help Melanie any way he could. Colin had felt a strange need to protect her from the moment he'd seen her running through the emergency room doors. He wasn't sure what her ailment was, but destiny was lending a hand, as it turned out. She was there to find out about her friend Charlotte whose death he was investigating. And even worse, her husband was the murderer. Piled on top of loss and grief, her sorrow had been endless. Once the case closed, he could not seem to forget her, but he'd been careful to give her space and time to heal.

Checking in with her now and then, he'd had from afar tracked how Melanie was faring. As someone who was used to dealing with death, he knew it took a while for people to accept it and move on.

Colin had been quite happy when her assistant, Lars, told him that she was working in India. It meant she was moving on with her life. He was eager to see her and found it unfortunate that the only flight he could get out of London was what he would later refer to as a "local" with two short layovers in Berlin and Istanbul. The inconvenience was that the London leg was delayed due to rain and thick fog, which meant he could miss his connections.

Ordinarily, this would not bother Colin, a patient man who might very well be one of the few people left on the planet who didn't mind layovers and missed connections. He'd traveled so much; it was the only time he got to catch his breath and a chance to catch up on his reading and finish reports. He even liked overnight layovers so he could explore new and exciting places. Right now, however, he wanted a direct flight to be with Melanie sooner than later. The fear he'd heard in her voice had made him more anxious to get to Delhi. Clearly, that was not going to happen.

Colin made a cup of coffee, settled in and tried to call Melanie. He called her cellphone several times before realizing his phone was not working well. He thought he needed a new phone but found someone at the help desk in his office who fixed the problem and explained that the weather had knocked out some service.

An hour later, Colin received a call and was told that the flight had been canceled and rescheduled for the following day. English weather and layovers. He wanted to reach out to Melanie and soon. Still trying but having no luck, Colin went to the lounge bar and ordered an icy cold martini. At that moment, he was not a happy man.

Pumpkin Cake

INGREDIENTS

- 4 eggs
- 1 C oil
- 2 C flour
- 2 t baking powder
- ¾ t salt
- 1 C raisins and/or chopped nuts
- 2 C light brown sugar
- 15 oz. pumpkin puree
- 1½ t baking soda
- 2 t cinnamon

Icing:

- 3 oz. cream cheese, softened
  ½ C margarine or butter
- 1 T milk
- 2 C powdered sugar
- 1 t vanilla

PROCEDURE

Preheat oven to 350°. Grease 15 x 10-inch pan. Beat eggs until foamy; add sugar, oil, and pumpkin. Beat 2 minutes at medium speed. Add flour, baking powder, soda, salt, and cinnamon. Beat 2 more minutes at low speed. Stir in raisins or nuts. Pour into prepared pan and bake at 350° for 40-50 minutes. Beat cream cheese, margarine, milk, and vanilla until fluffy in a small bowl. Add powdered sugar and blend until smooth. Spread on cooled cake.

Chapter 17

NEVER ENOUGH SHOPPING

Colin finally reached Melanie to tell her of the change of plans. Now that he wouldn't arrive until the following day, and feeling much less anxious, she decided to spend the day visiting as many markets as she could, including her favorites, Lajpat Nagar, the Khan market, and Qarol Bugh, and the Westside Ambience Mall. Most of this had to do with the palace and museum, but if time permitted, she'd drop by the two stores she'd passed when she had hurried back to meet Shiv. The jewelry store was close to the hotel she remembered. The beautifully decorated window of sparkling silver and brilliant gemstones would probably be a great place to buy a wedding gift for Lars and Dale. Maybe she would go there first.

After breakfast, Melanie logged onto her computer to map out a route that would cover as many fabric places as she could manage. She thought it best to hire a driver for the day. Her driver was outside waiting when she got to the lobby, and she handed him a list of the places she wanted to visit, along with pictures of the two stores she wanted to stop by before they started their day. He knew exactly where they were.

The first stop, of course, was the jewelry store. Melanie walked over to where the shop owner was crouched outside, smoking a hand-rolled cigarette. He rose as she approached and stubbed out his half-smoked cigarette.

"No need to rush. I'll just go in and look around."

Taken by her beauty and charm and wanting to make a sale, he said, "Thank you, madame. Something lovely for you today?" He ushered her into his shop.

"Yes, I'm looking for gifts for two very special people."

"Please take your time and look around." He hovered.

Melanie did just that. When she came upon a heavy silver bracelet, she stopped. "May I see this?" She pointed to the bracelet. "It's silver, right?"

"You have exquisite taste. That's a period piece from the early nineteenth. It's called a slave bracelet. Noblemen usually bought them for their wives as they acquired them. Look at the scrollwork. It signifies ever-loving devotion. It is one hundred percent silver," the man did a pure silver test by scratching a small blip into the bracelet and then dipping it in a solution labeled nitric acid. Many vendors tried to pawn off other metals as silver only to have their customers end up with green wrists, so she appreciated the authenticity test.

"I think I won't call it that. Perhaps in my case, it'll be a lovely masculine bracelet. It is for my close friends, two men, for their wedding. So, I will need two."

Melanie caught the discomfort of the man for a mere second before he quickly recovered his composure. Melanie picked up the piece, imagining it on Lars' arm. "I think it will work very well."

The proprietor frowned, seeing his sale in jeopardy. "Two, madame, but this is a rare piece." He looked then as if a light bulb had gone off. He paced for a few minutes while Melanie happily eyed all the other goodies in the store. He smiled slightly and said, "However, I believe you may be in luck. I have a friend with a shop who may have another bracelet. These rajahs had more than one wife, so they had to buy comparable pieces for each woman at times. Does it have to be an exact duplicate? No two pieces are precisely alike."

"As close as possible but, no. They don't have to be exact." After all, she considered, no two people are exactly alike.

Today, being a man of business, a customer was a customer, and this one looked and sounded wealthy, so the jeweler, despite his earlier hesitation, was pleased. He liked this pretty lady. And looking closely, he did believe she was a lady. "I will call my friend. It will, as I said, not be an exact match, but close enough. Where are you staying? I will check and get back to you."

Melanie left her contact information and headed back to the car.

Pleased to have found a solution to her wedding gift challenge for two men who had everything, she climbed in the waiting car, and they sped off to the next destination.

Their next stop was at the sari store. The colorful display of high-quality tunics was overwhelming. Expecting the prices to be quite high, she was thrilled to see the sign that said, "Everything under $25." In English, yet! Melanie immediately selected two tunics with matching pants threaded with a silver elephant design in a deep mauve color.

"*Ji*, that's Ganesh," the shopkeeper said, "Elephants, madame, symbolize new beginnings. Good choice. The mauve would bring out the colors of your beautiful eyes."

To Melanie, the words were music to her ears. She needed a new beginning and any compliment she could get. "Thank you," he reached for her credit card. I certainly could use new beginnings," she chuckled

Finally, they reached the textile district. Melanie darted into the store after store, each time toting an armful of pieces out to the waiting car. Her driver relieved her of the packages, and she was off again. She was having a field day.

Halfway through shopping Melanie began to feel her energy waning. She asked the driver to drop her at a teashop nearby for a good cup of tea and a snack to revive her.

"Suresh, go back to the hotel and drop off the packages. I will putter around some more and then find my way back. There is to need to come back for me."

As she entered the café, the heavenly smell of the hot scones coming out of the oven made Melanie even hungrier. For India, scones and tea, a leftover from English colonization, was not exactly foreign food. She ordered a pot of chai and a raisin scone. The waitress placed the tray in front of her. Melanie took a generous bite of her scone, ordering another. She drank her tea and felt her energy return.

After she finished, Melanie doubled back to Chandni Chowk, located in central Delhi. It was convenient with many good shops in the district, and because it was huge and busy, there were always fantastic textiles at unbelievable prices. She was looking for charming silks and satins with rich textures in various colors. Shiv wanted his palace to be bright and vibrant, and that's what he'd get. The Indian palate for colors was remarkable, and she wanted to take advantage of the wealth of fabrics. Kinara Bazaar turned out to be a real fabric jackpot. Immediately mesmerized by the fabrics, laces, and other items, Melanie stepped over to a salesperson and asked if she might take some samples with her. Because Melanie had been there before and because some people in Delhi knew who her client was, she was given carte blanche.

Her next stop was the Cloth Market. Once again, as Melanie walked in, she stopped in her tracks to admire the magnificent fabric colors lining the walls and stalls. She did not know where to look first. She took a deep breath and ventured to find the color palates she wanted to use in specific rooms. While touching fabric, she absentmindedly looked at her watch. She left her card with the manager at the front desk and ran out the door.

As she dashed out, intending to grab a cab for the ride back to the hotel, she saw her driver graciously waiting for her return, even though she had told him he could leave. How she would love to shop like this in New York City. "

"Suresh, how did you find me?"

"Oh, I just trailed behind you. I imagined you wanted to walk off lunch."

"Thank you. I appreciate your kindness."

He simply smiled and said, "Madame, you look like your tasks are completed. But *Ji*, the hotel is calling. Rajah Shiv is trying to reach you. Is your phone not on?"

Melanie quietly blessed him, handed him the last of her shopping, and checked her phone. It was on silent, and there were four missed calls from the Rajah.

When she called him back, she got a sweet scolding, "Melanie, my dear. Do you know how worried I was not being able to reach you? It's a good thing the hotel could reach your driver. I am not scolding, only concerned for you."

Melanie was touched. "My phone was on silent. I tend to get rapt when I shop. So sorry. I'm fine. I am heading back to the hotel."

"Good, you should rest. I'd like you to dine with me tonight. I have someone special for you to meet."

When Melanie arrived at the chic Spanish-themed Seville Restaurant at Claridge's Delhi hotel, she was beyond impressed. The alfresco tables, each overhung with a chandelier and draped with stark white tablecloths was, a stunning contrast to its electric blue interior. Melanie was led to a table where Shiv was sitting with a beautiful woman. She looked like the Russian model, Irina Shayk, but was more stunning and Indian. Shiv rose as she approached. He kissed her on both cheeks. The woman also rose. "Melanie Eagleton, this is Rekha Bali."

"I am so pleased to meet you. Shiv has spoken so much about you. I'd hoped to meet you at the welcoming party but had to miss it as I was delayed in London." She had no trace of an Indian accent. In fact, she sounded more like Colin than Shiv.

"Rekha is finishing her medical degree at Oxford. She had exams." Shiv was beaming.

Melanie was smiling inside. He'd known his intended *rani* all along! Melanie agreed as the night progressed that Rekha was Shiv's perfect woman in every way. Born in Britain of Indian parents, Rekha had the right combination of beauty, wit, brains, breeding and cosmopolitan exposure to be a Rajah's wife. Melanie texted Shiv her approval in the car on the way home -*You struck gold!*

Wired from her day of shopping and expectant of Colin, Melanie had a hard time falling asleep. The thought of seeing Colin again comforted and, for some reason, excited her. He'd turned out to be a great detective and a distant friend. They weren't close friends, yet he was the first person she thought to call about Victor. Probably because they'd been thrown together on the Marco-Charlotte mystery, and somehow, she felt they would be thrown together on this one too.

Thinking philosophically, she wondered if she had the right to get Colin involved in this? Was she being self-centered and selfish? Granted, she was apprehensive about the murders, and yes, she genuinely liked Colin's super-sleuth insight, but did she know him well enough to risk his safety to help her? If anything happened to him, she would never forgive herself. Still, she was also happy he would again be by her side.

Melanie, who always listened to her sixth sense, had had a bad premonition about his flight running into trouble. And so it had been. Rubbing her palm furiously on her arm to get rid of the goosebumps forming, she wondered if she was overreacting about all this, and perhaps, she simply wanted to see Colin again.

Colonial Scones

INGREDIENTS

- 1 C instant oatmeal
- 1 C cornmeal
- 1 t baking soda
- 1 C buttermilk
- ¼ C oil
- 3 T honey
- 1 C golden raisins
- ½ t salt

PROCEDURE

Mix dry ingredients, and then combine with wet ingredients. Mix well all together. Spoon the mixture into a heated, greased iron fry pan. Fry on low heat for 5 minutes. Place the pan in a 375° oven and bake for 10 to 15 minutes until it starts to brown and firm. Cut into wedges and serve warm from the pan.

Chapter 18

A Very Deep Sleep

When Melanie saw Colin coming out of baggage claim; her face lit up. She'd forgotten how attractive he was and moved hastily to greet him.

Colin rested his luggage and embraced Melanie. "It's great to see you, Melanie. You look amazing."

"You look amazing, too." Melanie found her composure. "The car is this way."

On the ride back to the hotel, Colin listened as Melanie explained the dramatic occurrences that happened in Delhi.

"I wonder if there is any tie to the reason I'm here. Recently Scotland Yard noticed an uptick in a global group called the 4Cs. A few of their incidents have turned violent, which is quite a departure from their M.O. Terrorist groups could have infiltrated them. The UK and India have a long-term agreement regarding assistance in times of global terrorism. Since this problem is adversely affecting the UK, India, and the United States, Scotland Yard has been given the authority to act in the best interests of these countries."

"Wow," Melanie said. "This stuff sounds serious."

"It could be, but I don't want to talk about that anymore. Tell me about you."

Chatter was so easy between them. By the time they reached the hotel, Colin had been fully updated on her life and she on his.

Colin checked in, and as they made their way to the elevator, Melanie informed him they were invited to dinner with the Rajah.

"Tonight? Please beg off for me. Maybe we can have breakfast in the morning?"

Melanie did not show her disappointment. She'd hoped they would have more time together, but she could understand…he'd been traveling for two days.

"Don't worry. Shiv is a very understanding person. Go on up. I am going to grab a bite before I head up. See you in the morning, and Colin, thank you."

After Colin went up to his room, Melanie tried several times to reach Shiv, but to no avail. She was sitting in the lobby when the hotel manager Mr. Rashid approached. "Ms. Eagleton, how are you today? Rajah Kumar instructed me to keep an eye on you and to make sure that you have everything you need. Just wanted to make sure all is well."

Though not in the mood to chat, Melanie knew this man was being very kind. Everything is beyond perfect," Melanie proffered. "But tell me, does Rajah Kumar always take such good care of his guests?"

"Always," Rashid answered. "Shall I send over some tea?"

"That would be lovely, but I'm headed to the restaurant. I'll get some there. Next time I'll take you up on the offer. I'm hoping since it's only 4 p.m. the restaurant shouldn't be too crowded. I could use a quiet restaurant."

"I can only imagine given these trying times. Follow me. I have just the place for tea and quiet. I will have the restaurant send you over whatever you desire there." He led her to a private room with its own tea nook.

"Oh, my," Melanie sank into the comfortable chair. "This is pretty special." She took a deep breath and began to relax. Just then, a text came in from Shiv. *"Stuck. No-can-do dinner tonight. Hope you and what's his name are not disappointed. Call you in a.m."* Melanie laughed. She loved it when he acted possessive How perfect she didn't have to cancel on him for Colin.

Rashid ordered a pot of chai and biscuits to tide her over until dinner arrived. The tea came quickly. The aroma, spicy and warm, was enough to make her eyelids droop. Melanie reached over to pour, but the hotel waiter stopped her. "Allow me, madame," he poured the hot liquid into a large porcelain cup. She took a sip of her fragrant tea, leaned back, and stifled a yawn.

"I will check in on you after your dinner. Mr. Rashid said, "I have the best sleep medicine. May I join you later? I, too, could do with a good night's rest," he winked.

An hour later, to his word, Rashid returned. He ordered two small drinks he called his 'relaxation special.' Post haste, two tiny gold-rimmed glasses filled with a sparkling golden liquid appeared. The waiter placed one in front of each of them and left. "To sleep." Mr. Rashid raised his glass and sipped his drink.

Melanie did likewise. It was so tasty she drank it all. That small drink was very strong, and as she sat back in the comfy chair, about ten minutes later, she began to feel a bit sleepy. "You're not kidding about this being a relaxation cocktail," Melanie said, "I'd better be going upstairs before I fall asleep right here." She could feel her eyes drooping and asked Mr. Rashid to guide her to the elevator. He did more than that. He escorted her to her room and made sure she locked and chained the door behind him.

Melanie didn't remember very much after that. She recalled kicking off her shoes, removing her outer clothing, and wrapping herself in a warm, comfortable silk robe. She remembered climbing into bed, pulling blankets all around her, and that was it. Nothing after that. She fell into a deep sleep from which she did not awaken for 12 hours.

Deep Sleep Relaxation Cocktail

For two

Powder a sleeping tablet such as extra strength Melatonin. Mix thoroughly with 1 oz. Cognac, 1½ oz. Triple sec, and 2 oz. Pineapple juice. Whip the white of an egg with a dash of cardamom and stir in gently.

Chapter 19

BREAKFAST WITH COLIN

The hotel telephone was ringing. Melanie stirred but, groggy, missed the call. She was listening to a bot say, "He-ll-o. Ms. Eagleton, you missed a call from room 1092." How efficient Melanie thought as she looked at her watch. "Eight a.m.! My goodness." Melanie turned on the 55-inch television and tuned into CNN, and sure enough, it was 8 a.m. Delhi time. "Good grief," she said, reaching for her cellphone. "I couldn't have been that tired." She'd slept almost twelve hours. There was a missed call from Shiv she'd slept through and the most recent from Colin. She was about to dial Colin when her cell began vibrating. Colin.

"Where are you?"

"Hi, Colin. I'm here in the room. I overslept. Did you sleep well?"

"I did. You?"

"Like a log. After you went upstairs, I had a magic potion with the hotel manager, Mr. Rashid, and I was out like a light."

"Remind me to get some tonight. Do you want to have breakfast?"

"I would love that. About an hour? I'll see if Shiv can join us."

Colin wanted to say just you and me but refrained. He wanted to discuss things privately with her before meeting the Rajah.

They hung up, and Melanie sprang into action. First, she called Shiv to invite him to breakfast at 9:30 a.m. and then jumped into a steaming hot shower. She sped through her routine: skin cream, face moisturizer, the works, and then she added a touch of makeup. She wanted to look good but not over the top, so she put on one of her favorites for every occasion jumpsuit and loafers. Dabbing a little perfume behind her ears and on her wrist, she gave herself a nod of approval. She looked natural and fresh but was unsure why she was going to such lengths for breakfast.

With time to spare, Melanie sat in the red Masanori Umeda chair with its classic rose petal design and set her phone timer for twenty minutes. Breathing deeply, she closed her eyes and allowed her mind to go blank. When the timer went off, she stood, patted the comfy chair and headed out the door. Maybe she'd get one for her home. In the elevator, she pushed the button for the 3rd floor, the restaurant floor, where she was meeting Colin and Shiv for breakfast. Colin had arrived before her and was seated at a table near the window. She watched as he smiled warmly at the waitress. He was, after all, a very friendly fellow.

Colin stood, came towards her, and greeted Melanie with a big smile when he spotted her. She was happy he was here, and for sure, she felt safer with Colin St. James Smythe before her eyes.

Melanie gave him a great big smile. "I am so glad you are here. Thanks again, Colin, for coming. Oh, here comes Shiv."

Strolling over to their table was the Rajah. He took Melanie's outstretched hand and kissed them before turning to Colin. She was getting used to the hand-kissing thing.

Melanie introduced the two men.

"Delighted," Shiv offered his hand. "So glad you arrived safely. I thought Melanie was going to be our next victim from worry if you hadn't gotten here," he flashed a smile at Colin. When Colin straightened up to shake Shiv's hand, he stood a good three inches taller. Not expecting him to be quite as good-looking or tall, Shiv felt a little irked. A guy thing, he was sure but nonetheless annoying. Shiv's instinct was to be a competitor, but he didn't want to offend Melanie or the guy who had flown long and far to be of help. Besides, he was out of the running with Melanie. She already knew about his "rani."

Colin looked in his early forties, with sandy hair falling over his warm, observant brown eyes. He looked fit and happy to see Melanie.

Colin noticed that the Rajah was eyeing his midnight stubble. "I am," Colin flashed a confident smile at Shiv, "growing a beard."

"Well, that stubble suits you," Shiv said casually. At least, he hoped it came out casually.

"What do you think, Melanie?"

"Yes." Melanie, who'd been eyeing it since yesterday, chimed in. "It does make him rather dashing."

For the first time since the death of Victor Gupta, Melanie could breathe more easily. She hoped the nightmare of seeing another death would fade much sooner than the last two. Now, if she could just get the recipe for that great sleep potion, she would be all set.

Shiv signaled the waiter, and in true Rajah style, he ordered for the table. In addition, Colin ordered black coffee, fruit, and an English muffin. Of course! His must-haves.

When they settled in with breakfast, Colin said. "Fill me in again on everything. Start at the beginning and leave nothing out."

Melanie began telling the story of Victor's collapse again, this time leaving out no detail.

"Anything or anyone out of the ordinary at the party?"

"It was a small party. Only twenty-six people." Shiv said. "There was only a couple, guests of Victor and Melanie, of course, whom I'd met that night. We have no new servants, and our cook has been the same for twenty years."

Melanie didn't like the sound of 'and Melanie, of course.'

"Tell me about the people you didn't know."

"As I said, there were two people who came with Victor. Since Victor brought them, I am sure he could have vouched for them. They were his colleagues. Unfortunately, as it turned out, one of them met the same fate as Victor. This entire thing is perplexing."

"Do you know why Victor chose to bring them to your party?"

"Victor was flying to America the following morning, and I think needed to meet with them about some last-minute details, so he invited them to the party. But he wouldn't have brought anyone I would not welcome. They both seemed nice and fit in well with the others. They did not stay all evening. They left relatively early."

"Anything to add?" Colin asked Melanie as he helped himself to an almond biscotti.

"I tried to find them both after the Holi celebration. I wanted to see how fellow Americans liked the celebration, but they were not around. So as Shiv said, I think they left early."

"How about anyone on your staff, Shiv?"

"No. As I said, there is no one new that I know of, but it's best to ask Mr. Mehta, my butler. Sometimes for parties, he hires temporary staff mostly from the Taj, but we were only twenty-six people, so I doubt it."

"A small party is twenty-six people? How many people constitute a big party?" Colin laughed.

"Three hundred or more." Shiv deadpanned.

"Anyway, the tactics these terrorist groups use nowadays are so high tech and unexpected, who knows. They have also been known to use infiltration tactics."

"My party wouldn't exactly be the place for someone to infiltrate since it was by invitation only, and the palace is quite protected."

"Right." Colin nodded. "After breakfast, I'll go to the police station, introduce myself, and hear what they've found. I'd like to visit the doctors too. It seems not so coincidental that both died hours apart."

"Yes, but coincidences do happen," Shiv said. "If by any far-fetched chance someone had tampered with the food, we all ate the same food, but nothing happened to anyone else. The police have already interrogated the other American who was closest to Mr. McKerny, and he seemed to have been ruled out as a suspect."

"I see," Colin said.

"Shall we come with you to the station?" Melanie asked.

"No. I have to go myself anyway. I made an appointment with one of the detectives. My coming here is two-fold. To help Melanie and to meet the Indian terrorist task force in Mumbai. So far, there are ten call centers in Bangalore where people have lost their lives in the past two weeks, and two additional people died at call centers in Hyderabad. It appears to be open season on call centers. We are keeping close tabs on this group of protestors called the 4Cs. They are pretty clever, and their methods are novel and different from the other attacks we've seen. We believe they have been infiltrated."

The Rajah was impressed. "We are eager to hear the results of your visit. Melanie and I will be together planning the décor for the palace. When you are done at the station, I would appreciate a call. I'll have a car readied for your use while you are here."

"That is very gracious of you," Colin said.

Shiv rose, pushed back his chair said, "Ready, Melanie?"

She nodded, and he took her elbow, steering her out of the room.

"Just a moment," Melanie beelined for Colin.

"I hope your day is productive. If you're late and you don't hear from me, it's because I've taken another of Mr. Rashid's magic sleep potions."

"Save one for me." Colin smiled and Shiv bristled.

"Sleep potions?" Shiv, who was in earshot, said.

"Yes. I hope Mr. Rashid is around tonight. His magic potion had me out like a light. I slept from 8 p.m. to 8 a.m. I barely remember how I got to my room."

"Out like a light." Colin's detective side reared. "What do you mean you don't remember last night?"

"I mean, I remember, but I had the best sleep since I've been here."

"Ah, you must have had sleepy-time liquor," Shiv said. It's a mixture of Indian juices, brandy, and a little something else."

"Just as good as my pills, and they last longer," Melanie added.

Colin seemed shocked, "Do you normally take drugs to help you sleep?"

"Not normally. Only on bad nights, planes, long bus rides, and strange hotels. Other than that, no."

"Hope you don't have too many of those," Colin admonished.

Shiv smiled at the Englishman's concern for Melanie and quickly escorted Melanie out of the restaurant.

*   *   *

Making his way through the crowded waiting room of the police headquarters, Colin nearly tripped twice over the haphazardness of the room. Stiflingly hot, it was filled with men, women, crying children, and even a tiny pet pig. The smell was overwhelmingly brutal, but he adjusted to it after a few minutes.

"I am Detective Colin Smythe," Colin presented his credentials to the sergeant on duty at the battered desk. "I have an appointment with Detective Malekar."

The sergeant nodded and said, "You are here because?" Colin explained his reasons for being there, and since he represented Scotland Yard, the detective said, "We are so glad to see you. Things seem to be escalating, and we are looking forward to your expertise."

Colin smiled.

Soon, a slender young woman, black hair in a tight chignon bun, walked up to Colin and shook his hand. She introduced herself as Prachi Malekar, the liaison to the police and an expert in terror and protest groups. "Please follow me." She started up an old, cracked marble stairway that led to a small room overlooking the plaza.

"Please." She pointed to a rather decrepit-looking wicker chair. Colin, not wanting to be impolite, sat. He hoped it would hold his weight.

Prachi took the seat opposite him. She crossed her long, slim legs at the ankles, drawing attention away from the stiff uniform skirt to the plain black service shoes. Her serious expression seemed never to vary and contrasted with her warm, intelligent brown eyes. She proceeded to open her iPad to display a map of the world with ten cities highlighted. She airdropped the map on a larger screen and retrieved a pointer from the corner of the room.

"These are pinpoints of where terrorist groups have been most active," Detective Malekar began, "As you might already know, there was a large demonstration last week in Manchester,

England. A sit-in at the Dallas headquarters of Tandy, protesting the offshoring of their helplines to India. Several large protests in New York, Los Angeles, and San Francisco. Smoke bombs here in Delhi, more serious bombings in Bangalore and Hyderabad, resulting in 12 deaths, and now two call center deaths that may or may not be related to each other. The terrorists appear to be expanding and escalating the severity of their actions. As call centers increase exponentially and take away more jobs from other countries, more people join these protest groups. There is one group called the 4Cs that is very vocal here and in the West."

"Yes. I am privy to this information and was present at the protest in Manchester." Colin outlined how Scotland Yard had addressed the Manchester sit-ins. "We had uniformed officers posted on the streets and several undercover people, but there was no physical violence, just name-calling and rather nasty posters. The group you mentioned, the 4Cs, has not been known for violence. At least not in the past. They could, of course, be changing their tactics. However, we believe there could also be copycat groups using their name because they get so much press."

"We have word on that too. They used social media techniques to draw in followers. We haven't been able to get a handle on them either. I hope to have more information by the time we get to Mumbai." The sergeant said.

"So, are you now calling Victor Gupta's death a homicide?" Colin asked. "From what I can ascertain, the method of the previous murders is completely different from that of Mr. Gupta's and Mr. McKerny."

"Yes. We are calling their deaths homicide. There seem to be something more personal to these deaths. Though we do have copies of the threatening emails sent to Mr. Gupta and four other heads of major call centers here in India, there is something off here. All the other call center heads were threatened with property damage, but Mr. Gupta's message said his life would be disrupted. We were concerned and offered him protection, but he insisted on living his life the way he always had." Detective Malekar said. "E-mails have been sent to Mr. Gupta for quite some time, but until now, none of the threats were carried through."

"I've made appointments tomorrow morning with Mr. Gupta's senior staff. Let me look at all this with a fresh eye. It's possible we are missing something."

"That's fine, but please let's keep each other posted on our findings." Prachi suppressed her irritation at being usurped by a foreign national on her territory.

"I will," Colin said, rising from his chair.

Almond Biscotti

INGREDIENTS

- 1 C sugar
- 3 T light rum
- 1 t vanilla extract
- 3 large eggs
- 1½ t baking powder
- 1 stick unsalted butter, melted
- 2 t pure almond extract
- 1 C coarsely chopped almonds, toasted
- 2¾ C flour
- ¼ t salt

PROCEDURE

Cream together butter and sugar. Add eggs and vanilla and almond extracts and rum, mix thoroughly. Add dry ingredients and nuts. Mix well—form two (16- by 2-inch) loaves on an ungreased large baking sheet.

Bake until pale golden, about 30 minutes. Carefully transfer loaves to a rack and cool 15 minutes.

Cut loaves into ¾-inch slices with a serrated knife.

Arrange biscotti, with a cut side down, on a clean baking sheet and bake until golden, 20 to 25 minutes. Transfer to a rack to cool completely.

Chapter 20

LUSH LUNCHEON

It was well after 5 p.m. when Colin finally called it a day. He'd met with the detectives who handled the Gupta and McKerny cases as well as the police examiner and hospital mortician. He agreed with Detective Malekar. Something personal was going on here. Years as a detective told him that. It was likely someone close to Victor and Albert whom the men trusted, someone with access. He took a deep breath and, looking at his watch, decided to check in with Melanie.

"We were just about to call you," Melanie said into the phone. "Shiv and I just finished up, and we are heading to his favorite restaurant. Would you like to join us? He has a private room there, so ask for him when you get here. This place has the best vegetarian samosas in all of India."

"Sounds great. What's the address?" Colin typed a memo on his iPhone. Though he knew they were working together, he found himself somewhat curious about Melanie and the Rajah's closeness, considering she had only just met. But he understood that becoming close with one's clients was an important aspect of how Melanie conducted business, so he busied himself thinking about how hungry he was and how good vegetarian samosas sounded right now. He waved down a yellow and green auto-rickshaw and was on his way.

The rickshaw pulled up to an elegant house with a sign that said Pandi Chat House. Nestled between boutiques and flower stands, it felt like Covent Gardens. A small sign proclaimed *Samosas* in English and Hindi.

"I am meeting the Rajah and Ms. Eagleton," Colin said.

"Rajah Shiv is on the blue patio. Just follow Sanjay and the sound of the fountains."

Shiv was by himself when Colin walked into the room. The two men began discussing what Colin had discovered or surmised, including that he believed these murders to be more personal than the most recent murders connected to terrorist activities.

"More personal?" The Rajah, a perfect gentleman, said, "I certainly want to hear about that, but let us have a pleasant dinner first."

Just then, Melanie came in from freshening up and joined the men. Shiv began to explain the menu. Melanie was suddenly quite hungry. The Rajah continued, "You'll like these; they are a little different from the peas and potato filling usually served in a chat house though, of course, they have that too."

After they finished dinner, Colin began again. "I met the detective in charge of the Indian investigation. There was a guest at your party with is a connection to the 4Cs."

"Impossible."

"No. Not at all. Mr. Orville, who was at the party, has ties to the 4Cs. As I was saying before Melanie joined us, they believe these murders fit a more personal vendetta than terrorist activity."

"But hasn't he been cleared?"

"Yes," Colin continued. "And his alibi is ironclad. He was at your party!" As I said, I am going to visit Victor's company and talk with the people there, including Steven Orville."

Melanie asked, "May I join you when you visit Victor's office?"

Colin nodded and said, "I do not believe the murders were coincidental. I am sure that both men had enemies because of their ties to the call centers, but there is more to this."

Shiv joined the conversation, "Victor owned many call centers, it's true. However, our experience in India has been that we do not kill people because we don't like them. It's not part of our culture. We much prefer to engage in a war of words. Of course, if the perpetrators were outsiders, that would be different," his thoughts drifted. "I still can't believe Victor is gone."

"You have my condolences," Colin said, observing him closely.

"Did Melanie tell you that Victor and I were boyhood school chums? We even passed our A levels at the same time. Victor, a Dalit, had a scholarship to our prestigious school. Under normal circumstances, our outdated caste system would not have permitted us to be friends, but Victor was a force to be reckoned with and would not be ignored. I couldn't ignore him because I, at times, wished I had the freedom just to be. Victor was smart, daring, and could care less about the status quo and his success proved that our system needs changing. A survivor and a self-made man with a heart of gold, he helped India's GNP a lot." Shiv paused. His voice was getting wobbly again.

Colin listened intently as Shiv was speaking. The caste system in India was so deeply ingrained that Colin was impressed that a man of his privilege recognized that it was outdated. It didn't escape Melanie that she and her close friend Charlotte had come from vastly different cultures and economic castes. Melanie, like Victor, was a scholarship student, though she rarely felt much different from the other girls in her school. Sometimes, though, Melanie thought she was treated well because she was Native American. She was sure that the guilt of the wealthy played a part.

"Rajah, was your sympathies why you became an investor? Your help was a big part of Victor's success, wasn't it?"

Melanie jumped in. "Shiv, I had no idea you were a big part of Victor's success." Melanie had been surprised to learn that Shiv was a silent partner in the call centers Victor owned.

Colin's sat observing the exchange. He was looking for someone Victor trusted with access. Shiv might very well qualify as a suspect. Especially at this point in the investigation.

"I don't advertise that. I wasn't really a partner. I had given him the startup money for his ventures, and he insisted on repaying me with shares in the company. I'd have helped him regardless, but I know nothing about how the company runs. Hardly ever been there."

"I assure you; we'll get to the bottom of this," Colin said.

Conversation ceased for a moment, and the room became very quiet. A waiter brought in trays of dessert. After eating and drinking pots of aromatic tea, Colin and Melanie said goodbye to Shiv and headed back to the hotel.

Shiv, as promised, had provided a car. As they walked into the hotel lobby, Colin stopped Melanie and asked. "Did you know before tonight that Shiv had shares in Victor's company?" He didn't want to have the conversation in the car in case the driver could be a plant.

"No, I didn't. It was quite a surprise but why are you asking? Do you…"

"Just asking," Colin interrupted.

They said their goodbyes when the elevator opened on Melanie's floor.

Melanie stopped in the midst of washing her face. Could Colin believe Shiv had something to do with Victor's death? No way! Then again, she would never have expected that Charlotte's death would be at the hand of her husband. This was getting bizarre. Getting into bed, Melanie noticed the message line on the phone was blinking. There were three messages. One from Lars making sure she was okay and to call him. Another from Shiv to make sure she'd arrived at the hotel safely. For goodness sake, she was traveling with a Scotland Yard detective!

The third message came as a surprise and filled Melanie with excitement. One of her dreams was coming true. It was a request from an academic dean at Pratt Institute in New York asking Melanie if she would consider part-time teaching beginning in the fall. One of their art and design professors had decided to return to her home abroad, and there was an urgent need to replace her position in the Culture-Based Interior Design course. Not only was Melanie a graduate of this prestigious school, but she also stayed an active alumna. She has been known as a mentor of young, talented people who'd traveled the same road she had and felt honored to have been asked. She would not say no. She'd make time in her schedule to teach in the fall. Professor Eagleton. That had a good ring to it. She bet this was the reason Lars wanted her to call him to let her know he'd given her number to the dean.

Eggplant Samosas

INGREDIENTS

Pastry

- ½ lb. plain flour
- 5 T oil
- 2 oz. cold water
- Pinch of salt

Mix oil and flour with fingers, adding salt. Then add water and mix quickly. Make small balls and chill.

Filling

- 1½ lb aubergines (long thin eggplant)
- 1 t chili powder
- 1 t cumin powder
- ½ t turmeric
- 1 t salt
- 2 chopped onions
- 1 chopped green chili
- ½ piece fresh ginger minced fine
- 5 T oil
- 3 medium tomatoes

PROCEDURE

Slice eggplant lengthwise and broil in a baking pan, skin side up, under the flame until black, then plunge in cold water, remove the skin, and mash. Mix in the rest of the dry ingredients.

Sauté onions, chili, and ginger in oil. Chop and peel tomatoes and add. Cook 5 minutes and combine the mixture with the mashed aubergines.

Roll out pastry balls as thin as possible. Place 1 round tablespoon of the aubergine mixture in the middle, fold in half, and press edges over and seal with the tines of a fork. Deep fry in oil for approximately 10 minutes or until brown. Drain on paper towels and serve.

Chapter 21

FABRIC & PATTERNS

Colin reviewed the conversations of the day. He was reviewing the possibility of the Rajah being involved in this affair. The way Melanie described him and what Colin had seen up until now made that theory unlikely, but in his line of work, nothing was a surprise anymore. But Shiv would not be so naive as to kill his good friend and business partner at his own party, but then again, it would be the perfect place. Why he would kill the American businessman was quite the question. That made zero sense. Colin was forced to postpone his visit to Victor's company as the key person he wanted to see, Steven Orville, had accompanied his boss's body back to the U.S.

New York City

Steven had made good on his promise to deliver McKerny to his family. Back in the U.S., he took the opportunity to shore up his position with his company, Aurora Technologies, if and when he returned. He also took the opportunity to scour the internet and hack into a few computers to wipe any resurfacing comments or damaging information about his mental health.

Regardless of whether he stayed or returned to the U.S., he would send his mother home. So, Steven took the time to look for a permanent place to relocate her. He needed and wanted to live on his own for the first time in his life. Especially with Melanie and Lorinda in the picture.

Steven's movements in New York were stealthy. Cautious, he had been circumspect when visiting the 4Cs offices and only did so late at night and in disguise. He stayed clear of the demonstrations that seemed to have intensified since he left. It was at the 4Cs office that he'd met the first woman beside Melanie Eagleton, who piqued his interest. When Lorinda told him she was a recent design graduate looking for a job, he had directed her to Melanie's company.

"I can't believe you know Melanie Eagleton." She gushed, all impressed.

"I don't know her, but I met her. It seems her firm is pretty impressive."

"It is, and I doubt they would even consider me."

"Never say never," Steven encouraged. Pity he had to go back to India, but he could use ears and eyes while he was away on both the 4Cs and his crush Melanie.

A week later, Colin got a call from the general manager at Victor Gupta's corporation to report that several employees who were out sick and Steven Orville were now back to work. "If you'd like to come today, we can accommodate you." The GM said.

Colin hightailed it down to Melanie's floor and rapped on her door.

"I didn't order anything," Melanie said to whom she thought was room service.

"I don't have anything. It's Colin," the voice responded.

Her face covered in a Korean green facemask, Melanie shouted, "Just a minute." She sprinted to the bathroom. A few minutes later, she opened the door and stood with a silly grin on her face. "Sorry, I was in the bathroom!"

"I heard you scampering around. Were you dolling up for me?"

Melanie looked down at her terry cloth robe and saw that she had missed a few spots of greenish glop that had smudged her robe. "Scampering, did you just say I was scampering?" She laughed out loud. "I haven't heard that word since you left America."

"It is one of my favorite words. Can you be ready in a hurry? The GM from Victor's company called. We can go today. Can you even make it?"

"I'm sure Shiv will be okay with it. I will meet you downstairs in twenty minutes."

Victor Gupta's business was a sprawling state-of-the-art facility on the outskirts of Delhi. Melanie and Colin were met in the modern and plush lobby by the general manager, who appeared tired, haggard, and still reeling from his bosses' death. "Please, come this way." He led them to an elevator.

Steven Orville and two of his colleagues were seated at the conference table when they entered the office. They looked from Melanie to Colin and back again. Steven smiled. "Ms. Eagleton, it's nice to see you again."

"Likewise, Mr. Orville."

"Oh, please call me Steven."

"I am Detective Colin Smyth," Colin said. "It's good to meet you all. He badgered the staff with questions, and when he was done, he turned to the American and said, "Mr. Orville, I will need to ask you a few additional questions since I understand you were with Mr. Gupta and Mr. McKerny at the Rajah's party."

"Yes. I was. They were my bosses. Unfortunately, I left early and did not hear what happened until the following day."

"Why did you leave early? I heard it was a very impressive evening."

Steven took a deep breath and began to speak. "I felt a bit out of place in a palace. It wasn't like I was an invited guest. Mr. Gupta invited Mr. McKerny because they had some things to go over before his departure the next day. I report directly to Mr. McKerny and as his 'boots on the ground' person, assigned to see if we could solve some of the issues we are facing back home. I was there to give that report. When I got a chance to make an early exit, I took it."

"Why couldn't the meeting be postponed until the next day?"

Steven stared at Colin for a few seconds. He felt his dander rising. Was this guy stupid or what? Didn't he hear what he'd just said? Trying to steady himself, he kept his voice low and began again. "Because, as I just mentioned, Mr. Gupta was leaving for America the following morning. He wanted to review the report before he left. And since it was also happened to be Mr. McKerny's birthday, Mr. Gupta thought it would be a fun thing for him to experience a Bollywood party."

"I see," Colin said. "What findings were you presenting?"

"I was sent here to find out if there was a win-win situation for America and India. I was a part of an activist group in the USA called the 4Cs. We were very vocal against companies like ours for outsourcing jobs overseas. Mr. McKerny, because of my background, hired me to come to India to see if there were other options that could work for both parties. He sent me here to figure that out."

"And what did you figure out?"

"Well, my report presented a hybrid model—a one-to-one ratio of Indians to Americans. We would send American workers here to India to work alongside their Indian counterparts in a one-to-one ratio. That way, both companies could win."

"That sounds like a good idea," Colin said. The guy was pretty sharp, if a bit impatient.

"I thought so," Steven said, pleased at the compliment.

"I also understand that you both brought gifts to the party."

"We did. Mr. Gupta explained to Mr. McKerny and me that it was the protocol that visitors bring gifts to the palace. Mr. Gupta told me the Rajah particularly liked a certain candy, and he told me where to find it, so I went there to procure the gifts for myself and Mr. McKerny. I bought four boxes. Two as gifts to the Rajah from Mr. McKerny and me. One for Mr. McKerny's birthday and one for my mother. She likes candy. Even Indian candy. The party was amazing and magical, but as I said, I felt a little out of place and so departed as soon as I saw an opportunity."

"Thank you, Mr. Orville. Thank you very much for your time. I am sure Mr. McKerny's family is grateful to you, too."

"It was the least I could do."

The other two employees had very little to add. They corroborated that Mr. Gupta had wrapped the meeting early and extended an invitation to Mr. McKerny and Steven Orville.

On their way back to the hotel, Colin asked Melanie, "What do you think of Steven Orville?"

"He's impressive. I thought he seemed honest if a bit nervous. Who wouldn't when being interrogated about a murder? But, honestly, what reason would he have to kill his bosses! There would be no benefit to him."

"You're probably right. And forthright. I liked that he didn't hide his connection to the 4Cs. Anyway, I need to change the subject because there is something I'd like to discuss with you."

"Now? About what?"

"Well, perhaps not this minute. Can we discuss that over dinner tonight?"

"Sure, but any hints? I hate surprises, you know."

"No hints."

"So, what are we discussing now?"

"Shiv."

Unfortunately, Shiv insisted on joining them for dinner, so their real conversation was tabled. Rekha had returned to London, and he was back to wanting to have Melanie at his beck and call. Melanie would have to figure out how to tactfully tell him that she needed some alone time every once in a while. Tonight would have been one of those nights, but she could not bring herself to uninvite Shiv though she couldn't wait to hear what Colin had to discuss. Alas, she would have to. Maybe Colin was right. Shiv was stuck to her like glue.

The following morning Melanie discovered by way of text from an Inspector Oswal that she was not a suspect in the Gupta death and was free to return to America. She was relieved. However, if Colin wasn't going to be leaving soon, and since she still had quite a bit to do on the project, there might be a reason to stay on through the next phase though there were things at home that needed her attention.

Melanie calculated how long it would take to finish everything that needed to be done for the palace. She wished she could just go home for good, but what was the point of making the long trek back since most of what needed her attention had to be done here in India. She would have to go and come back for the opening, but it would be one less journey.

"With the decision made, she texted Shiv to say she was on her way with the fabric samples she'd picked out to show him.

Shiv answered immediately, "Please come this evening instead. I'm having a few of my film friends from Mumbai over, and I'd love for you to meet them and get their take on your fabulous idea of a museum room. I'll pull together some of the costumes and posters to give you an idea of the treasures I have to go in the room."

"That's wonderful."

"By the way, if you want to bring the detective, you may."

"Thanks, Shiv, I'll do that."

Melanie very much wanted to go to the gathering because she was curious about Shiv's guests and realized that much of her business relied on referrals and word of mouth. Besides, it would be fun since she'd been watching a few Bollywood movies lately. If the gorgeous Deepika Padukone happened to be there, she would surely keel over and die! "Oops, bad choice of words" she tapped her lips. Melanie texted Colin and told him about the party.

"I hope no one dies at this party."

"Colin! That's insensitive. No one will die."

Melanie was glad to have the morning off and spent most of the day finishing her drawings and attaching the fabric samples to them. The main "museum" would be created in the large ballroom of the palace. From there, patrons would wind their way through smaller rooms, each featuring one of Shiv's major movies. At each entrance of each of the smaller rooms, viewers upon entry would be met with holographs of the characters he played, thanks to technology. They would literally be transported into the movie playing on a large LED screen. Should patrons wish to know more, they could don glitzy headphones for an explanation of the movie and the scene they were watching. In front of movie posters, life-sized wax figures would display the costumes worn in the movie. She'd been awed at the technology employed, but it was true that India's tech teams were legendary.

Before going up to her room after tea time, Melanie decided to stop by Colin's room to give him the party invitation that had arrived by courier. He answered the door topless.

"Looking good," Melanie said, walking into the room trying to avert her eyes from the six-pack muscles he sported at his age. Though she didn't think he was that old. Forty was the new thirty, anyway, and he looked great.

"So do you," he flirted.

"About tonight. Here is the official invitation. We can go together, or you can arrive as your schedule permits."

"Why do you think I am here getting all dolled up if not to go as your escort."

"Oh," Melanie said. Shall we leave at 6:30 p.m.? I'll meet you in the lobby."

"No, madam. I'll pick you up from your room. Since the Rajah Shiv is soooo very prominent in our lives, we should be on time. I'll fetch you at 6:15 p.m."

"Did you just say "our lives?"

"That was the dinner conversation I wanted to have, but your glue was so stuck."

Trying to avoid what she thought was coming—a kiss since he'd moved dangerously close to her, she said, "Of course, he is important in my life. Shiv is the reason I am here. He is technically my 'boss,' and he is my client, and he is paying me a lot of money. But why is he important to you?"

With a twinkle in his eyes, Colin said, "Melanie, nobody is your boss! Your client, maybe. But not your boss. And to answer your question, he's important to me because he's important to you."

Melanie smiled and said, "I'll be ready at 6:15."

"I'll see you then." Colin looked at her for longer than necessary, then gave her a megawatt smile and said, "Who could resist a Bollywood party?"

*   *   *

Several days later, Lorinda texted Steven that she had gotten the job as a temporary assistant at Diva Designers and thanked him for the lead.

Mango Smoothie

INGREDIENTS
- 2 C frozen mango
- 1 C yogurt
- 1 t honey
- 1 t lime juice

PROCEDURE
Blend till creamy and serve in a tall glass.

Chapter 22

An Evening of Stars

Colin and Melanie arrived at the palace at 8 p.m. True to Shiv's word, it was a Bollywood night to remember. Melanie, now an authentic Bollywood fan, spotted Katrina Kaif, Anushka, Sharma, Shahid Kapoor, Kangana Ranaut, Ajay Devgan, and many others whose names she could not recall immediately, but to her chagrin, no Deepika. "I hope you can dance the *Bhangra* or *Lungi Dance*," she whispered to Colin as they entered the ballroom.

He laughed and whispered back, "I'm a real Englishman. I can't dance. Maybe a foxtrot now and then."

Shiv saw them and immediately came over. Grasping both of Melanie's hands, causing her to nearly drop the portfolio tucked under her arm, he pulled her in for cheek kisses and then made a namaste gesture to Colin. Melanie thought the two men were preening like the peacocks in the garden.

"Everyone." Shiv clapped his hand to get their attention. "You must meet my fabulous designer, Melanie Eagleton. I can't wait for you to see how she'll transform this place into a first-class museum. The excitement of it all is unbearable," he said. "And this is Detective Colin Smythe of Scotland Yard, who is in India to investigate the loss of our beloved Victor."

The room was solemn for a few minutes before the buzz began again. Everyone at the party was only too aware of the tragedy.

"While they are chatting away," Shiv took Melanie by the elbow. "Let's sneak upstairs so I can show you some of the pieces I've gathered for the museum."

"Okay,"

Melanie informed Colin that she'd be with Shiv looking over some work before the party got going. Colin's face was unreadable, but she swore she saw a bit of annoyance in his eyes. As Shiv was dragging her by the hand upstairs, Melanie noticed that Kangana Ranaut had approached Colin and was now devoting his full attention to her. She would have frowned, but it left lines!

There were dozens of colorful costumes hanging on multiple clothes racks and a dozen more draped over the settee in the room where he took her. "Can I tell you again how I absolutely love the museum idea. Many of these costumes came from my family, so I know my grandfather is looking down right now with great pleasure that they will be displayed. He would have been proud of his legacy. Really, thank you, Melanie. I would never have thought of this."

"I am sure he *is*," Melanie said, knowing the importance of honoring ancestors from her heritage. "These are amazing," she said, staring at the beautiful cotton, brocades, and velvets. The colors were extraordinary. "May I?"

Shiv handed her cotton gloves, and she carefully picked up an exquisite sari for closer examination. "Simply marvelous," she replaced the sari and picked up a dhoti.

She asked, "Shiv, can you explain some of the pieces to me?

"The first piece you picked up is a pure silk *banaras* worn by women in the North of India." "This," he pointed to another beautiful sari "is known as *Kanchipuram*, mostly worn by women in the South." "And this," he points to yet another outfit "called an *Ikat,* is worn by women in the East. This *paithani is* from the west. See how they differ? So, like a name, it's possible to guess people's origins from the clothes they wear. Every region has its own style. You can also tell by the type of silk." "This," his eyes glittered, "is a masterpiece." The dress was the most elaborate and beautiful wedding gown Melanie had ever seen. "Look how fine it is," Shiva said, delicately and lovingly touching the garment. Today, we still respect the traditional ways of manufacturing silk where the matrimonial fabric is made only from double cocoons. But this is one of a kind. It was the betrothal dress of my grandmother; it came directly from the Silk Road."

"Ah, the Silk Road and Khyber Pass were a great source," Melanie said.

"Yes. And a very important part of our history. I know everyone claims it and rightly so because the trade route runs through all of Asia and the Middle East, but India was a central hub at the time."

"Nowadays, the most common way for women to wear saris requires wrapping it around the waist and draping it over the shoulder. Underneath, they wear a short-sleeved fitted blouse called a *choli*. The sari, of course, has become an emblem of Indian culture." He looked at the *dhotis* Melanie was holding.

"That is a *dhoti* men wear, *and similar to saris,* there are different styles for different regions. The tradition started in small hamlets where the original *dhotis* were simply a piece of cloth wrapped around men. Now we stitch them to look like *dhotis* and just step into them like pants. A Manipuri man wears a *dhoti,* a jacket and must have a white turban. In Bengal, *dhotis* are pleated and long so that one end is held in the right hand."

"You and your family deserve a museum for keeping this history alive for future generations. It is so important to have roots." Something her mother never allowed her to forget. Melanie smiled warmly at Shiv. She had grown quite fond of his charming personality.

"Shiv, on a more serious note, are these wonderful clothes insured?"

"Melanie, is the sky blue?" He raised an eyebrow, "I assure you, my dear, they are."

I know that we are going to have one fabulous museum! Perhaps it will be the quality of New York's Metropolitan Museum of Art's Costume Collection." Shiv beamed.

"That is my aim." Melanie concurred.

Shiv once again felt that choosing Melanie Eagleton as his designer was the best thing he had ever done for the project.

"Shall we rejoin the party? I don't want that Scotland Yard man thinking you've gone missing." Shiv winked.

Melanie felt her face flush as they exited the room. Once outside the room, Shiv retrieved a key from a chain around his waist and locked the door. They returned to the great hall and his other guests.

More people had arrived, but Kangana was still talking to Colin. And he looked rapt in their conversation. Had Melanie been more observant, she'd have noticed him looking at her from the corner of his eye. Melanie sauntered over, trying to look cool and unbothered. "Hello." Colin pulled her into the conversation. "This is Kangana. She has just returned from a trip to England to prepare for her upcoming role and wanted to confirm some details about jolly ole England. She needs to master an upper-class English accent for her next movie. Where better than Oxford?"

"Nowhere," Melanie proffered and then said, "but Colin, I thought you were Irish?"

"You are right. I am Irish, but I moved to Britain when I was quite young, so I grew up in Britain, which served to jettison my Irish brogue."

Kangana laughed, showing adorable dimples. "Ireland, Scotland, England, pretty much the same, right Colin?" she said, bringing in a bit of Indian sarcasm.

"Yes, but for the accents. So, you've got to stick with the Queen's English, I'm afraid."

"Oh, there you are." Shiv, who'd thought she was behind him, was once again pulling her by the arm onto the veranda of the great room. "Do come and meet my other friends."

Two very beautiful women were gracing the ottomans on the porch. One languidly rose, sweeping back shining black hair, and said, "I understand you're going to make a real palace out of this scary place. I can't stand this 17th-century rubbish."

"Pay her no mind," Shiv said. "Melanie Eagleton, this is Shamira Nehru. She's the female lead in my newest film, *Love Lost Among the Fountains*. Sounds more Italian than Indian, no?"

Melanie nodded.

Shamira, a beautiful woman in her early thirties, brightened up a bit, "Are you *the* Melanie Eagleton, aka the 'Decorating Diva?'"

"I am."

"I have seen your designs and positively adore them. Your work is so earthy and modern. You were recommended to me by a friend, but I had to run away to do this movie with Romeo here." She used an index finger to lift Shiv's chin. "I would love you to do my penthouse in New York. But tell me, how did you get dragged into historical work like the palace? It doesn't seem your style."

"By a very charming Rajah, who would not take no for an answer."

"We know." The women said practically in unison.

"So, where is your place in the city? I'd love to take a look at it when I'm back."

"59th and Central Park South," Shamira answered.

"Oh, my. I'll bet the view of Central Park is to die for!"

"It truly is, and I am truly serious about you helping me out."

"Let's make a date when we are both back in the U.S." Melanie smiled.

"This equally rude one here is my friend, Geetha Shetty," Shiv said.

"The Geeta Shetty who left me a message in New York? What a delight to meet you in person."

The woman nodded. "Yes. I am the one who recommended you to Shamira." They both laughed at the coincidence.

"How long before you are back in New York?" Melanie asked.

"Not for several months from the look of things here. I am booked for the rest of the year."

Good, Melanie thought. That would give her time to complete and decorate the horse farm living quarters.

Shiv then rang for trays of kebabs and drinks.

Everyone drifted towards the scrumptious-smelling food. Melanie looked around for Colin and spied him in the corner, chatting up another woman half his age.

"Does anyone here remember 'The Heroic Pilot?'" Shiv asked.

The room did a wolf cry.

"Well, for those who don't know, Shamira here," he held up the raven-haired woman's arm, "was my fabulous co-star then and will be my co-star too in the new movie. If you remember, I was a suave, irresistible Bangladeshi, and surprise, she was from an old Mumbai family. As with just about every Bollywood plot, her family opposed our marriage, but I, the irascible lover, whisked her away in my small plane. Unfortunately, before we could marry and consummate our relationship, the plane exploded into a fireball over a small lake in Pakistan. So sad, but it made millions. It is the first movie I will have in the museum."

"You are right. We make 845 versions of the same movie, but we always cry, and many do make millions." Someone raised a glass.

"Let's take a trip down memory lane," Shiv pulled open a vintage Vuitton wardrobe that had been wheeled in and unfolded the uniform he wore for 'The Heroic Pilot.' "Shamira, you should donate one of your costumes from the movie to my museum. How about the one you wore when I first encountered you at the debutante dance where we met? You looked magnificent."

"Absolutely. Can I get a tax break for the donation?"

"She has become so American." Shiv frowned.

Everyone laughed as they grabbed Indian kabobs off the silver trays being carried by white-jacketed waiters passing by. Melanie was happy for the lighthearted moments and slightly annoyed with Colin. Luckily, she would get over it quickly.

Four weeks went by fast, and Melanie couldn't believe she was finally going home. She'd said goodbye to Colin, who was heading off to meet up with a terrorist task force in Mumbai a week before. It seemed they had reached a dead end with Victor's and McKerny's deaths, and they had both been ruled unfortunate, coincidental death but not by foul play.

*   *   *

Steven was summoned by his CEO to make a trip to New York. He'd been pleased with Steven's proposal and wanted to discuss in person the ramifications. It proved timely as Steven had read in the paper that Melanie was leaving for New York until the palace opening. Maybe he could meet her on their territory, especially since Lorinda was in her sphere. He'd practically been talking with Lorinda on WhatsApp nightly and felt confused by the feeling he was developing for her. He would surprise her when he was in New York.

Lorinda was indeed surprised that Steven had returned so soon. She invited him to a 4Cs demonstration on Saturday, which he texted back that he would not be able to make it but would meet her for coffee. On Saturday, after the demonstration ended, Lorinda met Steven at a local coffee shop.

"Hey," he greeted her.

"Hi. You didn't wait long, did you?"

"No. I arrived just before you did."

Lorinda slid into the chair opposite Steven, her eyes sparkling. "I can't believe you're here. Now I can thank you in person." Lorinda smiled up at Steven. "I am indebted to you."

Steven looked at her over the rim of his coffee cup. "So, you got an interview. That's a good thing."

"It really is. But how did you even know about the Designing Diva?"

"Long story. Some other time. Let's order. I brought some homemade cookies to go with our coffee." He proffered a plastic container labeled "Butterscotch Wafers."

"The proprietor might get mad, but what the heck." Lorinda grabbed a cookie and bit into it… mmm, these are really good. Did you bake them yourself?"

"No. I got them from a shop known for homemade goods."

Did he live with somebody? Lorinda wondered. Though she was physically attracted to him, there was something mysterious about Steven. Maybe he was just really shy.

Lorinda was becoming a little impatient with Steven's hesitancy about moving the relationship forward. Still, just as her annoyance was building to a peak, he turned up his charm. They stayed at the coffee shop for an hour, much of the time him getting to know her better. She liked that as much as she liked him walking her to the subway, though she was disappointed he didn't suggest they get more intimate.

Lorinda caught the next train and waved goodbye to Steven. This was one strange guy, but she hoped she would see him again. She was indeed attracted to him and charmed by the fact that he had brought her a gift—no matter who baked them.

Steven stopped at a sandwich shop and bought a soda before walking to Jay Street, where he had left his rented car. He was heading back to the fancy hotel the company was footing the bill for in Manhattan. Things were looking up, he thought, as he climbed behind the wheel. Lorinda was going to be useful.

Steven crossed the Williamsburg Bridge and headed up Third Avenue. As luck would have it, he spotted the *decorating diva* emerging from a building under some man's umbrella, laughing with obvious delight in his company. Steven felt an irrational sense of ownership as the man gave Melanie a quick kiss on the cheek as she ran into a taxi. On a whim, Steven grabbed his cell and called Lorinda.

"Hello?"

"Hi, it's Steven. I was wondering if you'd like to have dinner with me tonight."

"Tonight?"

"I know it's short notice, but I can send an Uber for you. Can you make it?"

"Well, I think so. I was going to a movie with my friend, but I can cancel."

Lorinda was excited. She knew Steven would be leaving the country again soon, but she didn't want to make the first move. She was so glad he'd man up and asked her to dinner. Lorinda found the perfect outfit, went to the bathroom, and made herself beautiful.

Steven was sweating. He'd never been alone with a woman except for his mother. Most people wouldn't know this about him, but he had no idea what to do on a real date. Steven, ever resourceful, googled "first date" and wrote down a few pointers. Hopefully, they could have dinner and watch a movie together at the hotel.

Lorinda arrived at 6:00 p.m. Steven couldn't believe how good she looked. He'd never seen her with her hair out or with makeup on. "You look nice," he said, remembering his Google search that said to compliment your date.

"So do you," Lorinda blushed.

"I have made reservations for dinner downstairs in the restaurant. Then I thought we could watch a movie in the room if you want."

"I do. It sounds like a great plan."

All through dinner, Steven stared at Lorinda and looked a little uncomfortable.

Lorinda stifled a smile. He was nervous. Maybe she'd help him out a bit.

"Steven," Lorinda said softly. "All through lunch, we talked about me. Tell me about you."

No one had ever asked him about his life before. That made her feel special to him. He wondered how much he could trust the woman sitting before him. Would she bolt out the door if she found out about his sad life? And that he lived with his mother. When she touched his face ever so gently, Steven felt feelings he'd never felt before.

Lorinda watched as Steven paid the bill. All cash. What she didn't know was that he wanted to leave no trace of his movements. Even at the rental car place though they had insisted he leave a credit card, he'd convinced them to take cash when he left five times the amount of the cost of the car. All they needed to know was that his company had put him up at the Viceroy Hotel, should they check. His paranoia was clearly at work.

Indian Kabobs

INGREDIENTS

- 1 lb. minced lamb
- 1 medium onion minced
- 1 green chili minced with seeds removed
- ½ inch ginger root minced
- 1 cloves garlic minced
- 2 springs coriander leaves, chopped fine
- 1 egg
- Juice of ½ lemon
- 2 T breadcrumbs
- 1 t chili powder
- 1½ t ground pepper
- ¾ t garam masala
- 1 t cumin powder
- 1 t salt

PROCEDURE

Mix all the ingredients in a bowl and set aside for 30 minutes—grease skewers. Make long sausages with the meat and skewer. Brush with oil and grill 8 minutes per side, until slightly browned. Serve on a bed of coriander leaves.

Chapter 23

HOME AT LAST

Melanie had been home a week, most of her time spent catching up on emails, paying bills, and cooking herself an American meal! She felt bad that she'd waited to call Lars and had only gone into the office yesterday, but she'd needed the time for self-care and quiet.

Lars and the staff had been beside themselves when Melanie walked into the office. They hugged and hugged over and over again. Lars looked well, and it seemed married life gave him an extra glow. It had been several months since she'd seen him, and she was glad he was happy.

"So, partner," Melanie held onto him as long as she could. "How are things. My gosh, Lars, you look amazing. Work must be good for you," she teased.

"Well, of course, darling, you know how much I love my work."

"Let's carve out some time to sign our contract today. You've reviewed everything and no changes, the attorney said."

"Yes, yes, let's do that later. Now you have to tell me everything, and I want to see pictures and all."

One of the staff caught his attention and tapped her watch.

No sooner had she stashed her purse than he was perched on her sofa, ready to give and receive all the news that was fit to print.

Thank goodness he had an appointment…and an interview for his new hire for Decorating Diva.

"Want to sit in?"

"Not at all," Melanie said.

Back home, Melanie felt antsy. Was she even missed at the office? She needed a sugar high to console herself, so she went to the fridge to get some fruit. Hallelujah, there in the freezer was some frozen blueberry compote she'd made before she left for India. She took her compote, toasted brioche, and coffee to her desk and decided to reach out to her circle. Melanie had always been terrible at keeping in touch except with her clients, and that much her friends understood. Her mind strayed to Colin, wondering why he hadn't called. Was he as bad as she was with keeping in touch?

Ping: her text signaled.

-Hi. Calling to say hello.

Melanie brightened. She immediately pinged back.

-Hi, Colin. How funny I was getting ready to send you a message- and here you are sending one. I guess we are on the same wavelength telepathically.

- I could have told you that. I bet you were wondering why I hadn't called in a week.

-Precisely.

-I wanted you to have some quiet time. Are you doing okay?

-I am. I slept for two days, and it took some time for me. I didn't even go into the office until yesterday.

-Good. I'll call you now.

Blueberry Compote

INGREDIENTS

- 1-pint blueberries
- 1-pint raspberries
- 2 T blueberry jelly or jam

PROCEDURE

Mix and then chill. Will keep several weeks in the refrigerator. Pair with buns, brioches, or croissants.

Chapter 24

A DEMONSTRATION

Lorinda Murray was a lucky person. Her interview with the Decorating Divas was amazing, and she was getting ready for her first day at work. She dressed conservatively and was five minutes early. Lars, her interviewer whom she'd immediately liked, met her in the lobby. Her interview had lasted more than 45 minutes, and Lars had not seemed the least bit bothered by her tattoos, though she'd tried to cover up most of them, just in case. He seemed to like her credentials and personality, and the fact that he, she and Melanie had all gone to Pratt sealed the deal. Now here she was employed at Decorating Diva, and Lars said if she did a good job, the position could become permanent.

"Good morning," Lars greeted her with a smile.

"It is for me. A very good morning. Thank you again…Mr.….."

"Ahhh…ah…no Misters around here. You may call me Lars."

"Lars," Lorinda said, beaming up at him.

An hour on the job and to Lorinda's delight, the doyenne herself, Melanie Eagleton, the owner of Decorating Divas, walked through the door.

"Hello. You must be our new hire. I am Melanie Eagleton," the woman outstretched her hand. Lorinda felt the same warm energy from her as she did with Lars.

That evening Lorinda called Steven. After their night together, she felt less anxious. "I began my job today. Lars said if I do a good job, the position could become permanent. I am so excited."

"Lars?"

"Yes. He is a partner in the firm."

That must have been the guy he saw with Melanie. Steven suddenly became animated again and said, "Did you meet the owner?"

"You mean Melanie Eagleton. Only briefly. She was in and out of the office today. I think I'm going to be happy there, Steven. Here is the funny thing! Like you, she's working on a project in India! She's working on a major project for an Indian Rajah."

"Oh, when is she going back to India? Maybe I can meet up with her."

"I think in a month or so. I am looking forward to getting to know her better. She seemed just as nice as Lars."

Mom's Butterscotch Wafers

INGREDIENTS

- 1 lb. dark brown sugar
- 3 eggs
- 2 t vanilla extract
- 1 t salt
- ½ lb. (1 C) soft butter or margarine
- 2⅓ C un-sifted flour
- 2 C chopped nuts (or raisins or 1 C each)

PROCEDURE

Place all ingredients except nuts in a large mixing bowl. Beat by hand until light and fluffy. Stir in nuts.

Drop from teaspoon 2 inches apart on an ungreased cookie sheet. Bake at 375° for 8-9 mins.

Chapter 25

In Memory of Victor

Melanie's return flight was uneventful. In first-class, she hadn't noticed Steven just behind her in business class. However, as she made her way to customs, she noticed him and he her. He nodded but made no further attempt to connect with her, settling behind her as next in line for clearance. The Rajah had publicly announced the palace opening as publicity posters greeted her at the airport and the hotel. It was a big deal!

At the hotel, Melanie was greeted like a family. "You were gone too long," Mr. Rashid greeted her with a warm smile.

"Only a month," Melanie said. "It went by so fast."

"Well, we are glad to have you home."

"Ah, how sweet," She really loved the Taj.

Her phone trilled. "Shiv," Melanie answered.

"I hear you're back."

"Seems you have ears and eyes everywhere. I was trying to sneak back as I have some work to do before we meet. I'll take tomorrow off, and we'll hit the ground running bright and early the next day."

"Okay. That works as I have to do some media for my movie tomorrow anyway. You can be sure I'll talk about the opening of the palace too."

"Wonderful," Melanie said and rang off.

Melanie noticed a small replica of a snake charmer's basket and a beautiful vase of flowers on the table as she entered her suite. How special, she thought, pulling the card from the flowers. There was no note, but the card was signed with an "S."

"S, hmmm!" Shiv or from Smythe?

Melanie unwrapped the basket and admired the beautiful box inside. She opened the lid and found a box of Indian chocolates with edible gold wrapping. Melanie almost fainted. She knew the moment she saw the gold-wrapped chocolate that they were the same kind that had been given out at Shiv's banquet. The same kind that Victor ate right before he collapsed. This was creepy, and her heart was pounding from irrational fear. Why would Shiv nor Colin send something like this? They would never play such a cruel joke.

Melanie stood staring at the basket, trying to decide whom to call first—hotel security, police, Shiv, or Colin. She called the hotel security to find out who delivered it. They told her a local florist. Melanie, unsure of what to do next, was careful to touch nothing more than she had. She decided to call Shiv next.

Shiv responded immediately to her text by calling her. After listening to her babbling one, he could only say one word.

"What? Flowers and chocolates? I should have sent flowers. Forgive the oversight, but I didn't. I certainly would never send chocolates, not after Victor…." Melanie could hear the distress in his voice.

"I didn't think you would. But who would? For the same reason, I don't think Colin would be this inconsiderate, but I'll call him when I hang up. This is very upsetting."

"Call the police immediately. Let no one into your room, not even room service. I'll call Mr. Rashid and have him on alert. I'll be there after my interview if you are okay."

"I'm okay."

Melanie called the police the moment they hung up.

"Yes. Yes, Yes." The sergeant kept saying as Melanie prattled on. "This has to be quite upsetting. Please do not touch the "gift." An officer will be there shortly to inspect the premises and retrieve the gifts. I'll call you back shortly with the officer's name who will arrive…In the meantime, do not leave the premises or open your door to anyone."

Colin was beside himself. "Who would be that insensitive. He sounded very upset. Call the police now." He instructed.

"They are on their way here."

"Good. I will be there tomorrow. I suggest you leave the hotel and go to Shiv's palace."

"Colin, I don't think you need to come. Let's see what this could be all about first. And I think I will be fine here."

"I will be there tomorrow," he said with finality.

Her phone pinged with a message and the picture of Officer Patel, who arrived fifteen minutes later. Inside, donning cotton gloves, he inspected the room removing the candy and flowers.

Shiv arrived an hour or so later. "I am not happy with all this. Who on earth would be this crass? I just can't … look, let's go to my place. I trust my security more than I trust the hotels. You can't stay here."

Melanie and Shiv slipped into the waiting car parked at the entrance celebrities usually used at the back of the hotel. The driver put Melanie's overnight bag in the trunk and eased into traffic.

"I'm sure it's nothing," Shiv said. "But we can't be too careful. I'm famished. Haven't eaten all day. Could you use a snack? My guards will accompany us."

Melanie was not enthusiastic about eating again but appreciated the elegant old tea house. They were seated in a back corner away from any windows. Shiv ordered a pot of jasmine tea and crumpets. His guards took the table by the door.

The following morning Melanie joined Shiv very early as promised. "Let's take a look at what happened with the museum in the four weeks you were gone. The workers did a splendid job."

"Wow! Melanie was impressed. "This is impressive. The redesign and physical changes are done, and it's beautiful."

"What are your thoughts on the finishing touches for the museum? Let's get it done as quickly as possible."

"I'm going to recommend that we use the Morgan Library in New York City as a model. It incorporates the museum pieces in a living environment. We can use your family heirloom to give the feel of the Bengal period. Movie artifacts in each period room will bring it full circle to modern times. "Take a look at this." She showed him illustrations of how the five rooms would be decorated.

"What about the larger gathering space to host receptions and parties?"

"I have completed illustrations for that too."

"We are almost there, Melanie. Even in all the chaos, you've never missed a beat. Thank you. Now finish up your tea. You'll be very safe here, and I won't have to worry."

Melanie's room overlooking the garden was the respite she needed. Shiva even went so far as to post a guard outside her door.

Back at the hotel the next evening, Melanie saw the phone's message light blinking. It was a message from Colin. "I'm here. Where are you? Been trying to call your cell and your room. Why aren't you answering? Call me as soon as you get this message."

Melanie pulled her cell from her bag. It was dead. Wonder why he didn't call Shiv.

She plugged up her cell and dialed Colin from the hotel phone. "It's Melanie."

"Where have you been?"

"Shiv's. I took your advice and didn't stay at the hotel last night. I forgot my charger, so my phone was dead when you tried to call. I am just returning."

"Can you meet now?"

"I will meet you in fifteen minutes. Just give me a sec to freshen up. Where?"

"The Sapphire Bombay restaurant."

"Oh, fancy." Melanie decided on a change of attire. The Sapphire Bombay was a five-star Michelin-rated restaurant in the hotel.

When Melanie arrived, Colin was seated and sipping what she imagined was Chai tea, his favorite. He rose as he saw her coming toward him and walked around the table to give her a deep embrace. Melanie could have stayed in his embrace forever. She felt safe.

"You must be really tired," Melanie said, sitting in the chair Colin had pulled out for her.

"Yes. I am a bit tired, as I am sure you are."

"So, did the police come up with anything?"

Melanie shook her head. "Not that I've heard." "But I've been wracking my brain about who S could be. Giving some real thought to this, I think it could be Steven Orville."

"Steven Orville? How would he know where you were staying?"

He was on my plane back to India, although I didn't know it until clearing customs. He was right behind me in line and did acknowledge me, but he said nothing. But I'd forgotten to fill in my stay address on the immigration form, and the customs officer asked me where I was staying. I said the Taj. He might have heard me mention that I was staying here. The more I think about it; he is the only other S I know in India."

"You know I got the feeling that he admired you when we were at Victor's office. It does make sense if the symbolism of a snake charmer is that he likes you. The chocolates he probably felt if they were good enough for the Rajah, they'd be good enough for the woman he liked."

"None of this makes sense to me. But then again, none of the things that have happened in the past couple of years make sense either."

Colin agreed that indeed she'd had a stressful few years and hoped he'd be a part of the calm to come in her life. Some things were not coincidences but destiny.

Colin dropped by the police station.

"I know you've pretty much closed the case of Victor and McKerny, but at one point, you thought the 4Cs might somehow be involved. In light of this new development with Ms. Eagleton, do you think Steven Orville might be somehow involved? He is the only other S she knows in India and, as you know, has been connected to the 4Cs."

"How would he fit into a picture, but we can't see an immediate connection. We've known since the beginning that back in the U.S., Mr. Orville was a part of the 4Cs brain trust. That's what got him hired. He was the big data guy for them, but since he's been in India, we find no evidence that he has continued to be active with the group. He seemed to have moved on with his life which has become cushy. Man's nature for self-preservation. I am sure he doesn't want to go back to being unemployed."

"Could you spare a couple of eyes to observe him for a couple of weeks?" Colin requested.

"I'm not sure the police will approve such a request, especially without evidence. However, I will make the request."

At dinner that night, Melanie was pensive. Colin did his best to cheer her up. "Even if you are a target, we are on top of it now."

Melanie shook her head. "But why would someone target me? I am just a designer. I don't have anything to do with any of this. Maybe, I am overreacting, but if he did send me the basket and if he had ill intentions, surely he would be more circumspect?"

"I agree. But sometimes people get bolder when they think they've gotten away with something."

Melanie sipped her wine. All this was bizarre. Suddenly she felt tired. Tired of all the uncertainty, including what her relationship with Colin represented.

"I am fading fast," Melanie finished her wine and looked at Colin. "Shall we?"

Colin stood and took Melanie's hand to help her up. He didn't let her hand go as they headed to the elevator. Melanie did not object.

At her door, Melanie pressed Colin's hand to her cheek. "I am truly grateful to you for being here. You are a very special person, and truly…." She never finished her sentence as Colin covered her lips in an affirming kiss. Melanie felt the flutter, and before she knew it, they were deliciously wrapped in each other arms. Her exhaustion disappeared, replaced by desire.

English Crumpets

INGREDIENTS

- 2 C unbleached white bread flour
- 1⅓ C unbleached all-purpose flour
- ¾ t cream of tartar
- 1 3oz. cake of fresh yeast or 1 envelope active dry yeast (2¼ t) plus ½ t sugar
- 2¼ C lukewarm water
- 3½ t coarse sea salt, crushed or ground (use about half this if you're not grinding your own coarse sea salt.
- ½ t baking soda
- ⅔ C lukewarm milk

To prepare the crumpets, you'll need:
- A griddle or cast-iron frying pan
- 4 crumpet rings, about 3½ inches diameter, greased

PROCEDURE:

Sift together the flours and cream of tartar into a large bowl. Crumble the fresh yeast into a medium-sized bowl. Mix in the lukewarm water until smooth. If using dry yeast, mix the granules and the sugar with ¾ C lukewarm water and let stand until foamy, 5 to 10 minutes. Stir in the remaining lukewarm water.

Mix the yeast mixture into the flour to make a very thick but smooth batter, beating vigorously with your hand or a wooden spoon for 2 minutes. Cover the bowl with plastic wrap and let stand in a warm spot until the batter rises and falls, about 1 hour. Add the salt and beat the batter for about 1 minute. Then cover the bowl and let stand in a warm spot for 15 to 20 minutes so the batter can rest. Dissolve the baking soda in the lukewarm milk. Then gently stir it into the batter. The batter should not be too stiff, or your crumpets will be "blind" (without holes.) It is best to test one before cooking the whole batch.

Heat a very clean griddle or frying pan over moderately low heat for about 3 minutes until very hot. Put a well-greased crumpet ring on the griddle. Spoon or pour the third C of the batter into the ring. The amount of batter will depend on the size of your crumpet ring. As soon as the batter is poured into the ring, it should begin to form holes. If holes do not form, add a little more lukewarm water, a T at a time, to the batter in the bowl and try again. If the batter is too thin and runs out under the ring, gently work in a little more all-purpose flour, and try again. Once the batter is the proper consistency, continue with the remaining batter, cooking the crumpets in batches, 3 or 4 at a time. As soon as the top surface is set and covered with holes, 7 to 8 minutes, the crumpet is ready to flip.

To flip the crumpet, remove the ring with a towel or tongs, and then turn the crumpet carefully with a spatula. The top, cooked side should be chestnut brown. Cook the second, holey side of the crumpet for 2 to 3 minutes, or until pale golden. The crumpet should be about 3/4 inch thick. Remove crumpets.

Grease crumpet rings well after each use.

Chapter 26

ROMANCE BLOOMS

Waking up with Colin next to her felt close to heaven. It was the closest she'd come to feeling alive since Marco's death. She stared at the beautiful man, his sandy hair resting on the pillow. Could she afford to unbridle her heart? Could she dare dream of happily ever after? The thought scared her. Everyone she loved left her, and Melanie was scared to lose Colin. Yet she wanted to be brave. Easing out of bed so as not to wake him as she knew how tired he must be, Melanie went to the bathroom and quickly showered, donned her bathing suit and wrote Colin a note. "Going for a swim to clear my head, and if last night was any indication, need to keep in shape. Don't you dare leave before I get back. If you want, you can save Scotland Yard a few bucks and stay here with me." She left Colin, still in a deep sleep, and went to the pool.

Melanie exited the elevator on the lower level where the pool was located. She draped her cover-up over the lounge chair and tested the water with her toe. Perfect. Melanie jumped in and swam ten laps. At the end of the laps, she was slightly out of breath but was pleased she wasn't completely out of shape. Running between countries had taken a toll on her exercise and meditation routine, and she couldn't afford to go back to the state she had been in for more than two years; listless and depressed. If last night was a promise, she had a new reason to be in tip-top shape even though she and Colin lived on different continents.

Wrapping turban-style her hair in a towel, Melanie sat cross-legged in a corner garden that bordered the pool and began her deep breathing exercises. Twenty minutes later, she left her newfound sanctuary. She hoped by now Colin was awake. She wanted to have breakfast with him before heading off to the palace.

The elevator seemed to be stopping at the lobby level, so she pulled her cover-up closer and moved to the corner of the cabin.

"Well, well," the man getting on said. "Another coincidence!"

It was Steven Orville.

"Hello," Melanie spluttered.

Steven looked at her for a few seconds but did not speak. Finally, he said, "You know what they say if you meet a person three times, you're destined for love."

"Really," Melanie tried to stay calm.

"You know. Just a saying. It's good to see you again, Ms. Eagleton."

"Are you staying here at this hotel?" Melanie asked.

"No. I live across town. I have a confounded breakfast meeting. Hate it. Anyway, I hope you liked the gifts I sent you."

"Gifts? Are you the one who sent the basket and candies?"

"I am."

"Why?"

"You've been so kind and just a way of reaching out to another American. Not too many of us here. I heard you tell the customs officer you were staying here and remember how nice you were when we met and when you came to our offices with the British detective. A smile goes a long way."

"How nice of you." Melanie looked at the elevator dial that was pressed to floor 35. Whether he noticed or not, she was taking no chances. She would ask for a room change even though she had a keycard to get to the floors past 30.

"They're the same chocolates I brought to the Rajah's party. The shopkeeper recommended them. Apparently, all of India loves this gold-wrapped chocolate. Did you like them?"

"I haven't tried them yet, but I'll be sure to let you know. Thanks for being so neighborly."

"Do that." Steven stared at her and walked towards her.

"Well, this is my floor. You have a good day now, Miss Eagleton." He got off on the restaurant floor.

Melanie was shaking in her flip-flops. So, it was him, and as she guessed, he'd overheard her in customs. How creepy. She hit the close button and ran down her hallway to her room as soon as the elevator opened.

"There you are," Colin was awake. What's going on? Why are you out of breath?"

"I just sprinted down the hallway."

"Why? Swimming wasn't enough?"

"I just met Steven Orville in the elevator."

"What?"

"He was on his way to a breakfast meeting, he said, and Colin, it was he who had sent the gifts."

"Hmmm…did he say why?"

"He was being nice to another ex-pat."

"Well, that's nice. He wants to befriend you. At least we have an explanation, and there is nothing nefarious about it."

"There is something the matter with him. He is a bit odd. I don't know exactly, but he seems…don't you think?"

I have better things to think about at the moment," he pulled her close and kissed her, and I do plan to save Scotland Yard some money."

"My thoughts exactly," Melanie relaxed in his arms.

Colin headed to the police station to inform them of the latest and that they could pull the surveillance on Steven. Melanie went back to the markets to pick up more swatches to show Shiv. She took the opportunity while there to return the fabulous dress to the boutique, where she hoped to find an exquisite sari for the museum opening.

"Hello again," the owner greeted her.

"I remembered how lovely your clothing was! And the colors," Melanie said, touching the various fabrics in orange, blue, and green. They were of the best quality.

The owner, herself in a stunning sari, smiled and responded, "Aren't they delightful."

"They are, and these colors are extraordinary. I am the interior designer for Rajah Kumar," She handed the woman her business card. "I am looking for something to wear to the opening of his newly redesigned palace. And I need something special because I need to look beautiful."

"That wouldn't take much because, madame, you are beautiful. I will show you something special?"

The woman took her over to an exclusive section of one-of-a-kind designs, and Melanie picked out a stunning peacock-blue silk sari with silver embroidery on the sash and at the hem and a lace choli.

"I'd like to try this one on." Melanie pointed to the blue silk sari."

"Of course. Let me show you how to wrap it. Will there be someone familiar with draping a sari there to dress you for the reception?"

"I hope so, but I am not sure. I've done it a few times myself, but I'm never quite sure I'm doing it right. Let me just say nothing has fallen off yet." Melanie smiled. Colin, who she hoped would be with her, would not know how to wrap her in a sari no matter how smart he was.

"I'm sure Rajah Kumar will have someone for you if needed. Of that, I am sure. The young Rajah does not disappoint."

Melanie thought, how true a statement and how great it was that everyone who knew him thought the same.

"Come this way," the woman ushered Melanie into a small, lightly scented dressing room. The sari fit seemed perfect to her, but the owner said it needed some adjustments. With her measurements taken and a short refresher lesson in the wearing and wrapping of a sari, the proprietor promised to have the dress ready for pick up in a few days.

Melanie stepped out into the bright sun and called Shiv to say she was on her way. She spent the rest of the day with the Rajah, reviewing posters, picking movie characters for the holograms, and walking from room to room to decide on final touches. When the hologram set up ran into some glitches, she reminded him that it was his idea to have a life-sized hologram in every room! Melanie had to admit that the technology complemented and enhanced the museum pieces. They also reviewed the music and soundtrack that would play in each room and spent several hours poring over Shiv's family inventory of clothing, royal costumes, and artifacts such as paintings, pottery, and masks.

"You need a curator."

Shiv nodded. They wouldn't have time to hire someone right now, but at some point, an expert in the Indian Rajah period would be hired to help Rajah decide on the permanent collection and refresh the displays so they remain interesting and up to date. The first curators, Melanie and Shiv, went to town picking what they adored for the first rotation of the museum's art.

It was time to turn their attention to the food, and Melanie, the ultimate foodie, asked Shiv what he would be serving at the opening reception.

"How about samosas and fruitcake for a sweet. It's easy to eat and very English," he teased in an exaggerated British accent. "The chef has given me the menu." He handed it to her.

"Now that's more like it," Melanie looked over the menu and was already salivating at the various kababs, lamb chops, chutneys, and the samosas that were right on point, especially since Melanie loved them.

The menu for the museum tea bar included dishes served in his films. The last thing they had to do was to pick the lineup of films to be shown in the cinema for the next several months. Feeling accomplished, Melanie broke protocol and gave Shiv a big kiss. "Thank you, Shiv, for this great opportunity."

He smiled and blushed just a little. "By the time you get back for the party in a few weeks, I'll be over you." He winked. "I don't know why you just don't postpone your trip until after the party."

"No one would like that more than I but alas, meeting with the dean can't be postponed. Believe me, I tried."

Melanie spent two unforgettable days with Colin regretting getting on a plane and being separated from him. She felt herself blush like a schoolgirl every time she thought of him.

Melanie checked her email on her way to the airport that she'd only been too happy to jettison for time with Colin. There was a long e-mail from Pratt's president, Patty Brown.

Dear Ms. Eagleton:

We are delighted you have accepted our invitation and delighted to welcome you to Pratt Institute. We have tried to be reasonable given your hectic schedule. For the fall semester, you will be teaching a 3-credit course on Wednesdays at 2:00 p.m., once a week for 14 weeks. Your office and class will be at our Manhattan campus. Classes begin on September 8th.

This class will be face-to-face. However, if you must travel, we can arrange for some of your classes to be online. Please let your department chair know if this is necessary. The IT Department will assist with your credentials, and my office will assist you in developing the course if needed.

I am looking forward to meeting you again this Friday to brainstorm what we can do together to inspire the next generation of designers. I am also looking forward to your stories from India. Please find attached an invitation for tea and new teachers' orientation.

Cordially,
Patty Brown, Ph.D.

Melanie felt a wave, very excited. She was looking forward to the challenge. Professor Melanie Eagleton. It had a nice ring. She immediately emailed President Brown to confirm her attendance.

Light Fruitcake

INGREDIENTS

- 2½ C flour
- ¾ C chopped dried pineapple
- 4 t baking powder
- ½ C raisins
- 1 t salt
- ½ C brown sugar
- ¼ C shortening
- 1 egg, beaten
- 1 C chopped candied cherries
- 1 C chopped pecans
- 1⅓ C milk

PROCEDURE

Heat oven to 375°. Sift together flour, baking powder, and salt. Cream shortening and sugar together until light and fluffy. Add egg and milk. Then blend in flour mixture only until blended. Fold in cherries, pineapple, pecans, and raisins. Pour into a greased loaf pan. Bake for 1 hour 15 minutes.

If desired, replace 1/3 C milk with bourbon or rum

Chapter 27

A Sunny Day Spent Partly Indoors

India was coming to a close for Steven, who was to report to the office in New York City within the next four weeks. It had now been four months since Victor's death, and things had quieted down. Since Melanie would leave after the palace opening, he felt it was time to go if he wanted the slightest chance to get to know her better.

His mother, not realizing Steven had gotten his own place while back in the U.S., was preparing to go ahead of him to sort out the apartment he'd rented for her. There was plenty of time to tell her once they were home. His mind wandered to Lorinda. It was time to give her a call, too, though he was now only feeling tepid toward her. He was over-indexing on Melanie in the thought department, convinced she was the woman for him.

"Mother," Steven said before leaving for work, "the movers are coming to pack today. "And Mother," his voice took on a sterner note, "only keep what we need to carry on the plane. They'll send everything else to storage. Please, we need to travel light."

"I will, dear." His mother clasped her hands together. "Do you know what I am going to do today?"

"Meet your lady friends."

"No. I am going to make you peanut soup for dinner. How would you like that?"

"Sounds delicious, mom." He headed toward the door. This morning his head felt heavy, no doubt from all he had to think about to make the move home. He felt a little depressed, and once again, he was tempted to stop taking his pills.

His mother broke his stride. "Have a good day, dear. But Steven, what's the address I need to give the movers for delivery in the States?"

"Don't worry about it. I have to stop by their offices and sign some papers, so I'll make sure they have all the information they need."

Steven had mentally left his job, so he spent his days downloading files from the call center he wanted to take back with him instead of working. He suddenly stopped in his tracks. Something in his gut told him he needed to leave no forwarding address. No one in India needed to be able to trace him. It did occur to him that he might be traced to the New York office. But they would not have his home address but his mother's.

When he stopped by the movers, the address he gave them was the address of the storage company. There wasn't much to store as he'd instructed his realtor to furnish the apartment. As far as they would know, he would be occupying the same apartment.

Files downloaded and much on his to-do list accomplished, he called Lorinda from his burner phone.

Lorinda was very happy to hear from Steven finally. He'd been a little distant lately. She bombarded him with questions about why he hadn't called.

Steven didn't answer most of her questions. She was as bad as his mother with the twenty-twenty questions.

"So, when will I see you?" Lorinda asked.
"In about a month."
"Really. That's wonderful."
"And how are you? Do you still like your job?"
"More than ever."

Mom's Peanut Soup

INGREDIENTS

- 2 medium onions, roughly chopped
- 8 oz Brussels sprouts cut in half
- ½ lb. sweet potatoes or acorn squash cut into ½ inch cubes
- 2 carrots, roughly chopped
- 2 cloves garlic, minced
- 2 T ginger root, minced
- ½ t ground cloves
- ½ t salt
- ¼ t cayenne pepper
- 4 C vegetable broth
- 6 T creamy peanut butter
- 8 C chopped fresh spinach
- 2 T chopped peanuts for garnish

PROCEDURE

Coat large soup pan with cooking spray. Sauté onion and garlic. Stir in sprouts, potato or squash, and carrots, and cook until softened. Add ginger, cloves, salt, and cayenne and cook for a minute. Add broth and bring to simmer; stir in peanut butter until smooth. Reduce heat to low and simmer for about 30 minutes. Add spinach and cook for 10 minutes. Serve.

Chapter 28

PUTTING TOGETHER THE PIECES

Colin had not returned her calls informing him she was home safely. After her Friday meeting with the dean, Melanie decided to drive to her cottage in Newton. She would stay until Wednesday morning, returning for her first class at Pratt. On the way, Melanie contemplated the complexities of a long-distance relationship. She wished Colin was near and that she could share her slice of heaven with him. Would he fit in as Marco did?

*   *   *

Back in New York, Steven called Lorinda. He wanted to reassure her of his interest to make sure she was loyal to him and him alone. "How is it going?"

"Hi, Steven. Everything is great. How are you? Where are you?"

"I'm back in the city. We should meet."

"Sure." Lorinda was excited at the thought of seeing him again. "What do you want to do? I can make dinner at my place. I am so happy you are here, and I can't wait to see you again."

A few hours later, Steven was at Lorinda's door with a gift bag of gourmet popcorn and a bottle of red wine. She loved popcorn, and it seemed a nice touch.

"Hello Steven," Lorinda said, opening the door wide enough so he could enter.

"Wow, you look great." He handed her the gift. She did indeed look amazing in a short black dress. Her expertly applied make-up accentuated her green eyes, and her heart-shaped face glowed. Steven gave her an awkward hug.

"Dinner will be ready in twenty minutes. Make yourself at home and thank you for the gift. Red wine is perfect as we are having steak and popcorn…how thoughtful."

Steven looked around the very trendily-decorated place. He didn't expect it, but she was a designer. His eyes lingered on the very expensive-looking artwork hanging on the walls. This was not an apartment of a recently hired temporary graphic artist.

"Nice place." Steven walked through the rooms.

"Thanks to my parents. They didn't want me to have the total 'finding yourself' New York experience."

"So, where are you from?"

"Texas."

"And what do your parents do?" Funny, he'd never gotten around to these personal questions in the time they'd known each other.

"They're both heart surgeons."

"I see!" Steven headed toward the bedroom, and Lorinda followed. He liked that she was no ordinary girl.

Union Square Popcorn

INGREDIENTS

- 1 C butter
- ½ C light corn syrup
- 2 C packed brown sugar
- 1 t baking soda
- 1 t salt
- 8 C popped popcorn

PROCEDURE

Preheat oven to 200° F. Combine the first four ingredients over medium heat and boil for several minutes. Remove from heat; stir in baking soda. Stir well. Pour over the popcorn to coat well. Bake in a large roaster or pan for one hour, stirring every 15 minutes. Spread on waxed paper to cool and dry.

Chapter 29

SMYTHE

"Colin! Where have you been? Did you get my messages and text?" Melanie was relieved to hear his voice.

"Yes. My apologies. There was a bit of kerfuffle here, and every time I tried to call, something else came up. It turns out it was all for the good because I am on my way to see you."

"Seriously?"

"Unless you don't want me to come.

"Are you kidding, but what brings you this way?"

"Top secret."

"Wish you were here now. I am in Newton."

Colin listened but was not sure he would have liked being back in Newton. He much preferred the city. "When are you getting back to the city. I'll be there on Monday."

"What time?"

"My flight gets in at 6 p.m."

"That's perfect. My class is 2-4, which gives me enough time to come and get you."

Back in Manhattan early Wednesday morning, Melanie dropped off her car at the garage and took a cab, first to her favorite vegan bakery and then to the salon. She'd be well-groomed for her class and Colin. She wondered if she should drop by the supermarket to stock up. Colin hadn't said he'd be staying with her, but there was always that hope.

Dressing in a jade suit, she picked out a matching jade necklace and earrings set to go with the outfit. Gathering up her briefcase, Melanie headed to her first class. Arriving on campus with half an hour to spare, she darted to the campus café to get a cup of coffee. Booting up her lesson plan to the overhead screen, she sipped her coffee and felt excited to teach and see Colin.

Her students started coming in ten minutes early. The class was a hit, and her students seemed impressed with her. Melanie was also impressed with her students. These were young men and women who knew style and design and were eager for her to show them how to apply what they knew and what she would teach them to their careers. Melanie loved that the questions they asked were well thought out and right to the point. She found that she liked the first day of teaching and was thrilled at the possibility of a new niche. She hoped all her classes went this well.

Several students stayed after class to chat for a few minutes, so Melanie was delayed in leaving. A quick stop in the bathroom, she freshened her makeup and was off to pick up her boyfriend. Dare she think of him like that? She did a little jig laughing at her schoolgirl behavior. Melanie parked at Newark airport and ran into the terminal. Heart racing in anticipation, she ran to the arrival exit and there he was, right on time.

"Melanie began waving madly when she saw him, but he didn't seem to notice her, so she ran the length of the cordon until she was standing at the end of the line where he could meet her.

"Hello. Over here."

"I love this," Colin said as she gave him a happy kiss.

Grabbing his luggage in one hand, he held Melanie's hand in the other. "I booked a suite at the Parker Meridien."

Melanie was disappointed. "Oh, phooey! Why? I thought you were going to save Scotland Yard some pounds."

"Because I thought we could live it up on their pounds since we saved them so much money in India. How does room service every day sound to you?"

"Well, since you put it that way. I wish you'd told me. I could have saved a few hours and a few dollars. I went shopping. We'll have to stop by my place and pick up some stuff."

"I'd have been happy to stay at your place, but I was trying to make things easier for you, knowing your hectic schedule."

"The Parker Meridien is sounding good to me right now."

"As long as we are together, I am a happy man." He squeezed her hand.

A quick stop at her apartment, half an hour later, they checked in to the very plush suite Colin had booked. Large and airy with an enviable bathroom and lounge area, they would both be comfortable and not on top of each other. The thought made Melanie blush. She sidled up to Colin, who was standing by the window and snaked her arms around his waist.

"Views like this make me love your city. Such serenity and charm amid the bustle."

"It is spectacular, isn't it?"

"As are you," he embraced her, bruising her lips with a lingering kiss.

"So. What's the top secret that brings you here?"

"Top Secrets can't be told."

At 9 p.m., they entered the very attractive hotel restaurant where they sat next to each other in a cozy, round banquette. They ordered a light dinner of salad, small tea sandwiches, and two pots of tea. Once the waiter left, Colin drew closer to Melanie and kissed her, his hand resting on her breast, ever so lightly. If they hadn't been in the dining room, she would have climbed onto his lap. As she toyed with the idea, Colin suddenly became serious.

"Melanie," he held her hand across the table, "I have some serious news about Victor's case. The Indian police and Interpol now have clear evidence that Victor and McKerny were murdered. Traces of a poison called aconite was found in both men and is most likely the cause of death. They found traces of the substance in the chocolate the men ate. Though yours did not test positive with those Steven gave you, they wanted to speak with him again. It turns out he's left India. He was supposed to show up at his job in New York, but he did not. The authorities know he landed in New York, but the bad news is they have lost track of his whereabouts. The address he gave to his employer was that of the moving company. There is a good chance he is in New York City or came here to disappear. There is also a good possibility you could be in danger. That is why I came to New York. The incident with the snake charmer basket and chocolate he sent to you makes us think you may be in his sights. Why we have no idea, so it's best to be careful."

"Oh my god! This is bizarre. Colin, I can't believe this. I found out something interesting that may be useful. Lars hired a temporary assistant for our office. The last time I was here, I didn't have time to meet her. It so happens she is an alumna of my college, Pratt. I don't get to meet many alums from Pratt, so I decided to take her to coffee to get to know her better."

"That's nice, but...."

Melanie gently chided. "Well, it turns out she's acquainted with the 4Cs group. She is a lovely girl and the daughter of two doctors who rebelled for a while and somehow got involved with the 4Cs."

"Really? Now that's an interesting coincidence."

"We were talking about my time in India, and she mentioned she had a friend in India."

"Good grief, not Steven? What evidence do you have?"

"None. I didn't get to ask who, and she got a call and had to rush back to the office. But do you think…?

"It would be a coincidence. There are enough ex-pats in India to make it so, but…."

"I could talk with her."

"No, I wouldn't. If it is Steven, she could inadvertently tip him off that we were on to him. We'll get to her soon enough."

After he spoke to Melanie, Colin called his Indian police liaison and repeated what Melanie had said to him.

*   *   *

Four police officers, including a DNA expert, were immediately dispatched to Steven's old house in Delhi to do a thorough forensic search for any evidence that might have been left behind. There was an empty box from a chocolatier, the same one on the box they took from Victor's room. The police immediately realized their oversight. They had not visited the shop to ask questions as no evidence warranted it.

Immediately officers were dispatched to visit the chocolate shop. The shopkeeper, taken aback by the swat team, hurried from behind the counter.

"Welcome, constables. How may I be of assistance?"

The lead Inspector, Oswal, pulled out a picture and showed it to the store owner. "Has this gentleman visited your store?'

The proprietor pulled out a pair of specs and fitted it over his nose.

"Oh, yes. I remember him well, a lovely man. Why?"

"Can you tell us what he bought?

"He bought two different kinds of chocolates. These dark chocolate marzipans. And some of the chocolate for kings," he said, pointing to the gold foil-wrapped chocolates. He bought several boxes of these, five to be exact. He asked me to tie two with red ribbons and three with green ribbons, which I did."

"Anything else?

"No, that's all he bought."

"Did he seem at all suspicious to you?"

"Not at all. We even talked about his mother. Before he left, he asked me if I could recommend a hardware store near my store. I sent him to my friend on Rafi Marg Street."

After a few more questions, Inspector Oswal thanked the shopkeeper and headed to Rafi Marg Street.

The proprietor at the hardware store was equally surprised to see police officers coming through the door of his store.

"Good day to you, Inspector, sir." The proprietor said to the policeman who first entered. He knew he was an inspector because of the uniform. *What could be the matter? Why were they visiting him?*

"Good day to you too, sir. I am Inspector Oswal." He extended his hand to the gentlemen.

"Pleased to make your acquaintance, sir."

"We are here to ask you about an American who was referred to you by your friend from the chocolate shop."

"Ah, yes. Mr. Aziz."

"Yes," the inspector said, "he sent a gentleman to see you."

"Yes. Several months ago. Let me get out my notebook. I sometimes make notes about my clients, to remember, that is. Yes, here it is. He complained of a horrible rat infestation at his apartment and asked what I could suggest to kill them. I told him that I used aconitine as it seemed more humane than arsenic. We have infestations every so often. I sold him two bottles of aconitine trioxide. He seemed happy and satisfied. He left and was never back, so I guess it did the trick. May I ask why you are inquiring?"

"I am afraid I cannot," said the inspector looking at the store owner, knowing it was not his fault.

Inspector Oswal had a theory about what could have happened. Aconitine, a naturally occurring toxin from the plant Aconitum, kills without leaving a trace that a routine blood test would not detect. The symptoms the deceased experienced were also consistent with the poison: convulsions, ventricular arrhythmia, nausea, severe stomachache, etc. He could have injected it into the candy, and the chocolate masked the taste. If the boxes with the red ties were poisoned and the green ones were not, that would explain why the Rajah had not been sickened.

Back at the office, Oswal called out for food delivery. Stress always made him hungry, as did everything else. He selected that typically Indian snack, banana chips. Somehow, he'd suspected Steven from the beginning. The guy had a weird vibe. He had to be the killer, and, in his opinion, the killings were solved. Now, all he had to do was find the killer and bring him back. He had to locate Steven Orville.

Banana Chips

Ingredients

- Ripe or Green Bananas

PROCEDURE

Slice the bananas very thin (about 1/8"). Place banana slices on a baking sheet that has been lined with parchment paper. Brush the slices with lemon juice that has been mixed with a little water, and sprinkle with kosher salt and cinnamon. This coating will give it a crisp "chip" texture.

Bake at 250 for approximately 1 1/2 – 2 hours, flipping the banana chips over halfway through. The long baking time is necessary because, at this temperature, the oven will act more as a dehydrator than an oven.

Chapter 30

SOME SWEETNESS

Melanie and Colin, despite the bad news, spent five amazing days together. Ever since Colin spoke with the police in India, Melanie had been on edge. Figuring she'd be safer there, Melanie decided to leave the city and move to her cottage until things were more certain. On Wednesday, she'd drive to the city for her class and come right back. Melanie looked out over her lake of happiness and sorrow from the gazebo. Idly she wondered what it would be like being at the cottage with Colin. Could their love match that of hers and Marco? Surely, she adored Colin, and he did make her heart go pitter-patter, but Marco was that once-in-a-lifetime love. Annoyed that her mind had strayed back to her dead husband, she was about to gather her towels to head back inside when she noticed a car slowly driving by. Strange, she thought. They must be out-of-towners. Everyone around here knew the roads so well, and they breezed by. She wondered if she should offer help but decided they'd find the way as there was not much to getting lost in Newton.

She'd taken to going into the office on Wednesday morning before class. Colin had said no, but she had to find out if Lorinda's friend was Steven Orville. But how? Lorinda and Lars were in conversation when she arrived.

"Good morning." She sidled up to them.

"Hey, Melanie," Lars said.

"Ms. Eagleton," Lorinda brightened when her most admired person arrived. For a few weeks, she'd only been coming into the office once a week.

"So, what's all the news?" Melanie smiled.

"I was just telling her about the Rajah's project and how I can't wait to get to India."

"Ah. I see. Lorinda, maybe you'd like to come. It would give you a chance to see your friend. Oh, but is he in Delhi?"

"He is back from India. He came back going on a month now. Phooey, he was in Delhi too. Can I still go?"

"And who would take care of the office while I'm gone?" Did I tell you, Melanie, I think we should hire this young lady full time. She is an enormous help, and she knows her stuff." Lars said.

"Oh, don't be sad. There is always a next time." Melanie said. She was dying to ask more questions, but she had to be circumspect.

In her office, Melanie texted Colin. He immediately texted back. "Yes, professor."

"I am pretty sure Lorinda's friend is Steven Orville though I can't say for sure. She said her friend returned from Delhi a month ago. I didn't want to ask too many questions and raise suspicion. But I am going to find out more."

"You must remain clear-headed. And, you must be careful. Give me a day to think up a plan to get the information we need without tipping off Lorinda that we are looking for Steven."

"Okay. Thanks, Colin. I miss you so."

Melanie prepared to leave the office. Her mind was in turmoil.

"See you next week." She waved to the staff...and then to Lorinda. "Maybe your friend from India...what is his name...can join us for coffee or tea one of these days."

"That would be nice, but I don't think so. Steven is kind of shy and reclusive. Can you believe I've known him now for over six months and don't know where he lives!"

Bingo! This had to be Steven Orville. The guy she knew was definitely odd.

Pineapple Anise Bread

INGREDIENTS

- ½ C olive, corn, or peanut oil
- ½ t baking soda
- ½ C sugar
- 1 t baking powder
- 2 eggs
- 1 C crushed pineapple, drained
- 1¾ C flour
- 1 t anise flavoring
- ½ t salt

PROCEDURE

Cream sugar into olive oil; add eggs, and beat. Sift together dry ingredients and alternate adding with pineapple. Add anise flavoring. Pour into well-greased loaf pan. Bake at 350° 40-45 minutes.

Chapter 31

Around and About

Steven dropped by his mother before meeting Lorinda for coffee at their usual spot.

Sarah thought her son looked haggard, and he was not taking his medication from the looks of things. It had been hard on her not to observe him every day, but he'd insisted on a place of his own. She understood now that he said he had a girlfriend, but why was he reluctant to give her his address?

"Son, you should bring your girlfriend by sometime."

"I will."

"Steven, are you taking your pills regularly? A relationship might be stressful, you know."

"I know, mom. I have everything under control."

What bothered Sarah more than not meeting the girlfriend was that he was off his meds, and she might be the reason why. She said a silent prayer as he left her that day.

Lorinda was texting away to someone when Steven arrived. He felt his paranoia kick in and swallowed a pill before he got to the table. He knew better, but he just could not function as well when he took the pills every day. He'd get back on them as prescribed soon.

Steven had been working his magic on Lorinda, but she was beginning to whine about him not inviting her to his place.

"Who's got your attention besides me?" Steven slid into the chair opposite Lorinda.

"Oh, hi. I was just sending a message to Lars. Remember I told you Ms. Eagleton has been staying at her Newton home. She only comes in on Wednesdays. Well, she has to come in this Monday for an appointment, and I was giving Lars the details."

"Oh, she'll have to leave early to beat the traffic."

"I imagine she'd come into the city Sunday and stay at her place in the meatpacking district. I so want to be her when I grow up!"

"I'm glad you're loving your job."

"Are you feeling all right," Lorinda finally looked up from her screen and at Steven.

"Why?"

"Oh, nothing in particular. You just seem tired."

"I'm tired. Was up late last night." From being sporadic about taking his meds, Steven, sinking further and further into paranoia, had taken to keeping tabs on Melanie Eagleton. She was going to be the reason he no longer had to find a job. His intention; marry Melanie and use his financial acumen to make her company the best in New York City. Lorinda, his friend with benefits unbeknownst to her, was an information goldmine. Steven pretty much knew when, where, and how to find Melanie Eagleton if he wanted to. He'd thought about approaching her as ex-pats to keep in touch and to keep abreast of what was happening in India but felt their meeting needed to be more random.

Steven's mind veered off in a whole other direction. As Rajah's sidekick, he bet she'd know if things changed with the party incident. He had no idea what was going on back in India. Running into her by 'accident' was the way.

"Steven, Steven," He came back to reality as Lorinda began shaking his arm.

Melanie had her wish after all. Colin, missing her terribly, decided to visit her at her cabin. "I'm having a hard time staying away from you," he said, entering the cozy hideaway. "It's still so beautiful. I often think of this place when I consider redoing my home in England. It's why I was calling you in the first place when we reconnected in India, but we never got around to it. You were in India, where I was scheduled to go as luck would have it. Do you believe in destiny?"

"I do. But I'd hate to think that so much death will always be my destiny. Maybe I shouldn't believe in it." They both grimaced and headed to the bedroom.

They spent two glorious days together before they had to go to the city for Pratts's mid-semester reception for the new faculty. "Oh, God," Melanie groaned at the thought of going to the reception, but it was an important event, and she had to go.

"I thought you'd want to show me off. I'm a catch, you know." Colin hurried her out of bed.

Pratt had prepared a wonderful party for the new faculty. The Prosecco was flowing, model-looking waiters in tuxedos held trays of canapés high overhead as they glided between the patrons. An impressive three-piece chamber group played Bach's *Air on a G String* and one of her favorites, *Clair de Lune*.

"This is a grand event. I never dated a professor before, so I wonder if they do this in England?" Colin whispered as they walked around meeting faculty, students, administrators, and invited guests.

"Isn't your country the origin of such protocol?"

"There is that." Colin smiled and moved to the next guests waiting to be met. Colin was impressed with Melanie's whole life but felt this intellectual aspect of her career was more in tune with her essence.

Finally, the president of the college stepped up to the podium. She welcomed the guests and said how proud she was of the college's incoming faculty and hoping they'd adjusted well to campus life. Among a few others, she introduced Melanie as an important alumna who had gone on to make her mark and had made Pratt proud in the process. Invited up to speak, Melanie gave a few remarks, talking about her course and inviting any guests traveling to India to make sure they stopped by her latest work, Kumar Palace, the Museum of Rajah Shiv Kumar.

When she rejoined him, Colin was beaming. "This heady stuff is making me …." he trailed the sentence. "Excuse me, I need to go to the restroom. Can we leave right after?"

"I have to stay at least another half-an-hour, but why do you want to leave so early? He winked and said, "why don't you know?"

Lorinda approached a blushing Melanie. All smiles, she enthusiastically congratulated Melanie. "I am so honored to work with you."

"So, who is the brainiac now?" Lars and Dale sidled up, taking turns hugging her.

"Congratulations, mighty one."

"Oh," Melanie said. "I am so glad you were both able to make it. Dale, I haven't seen you in a long while. Belated happy anniversary!"

Dale smiled broadly. "Thank you, Melanie, for the honeymoon gift and for Lars's partnership. I wanted to call, but he said you were over the top busy."

"No need. You are family. We know how that is. Ah, here comes Colin now."

Melanie said as Colin rejoined them. "Colin, this is Lorinda. She is a Pratt alumna and coincidentally has a friend who lived in India." She was trying to tip him off without being blatant. "And these are my dearest friends Lars, my partner, and his husband, Dale."

"What an honor. I have heard so much about the incomparable Lars. I must say you look incomparable." Colin shook both men's hands.

"It's an honor. And thank you." Lars said. If Lars had smiled any more, he would have burst. "She so deserves all this and you," Lars whispered.

"Oh groan," Melanie grabbed a canapé of salmon mousse from a passing waiter. "Yum," she said, trailing behind the waiter grabbing four more. "Try this," she handed a napkin and a canapé to each of

her guests.

As they moved away to mingle, Colin said. "I have the perfect idea."

Salmon Mousse

INGREDIENTS

- 2 12-oz cans salmon, drained
- 1 C heavy cream, warmed
- 1 envelope unflavored gelatin
- 1 T dry English style mustard
- 1 t dill (dried or chopped fine fresh)

PROCEDURE

Mix and blend in a food processor until very smooth. Chill in a fish mold and serve with crackers and fresh dill for garnish.

Chapter 32

THE STUDENT PERSPECTIVE

Steven, unbeknownst to Lorinda, had followed her to the Pratt Campus party and was unrecognizable in a custom wig and mustache. He watched Melanie constantly surrounded by people showing off a man who seemed like more than just a friend. Steven was incensed. Then, as if a new person emerged right in front of his eyes, Steven felt a jolt of rage. That should be him who she was showing off. Here he was standing in plain sight but was invisible to his love. How could she not see him? Feel him? Steven took a few steps backward. The man was the Scotland Yard Police from India. What did this mean? Was he having feelings for Melanie, or was he here for another reason? Steven began to shake, sweat pouring from his wig. What should he do? What should he do? Steven, aware that his lifestyle would abruptly end in the next year, had to do something. He had saved up enough money for three years but having to keep two households was expensive, and since he hadn't and now couldn't go back to his job…the idea of a rich woman in his life who he could make richer than her wildest dream was his ticket.

Shaking, Steven went outside and dumped his wig and clothes. Get it together, he commanded himself. There was always Lorinda. Steven indeed liked Lorinda. She was the first-ever woman in his life, and from the looks of things, her parents were well to do but, Melanie was on another level. He knew he had feelings for her back in India, and that's why he'd given her the gifts, though nothing had come of it. Steven had stopped taking his meds for over a week now. He was beginning to feel bonkers. He knew the feeling well when the strange voices in his head began taking control of him. Pulling his pill bottle from his pant pocket, he swallowed two pills. It was too little too late to disrupt the full feelings of rage in his schizoid mind that once it latches onto something just spirals. He'd planned on bumping into Melanie tonight by 'accident'. That was his plan that had now gone awry.

As he descended into his darkness, he paced the grounds of Pratt. Then an ominous thought shot into his head. A lucid Steven watched as Melanie and the Brit prepared to leave. Putting on his thick wig, he threw a black hoodie over his head and proceeded to trail them to their car. On an empty, foggy street near campus, Steven watched as the Brit opened the door for Melanie and proceeded to walk around to the driver's side. Steven ran by, smashing a heavy glass bottle over Colin's head and disappearing into the darkness. As Colin fell to the ground, a loud groan left his lips. Melanie wondered what was taking him so long to get to the driver's side of the car look backward when she heard a thud. Colin, she called, winding down the window, and when she heard him groan, she sprinted from the car to where Colin, bleeding from his head, had collapsed. Frantic and scared, Melanie kneeled beside Colin. "Are you all right?" she hadn't seen the blood. Did you fall?"

"Call the police," Colin said.

A frightened Melanie kept looking around while dialing 911. She tried to raise Colin, and there on her hand was blood! Seven minutes later, they were in an ambulance on the way to New York-Presbyterian Hospital.

Heart-Shaped Cookies

INGREDIENTS

- 3¼ C flour
- ⅓ C sugar
- 2½ t baking powder
- 2 eggs
- ¾ t salt
- 3 t vanilla
- 1 C butter
- 2 C granola

PROCEDURE

Mix flour with baking powder and salt. Cream butter and sugar and beat until light and fluffy. Add eggs, one at a time, beating thoroughly after each. Add vanilla. Gradually add flour mixture, blending thoroughly after each addition. Stir in cereal. Chill dough and roll out dough on a floured surface until ⅛-inch thick. With a heart-shaped cutter, cut out shapes and place about 2 inches apart on greased baking sheets. Sprinkle with granulated sugar dyed red with food coloring or decorate with cinnamon heart candies. Bake at 375° for 10 to 12 minutes, or until edges are slightly browned.

Chapter 33

THE GAZEBO REVISITED, DOWN, BUT NOT OUT

Melanie felt shocked and sad about what had happened to Colin. Thank goodness, he was not badly hurt. The doctors at New York Presbyterian stitched up his head and ruled out a concussion. They stayed in the emergency room all night.

Colin had not seen his attacker. Neither had Melanie. The police surmised it could have been a mugging gone wrong when the perpetrator saw someone was in the car. Early the next morning, Colin was released from the hospital. Though he thought it best that they check into a hotel to be closer to a hospital, if necessary, Melanie felt he would be more comfortable in Newton and assured him that a hospital was nearby.

A pensive Melanie took the driver's seat as they made their way back to Newton. What had she done? Melanie felt a pang of guilt. She must have done something to be cursed because it seemed everyone she cared about sooner or later became a victim of violence. She didn't think she had bad personal karma, but what was it about her that seemed to attract catastrophe.

By 11:30 a.m. Saturday, Colin and Melanie arrived in Newton. Melanie pulled into her cottage driveway. The autumn leaves were still turning colors. She couldn't believe it was October already, and next to spring, this was her favorite season. This time the lake was so beautiful. The colors of the trees were spectacular. The weather was still temperate, and the holiday season was coming soon. She would have to miss Thanksgiving and Christmas as she was headed back to India for Shiv's palace opening. Melanie took Colin's arm and guided him indoors so he could go to bed.

The house was spotless. Nettie, her cleaning person, always had the house looking and smelling great. It seemed she'd been there yesterday. Melanie helped Colin settle in bed and went to make lunch, which she delivered to him on a tray. "Not quite breakfast in bed." She helped him to a sitting position. Even with a bandage wrapping his head, he did not look as pitiful as she'd expected. He looked pretty good. Melanie placed the tray over his legs. "You're feeling okay?"

"Pretty good. Thanks," he held onto her hand. "But if you keep pampering me this way, I will never be able to leave."

"That's the idea," Melanie said. "I don't want you to leave."

"So, was it you who hired the mugger?"

"Ha! Not very funny." Colin looked serious for a moment and said, "We didn't know something like this could happen, but Melanie," he took her hand, "it makes me realize how a moment can change a life and that we must seize every moment we have. Now that I am here, perhaps I will never leave. What must I do to keep you next to me? Tell me, and I will do it." Colin couldn't understand exactly what Melanie did to him but was grateful for it. He hadn't felt this alive ever.

"I'll take you to the airport Monday morning. Once we have a moment, let us figure out what the future looks like for us."

"Don't want to go. I can get sick leave. As the mugger made me realize, moments may be all we have, and I won't live them without you."

"I promise, you won't have to."

"Let's do what we can to wrap this case up in a hurry so we can start making plans of our own. Melanie, I think our next step is Lorinda. She may hold the key. This was the brilliant idea I had before I got mugged. What about inviting her here on Sunday? She'll be flattered, and I can tell how much she cares about you. We might be able to tease some information out of her without her even knowing what we are doing."

"I think it's a great idea. No. It's brilliant. And the train stops not too far away. How clever of you, Colin, and so much better than in the city or at my office."

"I like being clever," Colin winked.

Melanie hugged him. "Before we get too comfy, I'll run out to get a few more groceries. You can rest while I'm gone. I should be no more than an hour or so."

"Right," Colin said. "Off you go then."

Melanie locked the doors, windows, and anything allowing access to the cottage and drove to the small grocery store at the crossroads of Newton. Completely shocked by what had happened to Colin, she looked around nervously though Newton was hardly a place to be jittery. She bought just enough food to last through the week and into the weekend. It would take Colin at least that time to recover.

Melanie thought a striped bass would be more appropriate for Sunday dinner than beef. Somehow, she got the impression that Lorinda was not much of a meat-eater. Grabbing a couple of bottles of champagne, she headed for the checkout. Melanie had noticed that several bottles of her favorite North Fork wine she'd brought with her from New York for Lars and Dale were still there. They would be perfect to have with Sunday dinner. Enough to ply Lorinda and loosen her lips, she hoped.

Ed was backing out of his driveway as she approached the cottage. Melanie waved at him. "Hey, Ed, how are you, my friend?"

"Hey Melanie, it's so good to see you. Got in that exercise just before my arthritis started acting up a bit. On my way to the gym to stretch these old bones."

"Be careful. I hope you will soon feel better."

"Hey, just seeing you brings light into my world. How are you and Detective Smythe? Don't tell me something bad happened in Newton again?"

"Ed, nothing ever gets past you."

"I saw you both this morning when I was heading out. I didn't have time to stop but figured I'd bring you some pie later. But why is he all bandaged up?"

"He is fine. Come over when you get back, and I'll fill you in. He is resting."

Colin was asleep when she returned. Melanie tip-toed around putting away the grocery and then settling in with a book of final ideas for the Rajah.

Ed, to his word, dropped by after his gym workout. He brought homemade cookies and pies. Melanie was crazy for cookies and pies, especially homemade ones. His wife was an amazing cook too.

Colin, hearing the doorbell ambled out to see Melanie dashing off to open the door.

"What happened to you?" Ed said, looking at the bandage on Colin's head.

"Took a tumble on the uneven sidewalks of New York."

Melanie looked around at him. Good answer, she thought! He winked at her—no need to get into the real reason sand worry Ed.

"Are you stationed here again?" Ed asked.

"No. I'm just checking in on my old client here."

"Thank goodness. We can't take too much excitement in these parts." He smiled. "Well, I can't stay long. Saw you when you got out of the car and wanted to say hi."

Melanie knew better. Ed was a bit nosey and wanted to know why Colin was wearing a bandage. He also wanted to make sure Melanie was safe. Taking his leave, Ed said, "See you soon. Need a nap at my age."

"Aged to perfection," Melanie kissed his cheek.

Sunday morning, at the crack of dawn, Melanie was filling her water bottle for her run.

"Are you trying to leave without me?" A voice said behind her as arms encircled her waist.

"I didn't know you were a jogger."

"There is a lot you don't know about me, but that will change. Give me ten minutes to get dressed."

"Are you sure? With your head and all?"

"I am sure. The doctor said I was fine and could resume all activities." He stressed the all, and Melanie blushed. "It's only been 48 hours." Melanie added, "And Colin, I'll take bets the doctor would advise you to rest! But, if you feel good enough, why not."

Though Melanie was no slouch, Colin was a far stronger runner, and she had a hard time matching his long stride.

"Come on, slowpoke," he teased, running backward so she could catch up."

She did her level best.

Back under the pavilion, Colin joined Melanie in her meditation. Being with him was so easy and as close to perfection as she would ever have imagined. For Melanie, this was all turning out to be fine, even the bump on his head, which meant she had him by her side an entire week longer.

"I think you should take a rest now. Go back to bed while I make breakfast."

"I am not going back to bed unless you are beside me."

He moved in and kissed her gently. "What do you say?" Their lovemaking was slow and special. Melanie didn't want it to end. As they lay in the stillness of the late morning, listening to each other's breath, Melanie realized how much she cared for this man. She wondered if all that had happened with Marco was to lead her to meet Colin for, she felt a new love blooming in her heart. Sometimes things happen for the craziest reasons.

"I'll wash your back if you wash mine." Colin grabbed her hand and led her to the bathroom. "Shall we shower together? That will make everything official."

"I thought we were official back in India." She trailed after him.

"Official, official." That's what I meant."

"So, you are saying that you are free and clear to enter this relationship?"

"Absolutely free and clear. My on and off relationship is permanently off. I had the conversation with my former." Then, he slowed up a bit. "But Melanie, there is something else I want to tell you. Like you, I have been married before. I am a widower too. I don't discuss it much, but there you have it. I don't want any secrets between us, ever!"

Melanie didn't react. She just stared at Colin and was glad he was becoming more open. They were making memories, and they should have no secrets from one another.

"Not ever," Melanie whispered, all choked up.

Colin continued. "My wife, like you, loved to jog, and she meditated as well. We met at a running event. She was much more committed to being a physical person than I was, and I was devastated when she died during childbirth. My wife…and our daughter both." "I didn't think I would survive, and that's why I came to the States on a temporary assignment. I needed to be away from England for a while."

Melanie felt for Colin. "I'm so sorry. What a terrible loss. It's hard to fathom this life sometimes. Why things like this happen never seems to be for our good, but I know now that we learn and grow from the hard times and somehow find the courage to move forward. Sometimes it's hard to put one foot in front of the other, but we do." She squeezed his hand. "I am here for you, Colin, and I hope we will be looking after each other from now on for a very long time."

Over breakfast, Colin and Melanie shared their entire life stories before switching back to discussing the strategy to get Lorinda to tell what she knew about Steven Orville. Even though it meant traveling out to New Jersey, Lorinda had eagerly accepted their invitation for dinner.

On Sunday morning, Colin retired to read the papers, and Melanie decided she would serve the Banana Oatmeal Cookies Ed had brought for dessert. Maybe that would be all the truth serum she needed to get Lorinda to talk.

Ed's Wife's Banana Oatmeal Cookies

INGREDIENTS

- ¾ C shortening
- ½ t baking soda
- 1 C sugar
- ½ t baking powder
- 1 egg
- 2 t salt
- 1 C mashed bananas
- 1 t cinnamon
- 1 C uncooked quick-cooking oats
- ¼ t nutmeg
- 1½ C flour
- ¾ C chopped walnuts or pecans

PROCEDURE

Cream shortening and sugar until light and fluffy. Beat in egg, then stir in bananas and oats. Combine the remaining ingredients and stir into the cream mixture. Drop batter by teaspoonfuls onto a greased sheet. Bake at 400° for about 13 minutes. Cool on rack.

Chapter 34

GOOD FRIENDS HAPPY TOGETHER

Melanie and Colin picked Lorinda up at the train station around 3 p.m. Today, their goal was to get Lorinda talking about Steven and determine how much information about Melanie she had shared with him.

The tattooed lady looked gorgeous. She handed Melanie a wine bag that contained two bottles of very excellent, very expensive wine. One red and one white.

"Thank you. But wow, this is a lot of money for someone working as an assistant. It's perfect for dinner," Melanie smiled at the young woman and then reintroduced Colin. "You remember my friend Colin. You met at Pratt," she said, staring at her the whole time. She was from good stock.

"Of course, she does." After winking at Melanie, Colin did a very un-English thing. He took Lorinda's hand into his. He must have learned that from Shiv. "It is my pleasure to see you again. Melanie talks a lot about you and is very proud of how well you have fit in at Decorating Divas. I guess everyone from Pratt has that something special, huh."

Melanie could not believe how Colin was laying it on.

Lorinda's smile got bigger. "I do love my work."

As they drove the short distance to Melanie's cottage, Lorinda commented on the lovely town. "This is a great place. So peaceful yet so close to New York. I see why you want to escape here. Lars said it was heaven."

"Yes. I love it here. I felt the same way when I stumbled upon the place years ago. A friend invited me for a week when it was a total ramshackle mess of a place. I made some improvements. Now, whenever I come here, I feel as though I'm on a mini-vacation, and I don't have to travel too far to find my center."

"Speaking of travel. I'm so glad Lars is coming back on Monday. The office is not the same without him."

"Really?" Melanie looked through the rearview at Lorinda.

"He's just so much fun."

"And I'm not?" Melanie tried her best to sound offended. "And wasn't he gone for just one day?"

Lorinda smiled and said, "Yes, but I missed him anyway. It gets lonely in the office all alone."

"I can understand that too. I feel the same way. I will be going to India for the last time, and I will be taking Lars with me. I hope you'll adjust and miss us both." Melanie said, hoping Lorinda would add something about Steven. She did not—not yet anyway. Maybe we should just close the office and all go!"

Lorinda squealed. "Wow, that would be something."

The striped bass was a wonderful choice for dinner, and Melanie learned a lot about Lorinda. She was from money, hence the excellent and expensive wine selections. Her rebellious nature was due to her artistic tendencies in a household of scientists. An only child, she was always the shy, creative type picked on by classmates. Inwardly competitive, she'd won all the creative competitions at her school, securing her place and boosting her confidence. Her tattoos made her look a lot tougher than she was.

Melanie liked the occasional tattoo and said that she had wanted to get a small heart on her shoulder at one time. Colin added that his late wife had a small tattoo on her ankle. He had liked that about her.

"That's good. I think sometimes tattoos attract the wrong guys, but not Steven. He seems okay with my tattoos. I regret a few of them." Lorinda said.

"Steven? A friend of yours? A significant other?" Colin said teasingly.

"Yeah. He's the guy I was telling you about, Melanie. The one from India. We've gone out for a while. He's off-beat, but deep down, I think he's okay. I wanted to ask you if I could bring him with me, but I changed my mind. He's shy, a little anti-social and very private. He also has a mean temper and gets angry for no apparent reason. I wanted to come here, relax and spend a good Sunday with you, Melanie."

"And so here are we. Maybe next time, we'll coax your boyfriend into coming." Melanie said.

"Now that he is back for good from India, I hope to get to know him a lot better."

"I love India. When was he there?" Colin picked up the conversation,

"He was there for about two years or more. I'm not sure. I thought he would be there longer, but he just upped and came home. I guess there is no place like home. He was at a call center there trying to make peace between the 4Cs and the call centers. He was trying to bring jobs back to the United States."

"Well, that's a noble cause." Colin chimed in."

"Yes. I am all for it. Steven and I are both members. Most of the members were laid off because of tech outsourcing. Particularly to India. That's how Steven and I met. At a 4Cs rally.

Steven is well respected by the 4Cs. He brought us structure and even toughened us up a bit. He believes we must be more radical., louder, more insistent. He hasn't been as active since he got home, but I suppose he had to get his business in order. To be honest, he is kind of secretive. Can you believe I don't even know where he lives? I didn't know where he was in India either. I believe in New Delhi. He never talks about work or his personal life. I'm glad he's home. One day he'll trust me enough to open up. And to think I applied for the job at your place because of him."

"Really?" It was Melanie's turn to be surprised.

"Yes. When he came back from India, he told me he'd met a designer in India. It was you!"

Colin and Melanie exchanged discrete glances. They now knew for sure Steven was in New York.

At 8 p.m., they took Lorinda back to the train station. Though they hadn't been able to find out how much Lorinda had told Steven, they felt sure she had been his source of news about Melanie, especially now that she knew he had recommended Lorinda to apply for the open job at her firm. Maybe Lorinda was being used and didn't know it either.

Pistachio Encrusted Striped Bass

INGREDIENTS

- ½ C unsalted shelled pistachios, chopped
- ⅓ C fresh breadcrumbs
- 2 T grated Parmesan
- ½ t coarse salt; more to taste
- ⅛ t finely ground black pepper or more to taste
- 2 T olive oil
- 4 sea bass fillets, preferably loin pieces (4 to 6 oz. each)
- 2 T Dijon mustard

PROCEDURE

Heat the oven to 425°F. Line a small baking sheet with foil and lightly grease the foil (spray is fine).

Chop the pistachios into medium-fine pieces. Combine the nuts, breadcrumbs, Parmesan, salt, and pepper in a shallow bowl. Drizzle with the olive oil and toss with a fork until the crumbs are evenly moistened.

If using fillets with tapered ends, loosely fold the ends under to create a fillet of even thickness. Spread the top of each fillet evenly with the mustard. Press the mustard-coated side of each fillet into the crumb mixture to coat the fish generously. Set the fillets, coating side up, on the prepared pan. Sprinkle the remaining crumb mixture over the fillets to form a thick coating.

Bake the fillets until the topping is crisp and browned and the fish is cooked through, 10 to 12 minutes, depending on thickness. Serve immediately.

Chapter 35

OFF AGAIN

Colin was leaving to go back to India. Armed with some new knowledge from Lorinda, he was sure they would find Steven Orville soon. Though a likely suspect, they couldn't be sure he was a murderer, and they had no proof or motive. Why had he bought chocolate and tied them with two different ribbons? In India, buying poison to kill rats was somewhat expected even in the posh areas. In that respect, it was very much like New York.

They drove back to the city so Colin could check out of the hotel. "We have some time," Colin said. "I want to be able to envision you anywhere, so let's stop by your New York place. By the way, I've asked a friend, a private detective, to keep an eye on you for the time being."

Melanie smiled up at him, grateful for his thoughtfulness. Indeed, she was feeling apprehensive, and there were still two weeks before she had to go back to India for the museum opening.

"My, this is special," Colin entered the apartment and looked around. "You truly are talented. It's so very different from Newton and still very much you."

"I love my homes, and it's a shame I have to feel unsafe because of this nonsense. I see no reason for Steven to be interested in me, but clearly, he does. I think I am a bit worn out and tired of this whole thing," Melanie said, sitting on the bed.

Colin walked over and sat down next to her. "You are too precious to me to let anything happen to you. My detective friend is also going to tail Lorinda too. We'll find Steven soon. Still, he cautioned. "Please be watchful. Don't take any chances. Be totally aware of where you are and who's around you. I'll see you in two weeks anyway." He kissed her forehead, cheek, then found his way to her lips.

Melanie hated these constant goodbyes. She hoped after their last trips to India, the goodbyes would stop for a long while. He had become so much a part of her daily thinking, and she hoped life.

*   *   *

Lorinda had proven herself an excellent temporary assistant. Lars's offer to Lorinda of a full-time position was ready to be executed, but suddenly Melanie put the kibosh on the idea.

"Let's wait until after the Rajah's opening. She can hold down the fort while we are away, and do let her know we are very much ready to have her on board but right after India."

Lars wondered why the sudden change of heart but did not ask.

Melanie wanted to wait to see if anything developed now that they had a lead on Steven. She had to admit Lorinda was talented, and though she had none of Lars's flair and style, she had a style all her own, and it added value to Decorating Divas. Still, her connection to Steven was troubling. She was, after all, a part of the 4C's. Melanie wondered how much Lorinda actually knew and if she was a plant, more aware than they thought. Plus, if she were a plant, she would pass information to Steven Orville and stall the investigation even more. She would have to show her hand before Melanie could be fully convinced of what she knew and didn't know.

Lorinda sighed loudly. She was booking Melanie and Lars' flight to India. Unfortunately, they had too much follow-up work, so she could not join them.

The Rajah's splendid museum would be opening in four weeks, and Melanie had to arrive a week early to make sure everything was in order. She wished she didn't have to go back to India, but the highlight was she would see Colin. That perked her up. This time too, she'd have Lars for company on the trip, which made her happy. Today, however, she had to check in on her new project—the decoration of Shamira's 58th Street apartment.

Melanie grabbed a cab and headed to midtown.

"Good to see you on this side of the world," Shamira said, leading her to the living room. "Are you ready for the opening? You won't believe how many guests are coming over from Hollywood," Shamira said. "They'll be mixing with Bollywood stars, Indian politicos, and cultural leaders. This is the first time an opening of any sort will bring together this kind of crowd. It's so cosmopolitan and progressive."

"That it is."

"Don't get me wrong. I also love the old India when the Rajahs ruled. I suppose, though, I squarely belong to new India. I think it's going to be great. When are you headed over?"

"A week from today. I am really looking forward to it." She lied and suppressed a rising smile, thinking she'd taken on the white lying habits of Colin. "Today, I'll be quick. I just wanted to get some photos so I could start working on a concept during the flight."

"I hope you don't mind," Shamira said, "but I whipped up some Keema for a little snack. Let's have a bite before you start working. I hope you like it." She presented a silver bowl, a cocktail napkin, and dipping chips.

"It's delicious," Melanie said. "You must give me the recipe."

Melanie snapped photo after photo of the splendid apartment. The views were amazing, 270 degrees with Central Park to the North, the Hudson River to the West, where she could see a giant cruise ship making its way out to the harbor, the Empire State Building and The New World Trade Tower to the South. "Don't want to interfere with these views," Melanie commented. "I was thinking of bringing in some stills from your movies. How does that sound?"

Shamira smiled broadly and held Melanie's hands for a few seconds. They both loved the Rajah and his palace and India. They set a date to view the renderings, and Melanie said, "See you soon at Shiv's palace!"

Indian Keema

INGREDIENTS

- ¾ C chopped onion
- ¼ t ground cumin
- 1 T chopped fresh ginger
- 1 lb. ground turkey
- 1 t finely minced garlic
- 1 C chopped fresh tomatoes
- 1 T curry powder
- 1 T lime juice
- ½ t ground turmeric
- 1 t sugar
- ¼ t ground coriander
- Large leaves of lettuce for rolling

PROCEDURE

In a greased pan, sauté onion, ginger, and garlic. Add spices, then turkey until browned. Finish with tomatoes and lime juice. Remove from pan and spoon a small amount into a lettuce leaf, turn over the ends, and roll to make an elongated dumpling.

Chapter 36

THE PALACE OPENS TO THE PUBLIC

A week later, Melanie was on a plane to Delhi. She was only too happy to be a food guide for Lars. It turned out that Indian keema was the comfort food offered during the flight. Lars kept her amused, and with sleep time, time flew by fast.

As Melanie stepped into the terminal, Shiv was there with a small entourage of guards. It seemed no one was taking any chances anymore. He handed her the biggest bouquet she had ever seen, in all the colors of the rainbow. Embracing her in a bear hug, he kissed her cheek and turned to her companion. "Lars, we finally meet." Shiv bowed.

As did Lars. "It is my honor, Rajah. I feel I've known you for years."

"You have. We have talked on the phone enough. Only now I am in the flesh. Come, come, our car is waiting."

Melanie was beaming. "I really could never have done this without Lars, who, by the way, is now a proud partner in Decorating Divas. He was on his honeymoon, or he would have been here before."

"Congratulations. Ask Melanie. I'm looking for a *rani* myself," he said laughingly. "Anyway, I am beside myself with joy. This museum will be even more successful than we ever imagined or hoped. Thanks to our decorating diva. I can't tell you how many people we could not include in the private opening. Maybe we should have two openings!"

Melanie smiled and agreed. No honored guests should be left out.

Lars, who had never been to India, was lost in the sights, smells and sounds. When they reached the hotel, the Rajah reminded them that they were required to be at dinner the following night to meet and schmooze the big donors who would have an early preview of the collection before opening night.

"This is like living in a fantasy," Lars said as they were escorted to their rooms.

And Melanie said to herself, thank heavens we have time to rest. Remembering her first night in India at the beginning of the project, her lack of sleep and Victor's murder, she shuddered. Colin would arrive tomorrow. He'd pick them up for the party.

Shiv had left her a golden sari with dark green embroidery and emerald earrings for the event. Melanie took her time getting dressed, and by the time she met Lars in the hallway to take the elevator down to the lobby, she felt like an Indian princess.

"Oh my," Melanie burst into laughter. Shiv had obviously left him Indian formal wear too. He cut quite the gentleman figure with his blonde hair and *dhoti*! Lars beamed and glowed.

Melanie continued the laugh-fest. "I can't wait to see if Shiv sent Colin an outfit." She couldn't stop laughing. With their blonde hair, Lars and Colin could hardly pass for Indian. Regardless Lars looked darned good, and Melanie made sure there were plenty of pictures online for Dale to see.

Colin picked them up at 6 p.m., looking dashing in his tux. Melanie guessed that Shiv hadn't sent the Englishman Indian formal wear. She could understand that, after all, his ancestors were responsible for his ancestors' demise. Colin rushed to the driver's side, opened the door, and gave Melanie a very long hello kiss.

Lars was atwitter.

When Melanie walked into the palace, she was surprised to see the woman she had met on her first trip over, the one who had been peering at her drawings.

"We meet again," The woman smiled, offering her a namaste. Lata turned out to be Shiv's aunt. No wonder she had been so nosey and knew all about the palace.

"What a delight." Melanie returned the namaste greeting. "I didn't see you once the plane boarded."

"Oh, I took my plane. Was in the lounge meeting an old friend."

Well, there you have it, Melanie thought.

Dinner was magical. Melanie had never seen so much glitter. The opulence, apparently commonplace for Brahmins and Rajahs, the cream of Indian society, was still a new experience to behold. Unlike the Bollywood crowd, they were at once regal and royal—were well dressed, well-spoken, and well versed in the history of the Rajahs and their country. As a party to the coming attraction, Melanie was welcomed wholeheartedly as a part of this rarefied group. Was she glad she was wearing emeralds, even if they were borrowed!

Melanie pointed out people to Lars, who unabashedly awestruck was spiraling around the room. And Lars was the people's favorite. A man of deep charm and kindness, Lars was the immediate hit of the event. Even Shiv was impressed. What a team, he thought, Melanie and Lars.

At this once-in-a-lifetime event, the most famous Bollywood royalty, including Amitabh Bachchan and the one and only Shah Rukh Khan, mixed seamlessly with the younger jet-set Bollywood and Hollywood stars, the older and most distinguished Rajahs, politicians, prominent sportsmen and women, and tastemakers. As guests circulated through the rooms, they made a point of talking with her and complimenting her work.

"My dear," an old Indian royal and a relative of Shiv, standing next to her, observed, "how well you understand the sensibility of Indians."

"Thank you, you do know from my high cheekbones that I too am an Indian–Cherokee," Melanie said, feeling like she should curtsey or something. The lady looked sad. "Yes, we share the same fate at the hand of colonizers, don't we? No wonder your work shows empathy for times gone by. They should have something like this in the United States for your people too, don't you think?"

Melanie wanted to mention the Museum of the American Indian near Battery Park in New York but decided that was a conversation for another time and place.

"From what I hear, one of our more famous Hollywood stars wants a museum to celebrate his lifetime achievements, too. His agent is right over there. I think they are here to find you." She winked. "Shall I call her over?"

Melanie smiled while vigorously shaking her head. "I don't think so at this moment. I'm sure we'll talk."

After a few more minutes of chatter, Melanie went off to find Colin, whom she had not seen since they arrived. She was disappointed that he had just drifted off, leaving her to fend for herself. When she thought about it, she felt silly. Colin was talking to a younger Bollywood damsel when she spotted him. What's with him and young Bollywood starlets? Right next to him, Lars was laughing his way through the evening.

And, as they say, a good time was had by all. Ms. Melanie included. Melanie did notice one thing, though. There were no chocolates on the big round table. The only goody bags were perfume and special Indian teas.

A week later, the public event was even more spectacular. The world of luxe had come out to play. The museum was magnificent, with all old-world India joining with new-world India in splendor and grace. The paintings, costumes, and people represented India's glorious past and present. The museum was now open to all—no caste lines or financial requisites. Melanie's voice was almost gone from giving interviews with Shiv to the hordes of paparazzi. Finally, she was able to take part in the lavish party and feasted on fine wines, Indian and Western, sweet and savory *hors-d'oeuvres* that were freely passed. The tri-colored cauliflower skewers were her favorites.

Two days later, Melanie, Lars, and Colin boarded a plane bound for New York to her delight. Little did Melanie know that things were closing in on Steven Orville.

Tri-Color Cauliflower Skewers

INGREDIENTS

- 1 head each of white, purple and orange cauliflower, broken into flowerets
- 3 small red onions, sliced horizontally
- 1-pint cherry tomatoes
- 3 green peppers, cut into 1 – 1 ½ inch squares
- Olive oil for basting
- Salt and pepper to taste
- Wood or metal skewers

PROCEDURE

Insert the skewers into the vegetables, alternating for a pleasing color combination. Baste lightly with olive oil, sprinkle with salt and pepper. Grill for 10-15 minutes.

Chapter 37

SHIFTING ALLIANCES

Lorinda was hurrying to meet a girlfriend for a Saturday night movie at IFC. She was looking forward to the meet-up as she'd been blowing off her friends since her romance with Steven started. It was good to come up for air.

She stopped at the juice bar to get a green shake on W. 4th Street, and as she hurried along, she was thinking of Steven. Though always a bit unpredictable, he was getting more bizarre lately, especially when she said she would no longer divulge information about Melanie. She knew, of course, that this would make Steven angry. But she had to take that chance for several reasons. First, she had felt like a betrayer. Second, she couldn't figure out why he was so obsessed with Melanie's comings and goings. She was not about to jeopardize her position or relationship with Melanie and Lars by divulging information that was none of his business. Thinking about Steven's obsessions and her responsibility to Decorating Divas made Lorinda shiver and pull her coat closer to her body. It was cold. Thinking about all this drama, she was getting more upset and thought she should have stayed home.

"Over here," her friend June was waving madly at her. Lorinda crossed the road and hugged her friend.

"It's way too cold to be out here."

"Tell me about it. When the weather changes, there is just no looking back," June said. "You just missed a bit of drama. A couch just landed on the sidewalk about 10 minutes ago." June pointed to the ratty couch now smashed against the pavement.

"Landed?"

"Yup. Someone threw it off the roof. Good thing no one was passing by when it landed!"

"Lordy," Lorinda said to her friend as they slowed down. "There is too much craziness in the world."

"Talking about crazy, how is your man of mystery?"

"Worse than usual," Lorinda answered. "You know, I've been having doubts about Steven. The things he's been asking me to do at my office bother me."

"If you want to keep your job, you'd better fess up," June said. "If they find out you've been feeding information to Steven, who, as you well know, I've always thought of as more than a little unbalanced, you are toast." June shook her braids. "No, girl, you had better fess up and the sooner, the better."

"How can you say that? You've never even met him."

"I could only get it from you then, right?"

Lorinda gave June a long look and another hug.

The next day at work, Lorinda had pretty much made up her mind to tell Lars. Despite her nervousness, she asked Lars if they could talk.

"Yes, of course. What's up? Is something wrong?" he said, sensing this was serious. "You know I love working here, but …."

Lars' eyebrow shot up as he heard the "but."

"And I am grateful that you allowed me to show what I could do."

"Yes." Lars' voice second eyebrow shot up. "We certainly talked about that a lot. You've been a real asset to the office, so what now?" Lars could not imagine what was wrong. Was she going to quit?

"But there's something I need to tell you."

"Okay, what's so serious?"

"I have a friend named Steven Orville. I met him a while ago when I joined an action organization, a protest group called the 4Cs."

Lars had never even heard of the 4Cs. Not his lane.

"Well, in fact, he was the person who found out about this temporary position with your company and encouraged me to apply."

"Really?" Lars swung his chair to face Lorinda. This was going to be a long conversation and one he would have to remember when he retold Melanie. And he couldn't afford to stop Lorinda's train of thought by taking notes. "So, again, what's up?"

"When I first got the job, he'd constantly talk about Melanie, and I innocently give him information about her. It seemed odd, but it was more like harmless gossiping. Lately, though, I've started to feel that I was being pumped for information, and maybe that was why Steven was seeing me. He wanted to know her schedule and things like that. I thought it strange and decided I had to stop. It didn't feel comfortable. Plus, do you remember you offered me a full-time position? I told him I would have to sign a confidentiality agreement and could no longer give him any information."

"Who is he, and why would he want information on Melanie's activities? Has he threatened her? Or you?"

"No. Not that I know. He's just been very mean."

Lars was becoming concerned. "Let's discuss this with Melanie. This is her life we're talking about here. I am distressed about this, and I assume you will mention nothing further to this man again about our dealings or personal lives. Melanie may know him. Even if she doesn't, this may explain the strange e-mails."

"Strange emails? Lorinda was contrite and scared at the same time. She knew she had made a very big mistake in providing information to Steven. Perhaps endangering other people's lives. People she liked and owed much. She simply said, "Will I get fired?"

"I don't think so, but associating with him and involving him with Melanie and this company was a bad judgment call, don't you think?"

Looking properly chagrined, Lorinda whispered, "My loyalty is to Decorating Divas and always will be. I am so sorry."

*   *   *

Steven was sinking into chaos. With each passing day, his behavior was getting more bizarre. Furious that Lorinda would no longer share information with him about Melanie, he decided to take matters into his own hands. No one was allowed to interfere with him and his plans. If she was now of no use to him, he might as well get rid of her. And since Melanie was not shaking loose from her gent, she would have to go too.

Private Detective Bates watched as a rabid Steven Orville left his house in a huff. He followed him. Finally, he had a make on Steven Orville, and he immediately called Detective Colin Smythe.

Champagne Green Shake

INGREDIENTS

- 2 C fresh spinach
- ⅓ C rolled oats
- 2 C almond milk, unsweetened
- 1 T coconut oil
- 1 large apple, cored, any variety
- ½ t ground cinnamon
- 1 banana

PROCEDURE

Blend spinach and almond milk until smooth. Add remaining ingredients, and blend until smooth.

Chapter 38

Dangerous Love

Lorinda was getting dressed for work when there was a knock on her door. She looked through the peephole and saw Steven. Her first inclination was not to answer, but she thought it best to have a face-to-face conversation and end things, so she pulled open the door. "Why are you here so early? I have to go to work, so I don't have time to talk."

Steven's eyes flashed red, and before she could say another word, he had her in a chokehold. "If you play games with me, it could very well be the end of your life, you know. Do you know who I am?"

"Steven," Lorinda was flailing. "Please stop. What is the matter with you? Let go of me." She sputtered as his hold got tighter.

"If you do as I say, you will live to be a ripe old age, but your life ends here if you cross me. Where is Melanie?"

"Steven," Lorinda was pleading. "I don't know."

His hold tightened even more, and she could feel her eyes bulging.

"I said, where is Melanie this morning?"

"I don't know. She is supposed to be working on the Island." Lorinda could barely get the words out.

"Tell me where to find her, now!"

"Please let go of my neck."

"*I HATE TO BE BETRAYED, BUT I WILL GIVE YOU ONE MORE CHANCE TO GET YOUR ACT TOGETHER.*" He got very belligerent and looked like he would become violent.

"Please, Steven, I don't...."

Steven wasn't thinking about Lorinda. He was already rethinking his plans and decided to wait a few hours.

Steven let a limp Lorinda drop to the floor. "Go and find out where Melanie is this morning." He wagged a finger in her face. The moment you find out, text me." He also told Lorinda if she told anyone about him, she would die, and so would Melanie. Lorinda believed him. "I will go now and find out. I'll text you the moment I know." Lorinda scampered to her feet and headed for the door. She had to get back to the office to tell Lars. And fast.

A rabid and exhausted Steven sat down in Lorinda's chair and waited.

*   *   *

Lars looked at his watch. Lorinda had never been late since she started working there. "*Should he be worried?*"

"I am so sorry," Lorinda burst into the office. The train was stuck in the tunnel. Someone got ill, and we had to wait for EMS," she lied.

"Are you alright?" Lars asked. She seemed more frantic than she would be from just a stuck train.

Lorinda wanted to tell them what was going on, but she was scared that Steven would follow through on his promise. What was she to do? She had to tell.

"Honestly, I'm not alright," she burst into tears.

"What's happened?" Lars rushed over to her and grabbed her by the shoulder.

"He is crazy. He almost choked me to death this morning because I wouldn't tell him where Melanie was is. He is very dangerous. I'm so scared. He is a sociopath. He threatened to kill Melanie and me if I don't tell him within the next hour where Melanie is. Maybe we should call the police?" Lorinda was shaking so hard. Lars was afraid she would pass out. He placed her in a chair as Colin and Melanie, who had just returned from Long Island, walked in the door.

"What's going on?" Colin said, walking over to Lorinda. He looked at the red marks on her neck. "What is the matter?"

"It's Steven. He's threatened to kill Melanie and me too. I can't go back to my place. He's there, and he threatened to kill me if I told."

"Told what? We need to call the police right away." Colin pulled out his cell phone.

"No. Please. He said if I reported it, he'd kill us."

"How did you get away?" Melanie asked.

"I told him I would find out where you were and text him within the next hour."

"Okay. Let's tell him." Colin said, and Melanie almost fainted. "So, here is the plan," Colin hurried on. Let's put everyone on alert. It would be better for him to meet you at your class rather than to come here."

"But I don't have a class today," Melanie said.

"You do now," Colin said. It would be easier. He wouldn't do anything in front of a bunch of people, and the police and school security will be on high alert."

"What? I can't involve the school in this, Colin!"

"Please, Melanie. I will call the dean."

"But to put people at risk. I will not do that, plus it can't be good for the school."

Colin saw her point.

"I think Lorinda is right. He won't do anything in front of witnesses." Lars said. We need a public place but one where people are not likely to get hurt."

"Okay. Let me call the police and see what they suggest."

"Let's not do that," Melanie said. "We can't act as if we don't know anything? Your life and ours could be in danger too."

"The police agreed that Pratt could be the best place. They just had to call the dean and have all classes suspended so the building would be pretty much emptied of real students. Many police officers in plain clothes will act as students, so let's go to your class. Let us take care of calling the dean and setting up protocol."

"Lars and I will be there to keep watch for Steven," Colin said to an officer over the phone. "Lars, you could pass for a student too, right? We'll meet you two hours before the time we tell Steven."

Lars and Melanie looked at each other. If the matter weren't so serious, they would have burst into laughter. "I happen to be quite skilled at makeup," Lars said.

Colin stared at him. "That's a good idea. Should I be a student too? I'll need some jeans and a checkered shirt. A wig, make it brown and some spectacles."

"For you, we'll get a trench coat and hat. And a gun, I hope." Lars said.

With all set, Colin instructed Lorinda to call Steven. With shaking hands, she texted Steven the information as she dared not call—her voice would have been a dead giveaway. A worn-out Lorinda began weeping. She was the cause of all this.

Melanie left for her class with Lars. Colin went separately and earlier to meet the deceivers. When they arrived, the school was abuzz with police students, and one could not tell it was not an ordinary day. Melanie walked into her classroom expecting to see her fourteen fake students, but with Lars, there were fifteen.

Colin and another bunch of plainclothes cops were milling around outside. Lars, sitting in the back, seemed to fit right in. Melanie stashed her briefcase in the teacher's cupboard and greeted her class, trying her level best to appear calm and as normal as possible. "Today's topic," she wrote on the whiteboard, "is the FF&E (Furniture, Fixture, and Equipment) Designer."

As always, the class flew by. The students came up to talk with Melanie as they did after every class as Melanie had informed the policemen. After about fifteen minutes, they started to file out slowly.

Lars, who had been hanging back, seeing everyone leave, went out to talk with Colin. Melanie erased the whiteboard quickly, retrieved her briefcase, and was about to leave when someone came up from behind her. "Hello, I'm sorry I had to miss the class. Would you be able to give me the lecture notes?"

As she looked up and began to respond, a disheveled Steven was right in her face, in his black hoodie pulled up over his head. He handed her a small tin. "It's good to see you again, Ms. Eagleton. As I said, destiny is afoot for us, don't you think? Those," he pointed to the tin in her hand, "are special chocolate brownies. They are a token of my love for you. I've come to take you away with me. I know you've been swayed, but I promise I'll make you much happier than Smythe. Take that ring off your finger, and I'll replace it with mine. What do you say, my love, my love?" He took her by the hand and headed for the door.

Steven Orville walked into Lars, Colin, and the two detectives at the door. He let go of Melanie's hand and raced to the staircase. Colin and the two officers came back a few minutes later, without Steven. "Sorry, he ran too fast. Right out the door and into the street. But our men got him."

Melanie stood for a minute before fully grasping what had happened, and then she became hysterical.

Melanie gave the officers the small tin Steven had given her. "Chocolate brownies. A love token." Melanie turned the tin upside down and saw a note that said, "I love you. You're mine."

*   *   *

Steven was taken to the Police Department in lower Manhattan. Colin, Melanie, and Lars joined them. The officers asked to have Lorinda join them.

"We've sent the brownies to the lab to be analyzed. We'll know in an hour or so if there is any reason to be concerned."

A defeated Steven sat handcuffed to a chair. He did not seem remorseful and only smiled broadly at Melanie when she came in.

"You're here, my love," he said.

"Tell us, Mr. Orville."

"You can call me Steven."

"Steven. Why were you at Pratt today?"

"To see Melanie, of course. I need to protect her from," he looked up at Colin, "the man harassing her."

"And who would that be?"

Steven pointed to Colin. "Ever since he came to India, he had been interfering in our relationship."

"India. So, you met Ms. Eagleton in India."

"Yes. At a party."

"You mean the Rajah's party?"

"Yeah. Unfortunately, a man died there, and things became a little chaotic, so I didn't get to see her for a while. My boss also died, and I had to bring him back to the states, so we separated further. That's when this guy moved in." He gave Colin a look of utter disdain.

"I am sorry to hear about your boss."

"Well, he had it coming."

"What do you mean by that?"

"I overheard him and Victor Gupta in conversation discussing that my job in India was to shut me up about outsourcing American jobs overseas. I thought I was there to find a solution. They betrayed me."

"And?"

"Well, I had to let them go. They were a harm to the world."

"How did you do that?"

"I sent them chocolates. Poisoned chocolates."

Melanie gasped, and Steven looked up sharply.

"I'm sorry, my love. It's something that had to be done. I hate people who stand in the way of others. Don't you?"

"And was Ms. Eagleton receptive to your friendship."

"Of course. She spoke to me at the party and smiled ever so warmly whenever she saw me. She liked the gift I sent to her hotel and even thanked me. I just needed more time with her."

The police realized they were dealing with a sociopath or, at minimum, someone with borderline personality disorder and thought it best Melanie, Colin, and Lars leave. They would be in touch. Lorinda had not yet made it to the station, so Lars told her to meet them back at the office. Since Steven had already confessed to the murders, she was not needed anyway.

Back at the office, Lars was telling Lorinda what had happened. Lorinda burst into tears. "I am so sorry. I am so sorry. I will give my resignation today."

"There is no need for that," Melanie encircled her heaving shoulders. How would you ever have imagined?

Colin's phone rang.

"The brownies are being tested." He told them. "They were not poisoned. The Indian police have been informed of Steven's confession and seek extradition."

"That's a relief," Melanie said. Colin, I wonder where his mother is? I remember she was with him in India. Did you mention it to the police?"

"That's a new mystery."

Wickedly Good Brownies

INGREDIENTS

- 2 eggs
- 2 sticks sweet butter
- 1 T bourbon vanilla extract
- 1 C brown sugar
- 3 C sifted flour
- 1 T baking powder
- 1 t salt
- 1 C good bittersweet chocolate (Callebaut or Ghirardelli's) melted in a double boiler, so it doesn't burn
- 1 C Ghirardelli semisweet chocolate chips
- 1½ C pecan halves

PROCEDURE

Cream together butter and brown sugar until smooth, add eggs and mix until smooth. Add vanilla while mixing. Combine flour, baking powder, and salt, and add to sugar mixture about a half cup at a time while mixing, until all the flour is in and the batter is just smooth. Fold in melted chocolate, chips, and pecans. Spread into a shallow baking pan, about 1 inch thick. Bake in a

350-degree oven for 35 to 40 minutes, until the top is firm. Remove from oven and sprinkle with ¼ C Kentucky bourbon while still warm. Allow to cool a little, cut into 2-inch squares. Serve while still warm. A small ball of vanilla ice cream would be a nice addition.

Chapter 39

THE END IS IN SIGHT

Sarah Orville watched the news that night and went into shock. How could this be. Filled with rage, her son was spouting off as they led him to the police van to transport him to prison that America was failing its citizens and that people like him were needed. After recovering, Steven's mother rushed to the police station.

Her dear, sweet boy. What had they done to him?

Melanie watched the same broadcast. She felt sad that things had turned out this way. Steven needed to go to a treatment facility, not to jail. How could the world just discard people like Marco and Steven? They were both brilliant and both very ill.

Steven sensed everything in his life was falling apart. He was incensed that the country he was trying to save would send him back to India for trial. No way would he agree to that. Not far outside of the city, Steven told the two-armed guards accompanying him he needed to use the restroom.

When he seemed to be taking too long, one of the guards went to find Steven. Steven was ready. Using his handcuffs to strangle him…he dragged him behind the building and removed his shirt and pants. Approaching the guard waiting, with superhuman strength from his increasing madness, he was able to subdue him and dragged him too behind the building before he disappeared. He only hoped they wouldn't be found too soon.

Steven dared not go back to his house. But he had to find a change of clothes and get rid of his shackles. He had exchanged his prison clothes with the guard, but that was a dead giveaway. Until they realized he'd disappeared, he had some leverage. That night Steven broke into Lorinda's house. He figured she'd be too petrified to stay alone, and he was right. He changed into a green hoodie and a pair of Lorinda's sweatpants and pocketed a large black sunglass. Melanie's small office building had no security, so he waited until the streets got quiet and broke into the basement. Advancing up the basement stairs in the dark basement, he listened for any voices or movements. It was quiet. He took a flashlight from the bag he carried and quietly made his way up the dark staircase to the second floor. He looked around for security cameras, and when he saw none, he went to the second floor and called for the elevator.

Steven pressed the button to the Penthouse suite where Melanie's office was located. Right in front of the elevator was the door to her company. There was a keypad! How would he get in? He removed the batteries and picked the lock. By the time he made it inside, Steven was exhausted. He looked around for a place to hide to wait until morning when they would arrive at the office. Steven fell asleep in the storage room behind stacks of materials and other things. Voices awakened him. He held his ear to the door and heard a new voice—the one in his head.

At last.

Steven recognized Lorinda's voice. Then he heard Melanie's voice. And then two men, including one with a British accent. Steven's head felt like it would explode.

He heard someone coming toward the door as he was about to creep out. He jumped behind the door, so he would be hidden when they pushed it open. Readying his pistol, the one he'd taken from the guard, he waited for the door to swing open. Steven grabbed the person and raised his gun at eye level as the door swung open. It was Lorinda, and her eyes grew as big as saucers when she saw Steven. He cautioned her not to scream as he grabbed her, stuffed some material in her mouth, and tied her up.

"If you make a single sound, you're dead," he held the gun to her temple. Lorinda felt her heart drop to the ground. Steven pushed her in front of him, and they entered the outer offices.

"Hello." Steven walked into the room where the voices were coming from, his gun leveled at Lorinda's head.

Melanie spun around, and her eyes locked with Steven Orville. "Steven Orville," she whispered.

Then, everything happened fast. Colin jumped in front of Melanie and tried to grab Steven's gun.

"Do that, and everyone dies," Steven said.

"Steven, please," Lorinda was squirming. He punched her so hard she went flying across the room. Steven stared at her with a menacing look in his eyes, "Don't interfere, you bitch. You betrayed me, and I'll shoot you right here," he shouted.

Lars was trying to figure out how to get to the emergency button, but unfortunately, it was under the reception desk.

"Steven," Melanie stepped from behind Colin. "Please don't hurt anyone. I'll come with you if you promise not to hurt anyone."

"Step over here," Steven ordered. "Everyone else on the floor."

Steven grabbed her wrist and pulled her close to him. "Why must you make me so mad? Take that ring off now!"

Melanie did as he asked. She rested the ring on the table next to her.

"Give me your hand," he commanded, fishing into his bag for something.

Colin saw his moment. He jumped Steven, wrestled the gun away and got him to the floor. Lars dashed to call 911. Lorinda was curled up whimpering in a corner and did not move, and Melanie handed Colin duct tape. Steven was like a mighty ox. He knocked Colin to the ground and grabbed a box of chocolates from his bag. "Here, my love." He picked out a divinity and tried to force one into Melanie's mouth. He took another and ate it himself. "You must come with me, my love. If we can't live together, we will die together." He grabbed her hand again, but as they walked toward the door, he was gripped by excruciating pain in his stomach, his hold loosening on Melanie's arm. He then quickly fell to the floor.

The exact way that Victor had fallen.

The ambulance and police arrived practically at the same time, within minutes. Steven was still alive but writhing in pain. EMS quickly administered oxygen and hoisted him on a gurney. A policeman went with them.

Melanie, in shock, allowed Colin to lead her to a chair. Colin would call the Indian officials to apprise them of what had happened.

Another policeman riffled through Steven's bag, carting it and its contents as evidence. Before he left, the policeman looked at Lars and said, "We suggest you get a video lock for your front door, an individual alarm system, and a CTC surveillance or move offices to a place with more security."

Lars said, "But officer, there is one, an emergency system." The officer didn't skip a beat, "Then use it and next time, call us first." he ordered.

After the police left, Melanie, Colin, Lars, and a sniffling Lorinda sat together staring into space. Colin was the first to speak, "Well, I think we can now close the case of Death in Delhi," Colin said.

Lars asked, "Don't you mean Deaths in Delhi?"

"Okay, cases closed."

Two months later

Lars looked at the bauble on Melanie's second finger left hand that had replaced the friendship ring Colin had given her. "By the way," Lars whispered in Melanie's ear. "Congratulations on your engagement. Now I think we'll all live long enough so we can have a wedding."

"I'm feeling really sorry for Steven. Life can be so cruel."

"Well, you should be glad Mr. Orville acting up saved his life."

"I am so glad that they were able to pump his stomach fast enough to get the poison out of his system and also glad the judge saw fit to have him committed. I am sure his mother is relieved.

"Yes. It's admirable that India agreed to the sentence and didn't insist he be tried in India. "That he felt a sense of justice in taking his boss's body home even after he'd been the cause of his demise is something else. I hope he gets the help he needs. At least now the families can start to put this behind them."

Melanie's phone rang. It was Shiv. "My dear lady. You have been through some ordeal. I bet you need a vacation in India to recover."

"Shiv, thank you. It has been something else. I have forgiven you."

Colin cleared his throat.

the end

Divinity Fit for an Angel

INGREDIENTS

- 1 C sugar
- ½ C light corn syrup
- ½ C water
- ¼ t salt
- 2 egg whites
- 1 t vanilla
- ½ C chopped pecans or ½ C chopped cherries (optional) or both

PROCEDURE

In a 2-quart saucepan, combine ½ C sugar, corn syrup, water, and salt. Cook to the hardball stage (260°), stirring only until sugar dissolves. Meanwhile, as the temperature of syrup reaches 250°, beat egg white until stiff peaks form. When the syrup reaches 260°, gradually add the syrup to egg whites, beating at high speed with an electric mixer. Add vanilla and beat until candy holds its shape, 4-5 minutes. Stir in the chopped nuts or cherries, if desired. Quickly drop candy from a teaspoon onto waxed paper, swirling the top of each piece. Let cool. **Please do not add arsenic.**

Epilogue

Colin had driven them to Newton right after the incident. Curled up in a chaise lounge on the patio, Melanie was buried under a thick down comforter. Portable heat was blasting at full speed.

"I don't know why you have to be out here." Colin handed her a hot toddy.

"Because it's beautiful. Isn't it, Colin?"

"And cold."

"Then you should get under this comforter with me."

"How about you get in bed with me."

"Okay," Melanie said. "Did you call the hospital?" "I did."

"What of Steven?"

"He is being examined at Bellevue psychiatric. If proven sane, which I doubt, he will have to stand trial for attempted murder. Mentally incompetent, he should be committed to a hospital for a very long time. Since India had allowed America to conduct his trial for the murders there, now, it's up to the New York and Indian authorities to work out the details."

"Colin," she asked. "Do you think you should get mixed up with me? I am beginning to wonder if bad karma and death by poison follow me around."

"I've been thinking."

Melanie feigned surprise and sat bolt upright on the divan. "Are you going to leave me?"

"Where on earth did you get a harebrained idea like that?"

"Well, you said you were thinking, and that's usually dangerous."

"I thought that perhaps I should go back to London and resign. We make a great detective team, don't you think?"

Melanie laughed into her blanket.

"What'd you say we get married in the spring? Spring is always an opportunity for new beginnings."

"I'd like that, but I have had enough of small weddings and call centers and serial killers." Melanie pulled him under the cover with her. They were both safe. "Let's wait and do things right. Okay? Besides, I would love a long, dreamy engagement." That last thought was a murmur as she started to doze.

Colin watched as her eyes got heavy. She was one hell of a woman. He fully understood her concerns about what would happen to Steven and why it meant so much to her. He remembered her telling him that she never left her husband's side even after knowing what he had done because he was so very ill. That was loyalty. He was glad he had Melanie Eagleton in his life. He wondered what the next chapter of their life would be like and if she would move to London. Or would he move to New York? Either way, it was bound to be exciting and probably dangerous. Oh well, or as they say in New York, oy vey!

really the end